HOOK

ONCE UPON A VILLAIN

BIANCA COLE

CONTENTS

AUTHOR'S NOTE

Hello reader,

This is a warning to let you know that this is a **DARK** mafia romance much like many of my other books, which means there are very sensitive subject matters addressed and dark, triggering content. If you have any triggers, it would be a good idea to proceed with caution and read the warning below.

As well as a possessive and dominant anti-hero who doesn't take **no** for an answer and a lot of spicy scenes, this book addresses some sensitive subjects. A list of these can be found on my website: www.biancacoleauthor.com

If you have any triggers, then it's best to read the warnings and not proceed. However, if none of these are an issue for you, read on and enjoy this dark romance.

CILLIAN

ick Tock, Tick Tock, Tick Tock.

"Don't move, or you'll lose more than your hand."

"Jonathan! NO!" Ma tries to stop him, but it's pointless.

There's a crazed look in his eyes, no doubt a result of drinking too much alcohol. Outside, the brightest bolt of lightning strikes the earth, illuminating the room. Time appears to slow to a crawl as I watch the machete swipe through the air, slicing through my wrist. There's a sickening crunch of bone and splatter of blood as I watch my hand come apart from my body. The pain is so intense I no longer hear anything but the rushing of blood in my ears and my own scream. I think it's my own. It could be Ma's. The scream is unable to drown out the counting of the clock as everything fades to black.

"Sir!" Smyth's frantic voice pierces through my memories and brings me back to the present. "You're going to kill him before we get answers!"

I stare at the bloodied man before me, then at the ticking clock on the wall that shouldn't be there. It pulls me toward a vortex of violence and destruction. Toward an unstoppable rage that'll force me to obliterate this sniveling excuse of a man before I get what I need from him.

I glance at Smyth. "Why the fuck is there a clock in here?" That sound has haunted me ever since that night twenty years ago.

"Apologies, sir," Smyth says, retrieving the clock off "Apologies, sir," Smyth says, retrieving the clock from the wall. "I'll take care of it."f the wall. "I'll get rid of it."

"Make sure you do," I snap, glaring at him. "I don't want it within a hundred fucking miles of me, understand?"

Smyth nods and rushes away with it, leaving me alone with my target. A man who is officially employed by Piero but working for me. It appears he's trying to double cross me, feeding me bullshit information.

I walk around the man in the chair, eyeing him. He's shackled to a chair, his wrists already bleeding from struggling against the metal cuffs.

I want answers.

The floorboards creak beneath my loafers as I approach the table next to him. With a deliberate click, I unfasten my prosthetic hand and replace it with my infamous hook—the reason why they call me Hook. The cold steel of my weapon glitters under the faint light coming from above us.

He glances up at me through one eye; the other swollen shut after the two days of merciless beating he'd endured at my hand.

"Do you enjoy being able to see?"

His lip trembles. "Please," he begs.

Pathetic.

Moving closer to him, I bring the back of my good hand across his face in a hard slap. "I asked you a question. Answer me or I'll prick your good eye from its socket with the tip of my hook," I slide the flat edge of the metal across his cheek, watching him tremble in fear.

His entire body is shaking. "I told you all I know about Pierro and his operation. Please, stop this."

"You told me nothing other than lies." I trail the sharp point over his skin, drawing a thin line of blood. I watch as it trickles down his face.

"They weren't lies, I swear."

"Another lie. You've sent me on a wild goose chase—one that will cost you your life."

The man before me turns ghostly pale. "I swear, whatever Kevin told you, it's a fucking lie!"

My fist collides with his jaw, and a sickening crack pierces the silence in my basement. His jaw is now broken and he can no longer talk. Although talking isn't necessary as long as his right hand remains intact.

"Alright, since I broke your jaw, you'll write everything I want to know." Reaching into the pocket of my jacket, I pull out a pen and crumpled paper and slap them onto the small, musty table in front of him. "Write it all and don't leave any details out." I unfasten the chains around his wrists and stare at him expectantly.

His eyes are dull from fear and pain as he picks up the pen with a trembling hand. He struggles to form legible words on paper. The handwriting looks childish, but I don't care. All I need is for him to tell me what he knows about Piero's next moves so that I can move forward with my plans.

My blood boils as I watch his pen scratch against the paper. Rage floods through me because he's been keeping information from me this entire time, and I have to grit my teeth to stop myself from ripping the paper out of his hands before he's done. Every second feels like an eternity until he drops the pen.

I snatch the paper away from him, and the information on it makes my fury double. He's been lying to me all this time. The rage explodes within me like a volcanic eruption and I bang my palm on the table.

"Did it amuse you? Sending me after those men who had nothing to do with Piero's operation?"

My voice holds a calmness that makes his entire body tense. He can't answer, but I don't want his answer. This man dared to underestimate me, and that will be his downfall.

My hook glints in the light as I bring the tip closer to his face, sliding it lightly across his cheek and leaving another shallow cut to match the other.

"People that mess about with me always die."

His eyes dart around, looking for a way out, but there's no escape.

I drag my hook harder across his face, taking pleasure in the way he quivers.

His sobs fill the room and I can see the fear in his eyes; it's an emotion that I love to witness.

I continue to carve deep gashes across his body, all the while admiring the way he bleeds. He can't speak because of his broken jaw, but his muffled screams are like a symphony to my ears. If he was able to speak, he'd beg me for mercy.

But cowards like him deserve punishment for trying to deceive me. Pressing the sharp point of my hook between two of his ribs, below his heart, I twist it with vigor as he screams in agony. That dreadful ticking noise still resonating in my head, driving me fucking insane. It may be gone from the room, but the sound never left my mind. I don't understand how a clock got into my establishment in the first place.

With each stroke of my hook into his skin, more blood oozes out, and he shrieks louder.Satisfied with my artwork of carnage, I take a step back and grin at my handiwork. A barely conscious man lying in a pool of his own blood.

This is what happens when someone crosses me.

Reaching into my pocket, I wipe off the congealed blood from my hook before unscrewing it and stowing it away.

Then, reaching for my prosthetic arm, I fastened it back on; my limb's absence still causes a dull throb inside me.

I turn around to find Smyth standing in the doorway. His face is a mask of fear and his mouth set in a grim line. "Leave him to bleed out and deal with the body later. Make sure you get Frank and Shawn to help, as I don't trust them. Tell them what happened."

"Yes, sir," Smyth walks into the room.

"Let this be a lesson for all the idiots who consider crossing me," I snarl.

I feel his eyes on me as I pause at the threshold of Neverland's basement before glancing back. "And Smyth," I say, my voice low but laced with menace.

He swallows. "Sir?"

"Never leave a clock in the room again... or it might be you sitting there."

My gaze skims his shaking body before I spin around and climb the steps into my sex club, Neverland.

The darkness still lingers even though it's morning. My rage feels so vast I can barely contain it. Reaching for a tumbler, I pour myself a large scotch and take a gulp, letting it wash away whatever shred of humanity remains. Alcohol is the only thing that can silence the fury threatening to consume me. I guess it's one thing I have in common with my father.

Piero Panarello deserves to rot in hell for all he's done to me. He's the one who stole everything from me and left nothing but a husk of a man, seething with anger at the world.

Losing my hand was the beginning. It made me angry, but Piero's actions sent me spiraling into hell ten years later.

Our families were rivals in Los Angeles, but uniquely, we had a comfortable pact and got along well. In turn, Piero and I were close friends as kids. We both grew to be highly respected members within our families and had a great deal of influence.

For a time, we worked together to strengthen both our organizations. We controlled different parts of the city, split it down the middle so that each family could have a slice of power. Together, we set up clubs, casinos and organized crime schemes to bring in more money for both outfits.

But then Piero betrayed me. He orchestrated an attack on my family's headquarters while I was away at a meeting out of the city. The moment he betrayed me, I set up again with the funds I had in my name. This time I was forced out of my city, Los Angeles, to San Diego.

There was less competition and I setup my organization under a new name, The Rogues. No family name. No way to tie it to me. I knew if Piero heard I was so close, he'd come and hunt me down. And now, The Rogues are going to return to Los Angeles to steal back what's rightfully ours from that slimy son of a bitch.

"Hey, Cillian," a feminine voice calls from the entrance.

It's one of the bartenders, Crissy, or is it Kirsty?
Fuck.

I don't know, but I've fucked them all.

"Hey," I say gruffly, tossing back the rest of the scotch. "I was just leaving." I'm about to walk out from behind the bar when she steps into my path and places a hand on my chest, arching a brow.

"What's the rush?" Her lips purse temptingly and I know that fucking this piece of ass over the bar might well help take the edge off the day I've had.

I grab her wrist and yank her toward me, knowing full well that most of these women hope I'll make it a regular thing. The fact is, I don't even remember if I've had sex with this one or not, or what her name is.

Her lips purse and eyes dilate as she pushes her chest

into me, trying to draw me in. And as I gaze at her, the desire to fuck her diminishes. "I'm not feeling like it tonight, sweetheart." I release her wrist. For a number of months now, something has been off.

Perhaps I've grown tired of fucking these girls. They're all the same, desperate and greedy for money. I need something fresh to pull me out of the rut I'm in, and if the information Luke provided me is true, I'll get that from Piero's fiancé, who I intend to snatch from under his nose and make mine.

"Oh, okay," she says, looking disappointed.

I can't say I care too much, as I've got a plan to get in motion. Kai, the man I killed, gave me the most important piece of information yet—information that isn't common knowledge.

Piero is engaged. And while he may have stolen my world from me, I intend to steal it all back, starting with his innocent little fiancée, Gwendolyne Tesoro, princess of the Tesoro mob. It's time to go on a hunt for Piero's most recent and prized possession.

2

GWENDOLYNE

The dining room is aglow with the flickering candles, their soft light illuminating the room. A crisp white cloth is draped over the mahogany wood table and a bouquet of fresh roses sits in a vase, the sweet smell of their perfumed petals filling the air.

Italian classical music plays in the background to add a layer of romance to the already romantic atmosphere.

My gaze shifts to my fiancé opposite me, his dark eyes locking onto me with an alluring yet predatory gleam.

My heart races at the sight of his devilish smile, which is sinful and intoxicating. I force out an awkward grin in return.

Two weeks ago, my father announced our engagement to unite two of California's most powerful mafia families: The Panarello family and ourselves.

It's my destiny to marry Piero Panarello, Don of the Italian mob in Los Angeles and fifteen years my senior, yet he looks as if he has stepped off a fashion magazine cover.

"How is your food?" He asks, sipping his wine.

My throat suddenly feels dry, but I nod. "Delicious." I stab my fork into the center of the spaghetti and twirl the pasta onto it along with the rich ragu sauce.

Piero licks his bottom lip, his gaze burning into me. "Not as delicious as you look in that dress."

Fire spreads through my veins and I glance away, unable to look at him for too long without being overcome by too many confusing feelings. "You look pretty amazing, too." I take a long sip of the fancy Italian wine, savoring the taste. "This wine is one of the best I've ever tasted," I say, in an attempt to divert the conversation.

His smile widens. "I should hope so. It's fifteen hundred dollars a bottle."

My eyes widen as I stare at the glass, unable to fathom how anyone could justify spending that much on one bottle of wine.

In the two weeks since I met Piero, he has revealed himself to be someone who likes overindulgence and extravagance. A common trait in our world, but he takes it further than anyone else I've ever met. A feeling of unease unfurls within me, as I remember we're soon to be married.

"Has my father mentioned a date for our wedding?"

His smile deepens into a sultry smirk that sends warmth cascading down my spine. "Not yet," he replies, swirling his glass before taking a sip of the rich liquid.

12

"But I'll recommend the date is sooner rather than later."

I suppress a shiver. "Why's that?"

He stands and strides toward me like a hunter stalking his prey. "So delightfully innocent, Gwen. Because I crave you." His hands grasp my shoulders as he kneads the knots in them.

Pleasure ripples through my body, and I give out a moan of appreciation. "What are you doing?"

"Am I not allowed to touch my fiancée?" His voice oozes with authority. This is the first time a man has touched me, and it's sending sparks of pleasure all over my skin.

"Y-yes…" I mumble.

Piero leans down and places a searing kiss on the back of my neck, making me moan. I shuffle in my chair, suddenly painfully uncomfortable.

"Turn and face me," he orders.

I turn in my chair to look at him. Without asking permission, his mouth is on mine. He takes everything I have to give, thrusting his tongue into my mouth as he explores it possessively. His lips are demanding yet gentle, possessing me in a way that makes me feel desired and protected.

It sends a spark right to my core as I deepen the kiss, lacing my fingers in his thick hair and pulling him closer. He groans when I tug at his hair, and I'm emboldened by his response.

He makes a deep, growling sound as he pulls away to whisper against my lips, "You taste so sweet, Gwen."

Suddenly, he drags me out of my chair and sits on a

nearby chair, pulling me onto his lap and kissing me again.

Piero's hands roam over my body, caressing me through the thin material of my dress. I'm melting from his touch, my body responding eagerly to his every move. He breaks the kiss only to trail kisses down my neck and onto my collarbone, nipping at my skin and leaving marks in his wake.

Piero's lips continue to move across my skin, stoking the fire within me. His touch is commanding, but it's not unwelcome. It's like my body is responding instinctively to his every touch, desperate for more.

His gravelly voice sends shivers down my spine as he breathes against my ear. "You belong to me now."

As his hand slips beneath my panties, that's when I'm brought back to my senses. "Wait," I gasp, pulling away from him and looking into those alluring hazel eyes. "We can't, not until we're married."

Piero huffs out a low laugh, the corner of his lips curling into a smirk. "Do you always stick to the rules, Gwen?"

My cheeks heat and I glance away, not wanting him to see how much he affects me. "Yes," I squeak. "Most of them. Is that so bad?"

He grabs my hand in a tight grip, making my entire body tremble with desire. "No, but it won't get me what I desire the most." With a glint in his eye, he motions toward his crotch and the obvious bulge there. His words leave me liquified with heat. "But I'll have you soon enough," he whispers against my ear. His eyes have a wicked gleam and I can't look away, no matter how hard I try. "Your obedience won't save you when I finally have you beneath me. You won't be to stop screaming my name when I make you come over and over again."

"Piero!" My voice shakes.

"Exactly. Just like that, Gwendolyne," he purrs, as he lifts me off of his lap and steps back, winking at me before returning to his seat.

We resume eating our dinner, but he lifts his glass of wine in a toast first. "To us and the amazing sex we're going to have."

"Seriously? I've never met a man as forward as you."

He cocks an eyebrow. "Then you've never met any man worth knowing. A real man makes it clear what he wants and he takes it."

I swallow hard as I wonder what exactly he means by that. Piero comes across as the type of man who wouldn't care if a woman is willing or not—a thought that sends a chill down my spine.

"How many children do you want, Gwendolyne?" His voice is a deep rumble that makes my stomach twist in knots.

I know why he's asking—to ensure his family line has successors, but I hadn't expected the question so soon.

"Honestly, I'm so young. It's not something I've thought about."

The arch of his brow makes me sink deeper into my chair. "I want four," he proclaims. "Big families are the best."

I place a hand on my stomach. I'd always thought I'd have two children; four is too many.

"We'll see what happens after we have our first, no?"

He laughs and leans forward. "Indeed, I can't wait to breed you."

My entire body ignites in flames. Every time we've met he has been around my family, so it appears his true colors are showing tonight. "Are you always this crass?" I ask.

He gives me a sly smirk. "Of course not, but when I'm sitting opposite my drop dead gorgeous fiancée, who can blame me?"

I hate how inexperienced I am with men. Dad has kept me too sheltered, locking me away to protect me.

I bite the inside of my cheek. "Can we change the subject?"

"Of course." I sense a hint of disappointment in his tone. "Besides enjoying having dinner with me, what are your interests?"

His arrogance never ceases to amaze me, but of all the things he could have asked, that's the one thing I wish he hadn't.

"Well," I pause. "I love nature and observing wildlife."

When his expression remains neutral, I feel comfortable enough to continue. My dad has always called my love of wildlife photography silly and a waste of time.

"I find peace in taking photos of landscapes and animals." There's something extraordinary about capturing the beauty of this world which has existed for countless years. It's when I'm surrounded by nature that I discover a tranquility that can't be found in anything else, especially bird watching; there's something magical about seeing a gorgeous bird soaring through the sky and witnessing the colorful feathers in motion.

"A photographer?" he asks, his eyebrow arching in intrigue.

I nod. "Yes."

He grins. "How about you capture shots of me naked?"

My mouth dries and heat rushes through my body. Taking photos of this irresistible man nude? I can't even begin to imagine how I'd focus. "I don't think that's a good idea," I say.

"Come on, relax. Tell you what, let's take a stroll in the garden. It's a lovely evening and you do like nature."

I smile at the idea of getting some fresh air. "That sounds lovely."

Piero stands, offering me his hand. "Shall we?"

I take his hand in mine and he pulls me to my feet, smiling at me.

"You are the most stunning woman I have ever seen," he breathes.

My heart flutters at his words and I remember all the stunning models he'd been linked to in the past.

What an absurd lie.

"I hardly believe that's true, considering all the models you've dated in the past."

His past conquests are common knowledge and plastered all over the internet. It makes me wonder whether he can be a faithful husband or not.

"Nothing compares to you, tesoro mio." His sexy accent does funny things to my insides.

I pinch my lips together and shake my head, struggling to believe him. "Don't be ridiculous."

"My sweet Gwen," he continues, gazing into my eyes with an intensity that makes me tremble. "They were nothing but pale, stick-thin ghosts with no personality whatsoever."

The moon casts a soft light over us as we step out onto the stone patio, stretching around the house. "You're a rare beauty with the best fucking figure I've ever seen. And you're special, not like other girls your age."

My stomach somersaults at his words as no one has ever paid me compliments like him.

Ahead of us stands an old fountain, gurgling peacefully in the night air. The stars twinkle above it, giving it a magical feel. "This place...it's breathtaking," I whisper in awe as he leads me closer to the fountain.

He steps closer, radiating heat.

"The sound of running water always calms me," I say.

In a split second, Piero grips my hips and pulls my back tight against him. I can feel the hard bulge in his trousers as it rubs against my ass. His lips brush my earlobe as he speaks in a low voice. "There's something else that's calming…"

A shiver runs down my spine and I feel my heart skip a beat. "What?"

"Kissing," he responds in a seductive tone before

spinning me around and pressing his lips to mine in a passionate kiss.

I melt in his arms, unable to resist the overwhelming desire for him.

Piero wraps an arm around my waist and uses the other to press my hand against the steel pole of his huge cock. My eyes widen as I realize how aroused he is, and I ache for him in response. He pulls away to whisper in my ear, "Do you feel what you do to me, Gwendolyne?"

I'm speechless. All I can do is nod slightly, making him groan and kiss me harder.

"Fuck, I need to be inside you right now," he says gruffly, pulling back before I can respond.

My entire body burns at the thought. "Not yet, Piero, please wait."

He chuckles again. "Don't worry, sweetheart. I know better than to fuck you before marriage. Your father would murder me."

We both stand silent for a moment and I can't shake the disappointment that he didn't insist we take things further.

What the hell is my problem?

He kisses me one last time and then glances around the patio. "We didn't get far on our walk, did we?"

I shake my head, apprehension gripping me. "It's getting late. We should call it a night."

He nods reluctantly. "Your father will be suspicious if he gets reports from your bodyguard that you are staying here too late. I still don't understand why he wouldn't let you stay here where we can get to know each other more easily." His smirk is telling and my resolve weakens in silent agreement.

"It's his rules," I reply, the words uneasy on my tongue.

He grins, moving closer until there's no space between us. "Yes. You definitely don't like breaking them, do you?" He leaves a trail of kisses on my neck before raising his gaze to mine, stealing away any remaining breath from my lungs. "Enjoy making your pussy come while you think of me," he breathes against my lips before pulling back and striding away without another word.

Shaken, I barely notice Anton, my bodyguard, stepping forward to lead me to the driveway. His heavy footsteps thudding on the path fills the silence until we reach the car.

"Let's get you back to the hotel, miss." He opens the back door.

I take a seat in the town car and cross my legs as heat curls through my belly and shameful wetness soaks my inner legs. Our first time alone, and it's clear my attraction to Piero is overwhelming. It feels as though if we don't marry soon, I'll get so desperate that I'll beg him to fuck me, married or not.

3

CILLIAN

$\mathcal{M}$y cell buzzes, its vibrations resonating against my ribcage as I turn the corner toward Piero's engagement party.

I pull it out to answer the call.

"What?"

"Sorry to bother you, sir, but I wanted to check if you'll be attending tonight's monthly meeting?" Smyth's voice crackles through the receiver.

I squeeze my eyes shut and pinch the bridge of my nose.

Damn!

I had forgotten about the meeting. "No... I can't make it tonight. Sorry, Smyth."

He sighs on the other end. "Alright, I'll take notes for you and tell you what happened tomorrow."

"Do that," I say before ending the call, not wanting to explain why I wouldn't be there.

Stuffing my phone back into an inner pocket of my

jacket, I pull out an invitation that a contact obtained for me.

I approach the entrance of the building. A line of people form a queue waiting for security clearance, and I join the back, tapping my foot against the ground.

Smyth would flip if he knew what I was planning to do here tonight.

He's always been one for caution, but after all these years of planning and waiting, I intend to take my time over this and make sure I get it right.

The guard stares at me with a bored expression as he holds out his hand, expecting an invitation in return.

Without saying a word, I pass him mine and he waves me through. It's too fucking easy to get inside this wretched party.

Tonight, it's all about the prize. Gwendolyne Tesoro, the wife-to-be of my nemesis Piero.

A woman who her father, Jovani Tesoro, has kept well hidden over the years. Rumor has it she's a true treasure, as her name suggests. And the thing about me is I can't keep my hands off treasure, especially treasure belonging to Piero.

The ballroom itself is awash with decadence; chandeliers drip from the ceiling like diamonds, casting an ethereal glow over everything below. The string quartet plays music in the corner, adding to the ambiance.

The attendees are nothing short of perfection. Each one decked out in their finest tuxedo or gown, sipping champagne while chatting away like old friends.

The place wreaks of Piero and his over-inflated ego. The crème de la crème of society has come out tonight;

from influential families to powerful business magnates, all gathering at Piero's high-class party. It makes me want to puke.

I scan the room for my target, excitement rising as adrenaline heightens in my veins. Seeing Gwendolyne is worth the risk. She'll be mine before Piero can utter his wedding vows.

I linger on the sidelines of the glittering ballroom, my gaze skimming past the guests in search of the man of the hour. It's dangerous to be here. If Piero discovered my presence, there would be no escape.

That's all forgotten when my gaze falls upon a tall figure with golden brown hair across the room. Resentment bubbles in my veins as I spot him, the man who took everything from me. He has a young woman on his arm and she has brown, sun-kissed hair that shimmers in the light, stretching to her waist in luscious curls.

This must be Gwendolyne Tesoro. From behind, she's utterly breathtaking. Her form is curvaceous in the most delightful way, her long legs visible beneath her knee-length evening gown. She has an ethereal beauty, with a grace and poise that's out of this world. Even before I've seen her face, it doesn't take much effort to imagine spanking her pert ass while I fuck her senseless.

Turn around.

She's facing away from me. Disgustingly, Piero lowers his hand to caress her ass and she shudders.

A server stops by my side to offer me champagne on a silver tray. "Hello, would you like a drink?" She bats her eyelashes at me flirtatiously.

I force my lips into a hint of a smile. "Sure, thanks,"

I say, suppressing the urge to flirt back. I have a job to do, and I can't jeopardize it for a fleeting moment with a pretty girl.

Taking the flute, I step away from her and toward Piero.

My eyes narrow in hate and contempt at the sight of him. My arch-nemesis. Yet, even as I try to focus on him, my gaze moves back to the woman by his side — a pretty thing whose delicate shoulders are exposed by the low back of her dress.

My fists clench and my pulse races as Piero leans toward her, whispering something in her ear. She turns her face to the side and I see the responding blush creep to the tip of her ears.

A raging storm brews within me. He doesn't deserve her perfection.

Mesmerized, I watch as she turns my way, revealing her beauty in full. Hair like soft brown velvet cascades across her heart-shaped face; rosy lips curve into an alluring smile that reveals perfect white teeth; emerald eyes pierce through my soul.

An obsession solidifies within me. Gwendolyne Tesoro will be mine.

Piero makes her laugh, and it makes me sick. He's so sure of himself—of his power and his wealth, so certain that no one would dare stand against him.

But he is wrong. He doesn't see me standing there watching them. Observing as they greet their guests with smug self-assurance. It makes my mission more urgent. To take Gwendolyne away from him, to make him pay for all he has cost me.

The temptation to approach her, to make my presence known, is too risky right now. Piero would recognize me if we came face to face, and I know my time here won't end well if that happens.

"Excuse me," someone says, clearing their throat behind me.

I turn around to find myself facing one of Piero's men—his loyal man since before Piero ruined my life.

"Yeah?" I ask, trying to keep my cool.

The man narrows his eyes, squinting as though trying to place me. "Do I know you?"

I shake my head. "I don't recognize you, no."

His lips purse together and he holds out a hand. "Dario," he says. "And who are you?"

"Henry," I say, thinking of a name.

He shakes his head. "No, I don't know a Henry, my bad."

"No worries. See you around."

He looks at me skeptically for a long moment, then steps back and waves his hand dismissively. "Yeah, see you around." I watch him walk away, my heart thumping against my ribcage. When I turn back to look for Piero and his fiancée, I find Piero but not Gwendolyne.

I stride toward the restroom, eager to get a moment of privacy with Gwendolyne before she returns to her fiancé's side. The worst thing in the world is a beautiful woman who is a complete airhead and I want to speak with her.

As I'm about to walk past an archway that leads to a back alcove, I come to an abrupt stop.

My sixth sense screams at me that she's in there, not in the restroom. With my heart pounding hard, I peek into the alcove and find Gwendolyne sitting in a plush armchair, her eyes closed, her head resting back. God damn it, she's even more beautiful this close.

I clench my jaw as desire coils through me, hot and heavy. This woman is going to be the death of me. I feel it in my bones. She's bad fucking news. It doesn't stop me from moving closer. I stop when I'm mere feet away from her. She hasn't yet noticed me.

What kind of spell has she cast upon me?

My throat tightens as I sink into the armchair next to hers and admire her peaceful expression for a moment. "You look peaceful, princess," I murmur.

Her eyes snap open and lock onto mine with electric force. She scans my face before shifting upright to take in our surroundings, noticing it's only us two here in this intimate space. "Sorry, I didn't hear you sit." A touch of surprise lingers in her voice.

I smirk, loving the way her cheeks flush. "No, you were wrapped up in your own little world, weren't you?"

She swallows, her throat bobbing as she does, drawing my eyes to it. What I'd give to reach out and wrap my palm around it while kissing those pouty, red lips. "The party is overwhelming, and I wanted a break," she says, meeting my gaze.

"This party is being held to celebrate your recent engagement?" I ask, teasing her.

"Yes, I'm Gwen." She holds her hand out for me to shake, but I have other ideas.

A devilish urge surges through me as I kiss the back of her hand. I want nothing more than to pull her into my lap and devour her. She's fucking exquisite. "It's a pleasure to meet you," I say, not giving my name on purpose.

Her eyes flash in irritation, but she doesn't ask me my name. Instead, she tries to reclaim her hand from my grasp. I'm not ready to let go.

A crease forms between her brows as I stand and yank her to her feet, pulling our bodies together.

"What are you doing?" she asks, breathless from the sudden proximity.

"Do you dance, Miss Tesoro?" I ask.

My grip tightens around her delicate waist as she tries to resist me. She can fight all she wants, but I know that at the end of this sweetly torturous game, she will be mine.

She shakes her head hesitantly and responds, "No, I'm a terrible dancer."

I draw her closer to me, relishing the sensation of her body pressed against mine. I feel the fire between us ignite and my cock harden in response to the challenge before me.

Her nostrils flare and eyes dilate, betraying her arousal as she battles with her own desire.

"Well, I'm not entirely sure I believe that, princess," I whisper seductively into her ear.

She shivers in response, and my amusement grows.

"Dance with me," I demand, infusing my tone with dominance.

"I don't think it's right for me to dance with someone other than my fiancé," she stammers out.

The thing is, I don't take no for an answer. I always get what I want. I move even closer so our bodies are flush together, allowing her to feel my hard cock against her abdomen. The heat on her face tells me Gwen knows how far I'm willing to go for her.

"It's not a request," I growl in warning. "But an order." There's no denying it now—she is mine and there is no escaping it.

4

GWENDOLYNE

My breath hitches, my heart thunders as he ensnares me in his dark gaze. His powerful muscles press against me as he twirls me around the floor in an intimate dance. A part of me wants to break free, but I can't—not even when my fiancé's name crosses my mind and brings with it an overwhelming sense of guilt.

I relish the forbidden thrill between us, despite knowing it's wrong.

This man, whose name I don't know, is persistent. His hard dick grinds against my stomach, making me ache.

I came to this alcove to escape the chaotic party, only to be confronted by a mesmerizing stranger who is intent on seducing me. His smoldering gaze burns right through me as he pulls me closer, as if he's trying to meld our bodies together.

"I came back here to get away from everyone," I say,

trying to pull away from him. The man doesn't budge an inch.

"Is that so? And yet you found me. Isn't that a happy coincidence?" He grins at me, and my knees tremble.

I can't gather my thoughts. "Who are you?" I ask, my breathing shallow and uneven. If this man is Piero's friend, then he's a bad one for coming on to his fiancée.

"That doesn't matter," he murmurs against my ear, sending a chill down my spine. "What matters is that I'm here with you now." The warmth of his body surrounds me as he continues to sway us to the music, our little alcove becoming our own private world where time stands still.

My heart thunders in my chest at the intensity of his chestnut eyes. He's as devilishly handsome as Piero, but there's something more menacing hidden in his gaze. A warning that I should steer clear of him.

"So, you won't tell me your name?" I ask.

"Isn't it better this way? More mysterious without names." His arm snakes tightly around my waist as he pulls me closer.

My eyes narrow. "You know my name."

He presses his lips to my ear. "Everyone here knows your name. But, does everyone appreciate how fucking gorgeous you are?"

A thrill shoots through me at his words, both illicit and forbidden.

"That's inappropriate, considering this is my engagement party," I stammer.

I pull away from him, but he holds firm.

"You're not claimed until there's a wedding band on

that finger." He nods toward my hand, keeping me tight against him. "And until then you're fair game, princess."

"Don't call me that."

His lips move to my neck and he nibbles the skin, making me gasp. No man other than my fiancé should make me feel this way.

"Why not?" he asks. "Is it because your pussy is dripping wet for me?"

I shake my head in disbelief at his crudeness, yet my thighs tremble in response.

What is wrong with me? If Piero were to find us, like this....

"Let go of me. You're being disgusting."

"No, princess," he growls, pressing tighter against my body. "Why would I do that when I love feeling your sexy curves pressed against me?"

My throat constricts with fear as his eyes alight with dark emotion. Terror fills me. I want nothing more than to sprint away from him and never look back. There's something unhinged about him. I sense he's far more dangerous than Piero, who's a mob boss.

"Please let me go," I beg.

He bites on my earlobe hard enough to leave a bruise and a sharp shock shoots through the middle of my spine.

"Only once I get a kiss."

"A kiss? I'm engaged!"

"Come now, Gwendolyne." His husky voice feels like a caress against my skin. "Surely you want to have kissed more than one man by the time you get married?"

I swallow hard, hating that this stranger is right. I'm going to be bound to Piero for life and have never kissed another man. A thrill runs through me at the thought of breaking the rules and doing something because I feel like it. Before I know what I'm doing, I lift onto my toes and press my lips to his for a chaste kiss.

When I try to pull away, he keeps me tight against him and deepens the kiss. His tongue thrusts into my mouth, sending sparks racing through my body. Moaning, I relax into his arms as he grabs a fistful of my hair and devours me as if he's trying to drink me in. My knees grow weak with desire as an ache pulses between my thighs. All I can do is melt for him.

The sounds from the ballroom drift in, snapping me back to reality. Yanking away, I glance at him in shock, shaking my head rapidly. "Oh my God," I whisper in disbelief. "I don't know what got into me! Please don't tell Piero."

He chuckles. "I'm not telling him anything, but I do intend to steal another kiss or two before you're married to him."

I shake my head. "No chance. I don't want to see you again."

Without looking back, I spin around and run. My heart races in my chest at superhuman speed. Eventually, I stumble into the restroom and lock myself in the nearest stall, collapsing onto the toilet seat with my forehead against my hands.

What was I thinking?

The way Piero makes me feel when he kisses me is nothing compared to the way that stranger made me feel.

It means what I feel for Piero is nothing but infatuation.

Taking a deep breath, I open the stall and stand in front of the mirror, examining my reflection closely.

My lips are swollen from the passionate kiss, so I try to use lip gloss to cover it up. My hair is a little tousled because he grabbed it, so I run a comb through it before returning to the ballroom.

I'm tense and on high alert, hoping I don't run into that mysterious man again.

Piero is nowhere in sight when I enter. The room is full of music and joyous laughter. It's meant to be a celebratory party, but as memories of my moment with the stranger refuse to leave my mind, my feelings are all over the place.

Did he do this on purpose? To deter me from marrying Piero? No matter what his plan is, it has made me rethink everything about our union.

I shudder as I hear Piero's gruff voice call out, "Ah, there you are, darling."

I whirl to face him. Our eyes meet and instantly I wish I hadn't given into temptation and kissed another man. The guilt I feel is sickening.

I plaster on a smile. "Yes, I just went to the restroom."

Piero pulls me close and kisses me. Even though his kiss is full of passion, it makes me feel dirty inside because it's nothing like the kiss I shared with the stranger. He grabs my hand and guides me through the crowd.

"Where are we going?" I ask.

"I want you to meet my friends," he says, as if I'm a flashy possession he wants to show off. I can't deny it makes me feel special, something I've never felt before we met.

Piero waves his hand at a short, stocky man. "Elio and his wife, Alina."

Elio forces a smile, eyeing me suspiciously. His wife's brown eyes scan me with disapproval before she smiles briefly.

"And Tino, my second-in-command." Piero gestures to the tall lanky man with jet-black hair and dark eyes, who bows to me in greeting.

"Alexander works for us too," Piero adds.

The silver-haired man gives me a curt nod.

He points to a woman. "Kira is a freelancer I hire on occasion."

Kira takes my hand and shakes it. "Pleasure to meet you, Gwen... I've heard so much about you." She smiles genuinely, which is nice after the cold reception from Elio and Alina.

Alexander steps closer and takes my hand, kissing it softly. Before he utters a word, Piero smacks Alexander on the back of his head.

"What the hell was that for?" Alexander asks.

"Keep those filthy lips away from my fiancée," Piero says sternly, as Alexander rubs the back of his head.

"Apologies, boss," he says, giving me a toothy grin.

I'm relieved to see that the man I kissed isn't here, so hopefully, I can pretend it never happened and go back to normal.

"So, Gwen, what do you enjoy doing in your spare time?" Elio asks.

And that's when I realize they're all staring at me. "I'm a wildlife photographer," I reply.

Alina rolls her eyes. "Photographer? That's so unoriginal."

I don't like this woman already. "How is it unoriginal? I enjoy taking photos and, therefore, do what I enjoy. I don't care how many other people also do it."

"Well said," Kira agrees, glaring at Alina. "We should all pursue our interests without fear of judgment."

I smile, knowing that I'm going to get on well with Kira. So far, Tino and Alexander seem alright too.

"I agree," Tino chimes in, looking slightly embarrassed. "I enjoy reading whenever I can find the time."

"What genre do you prefer?" I inquire.

He grins at me. "I love science fiction because it gives me the chance to explore new worlds."

Turning toward Piero, I gaze into his eyes and ask him, "What about you? What's your favorite hobby?"

"My work is my passion," he responds coolly. "There's nothing more rewarding than expanding my empire."

I frown. "You find working fun?"

He shrugs before taking a sip of his drink.

My mind reels with doubt as Piero's response echoes in my head. My thoughts slip to the stranger from earlier who stole a kiss; his smirk and mischievous eyes playing tricks on me.

Piero is great, but suddenly I can't help longing for

something more—longing for that spark of connection I felt with him. A deep, indefinable anger simmers toward my dad for forcing me into a marriage devoid of experience.

Pushing away my thoughts, I try to recall why I was so thrilled to marry Piero before tonight. But no matter how hard I try, all I can see is the handsome stranger who has gotten under my skin with one stolen kiss.

5

CILLIAN

J stalk through Macy's, never taking my gaze
from Gwen. She's wearing a simple indigo
summer dress with floral pattern, and her hair is
styled in a modest updo. She looks different from the
party but breathtakingly beautiful.

With every step I take, her fear intensifies as if she
can sense me nearby. Each time, she spins around to try
to locate me. She turns in my direction again and I slip
behind a mannequin, my heart racing with the thrill of
the chase.

"Are you okay, Gwen?" one girl asks.

She clears her throat. "Yes, I just... Never mind."

They continue flicking through the rows of dresses
in silence.

For the past week, I've been following Gwendolyne
Tesoro and her pesky bodyguard around Los Angeles. It
appears she's staying at a hotel in the city to remain
close to Piero before the wedding, even though she's

seen him a handful of times. My following her is escalating my obsession with each passing day.

And today is when it will reach its climax. I will reveal myself to her for the first time since our kiss.

It's not my style to strike too soon; building suspense and tension will make it far more gratifying when I take her.

Ever since we first met, I've been unable to focus on anything but her. She haunts my thoughts and even in sleep, I can't escape. Her emerald eyes feature in every vivid dream I have.

The three girls finish looking at the dresses and head toward the dressing room to try them on. Her bodyguard, who is incompetent, remains near the front entrance of the women's clothing floor, watching a woman who has been making eyes at him since the moment they entered.

I make my way toward the fitting room entrance, where I stop and peer inside. Gwen sits alone in the waiting area with a bridal magazine open, which means that she's not trying dresses on today.

The shop assistant clears her throat behind me and I straighten, turning my head and studying her for a moment. She's young and doe-eyed. "Can I help you, sir?"

I flash back one of my most winning smiles. "No, I'm waiting for my fiancée and her friends," I tell her.

Her cheeks flush, but she smiles. "A real shame. If you weren't taken, I'd ask you out."

I chuckle. "Well, nothing is ever set in stone until the wedding day."

Her brow creases as she sizes me up. "Men like you are too dangerous," she says before moving to straighten clothing on a mannequin nearby.

As soon as she leaves to assist another customer, I move back to the opening of the dressing rooms to watch my prey from afar. The little princess fidgets while flicking her hair back from one side of her face to the other. She glances around the room as if sensing me watching her, so I dart out of sight.

"Gwen," I overhear her friend call. I peek through the doorway and see Gwendolyne standing there with a girl.

"What do you think?" She asks, strutting about in a powder blue dress and twirling around.

"I love it," Gwen replies, nodding. "It's my favorite."

The other girl comes out wearing the same dress, confirming my suspicions. These girls are Gwen's bridesmaids. I don't know who they are as my research on Gwendolyne suggests she doesn't have friends, not by choice, but because of her father's rules. Perhaps they're family members.

"Agreed," the first girl says. "Let's get this one. It's perfect."

My pulse quickens as Gwen stands up, handing over her credit card to one of her friends. "Pay for them both. I need to use the restroom."

Jackpot.

My blood burns with desire as I'm presented with the chance to speak with her again.

I move away from the entrance of the changing area and hide behind a mannequin so Gwen doesn't notice me. The opportunity I've longed for since we last met—a moment alone where her attention is on me.

Gwen walks toward the restrooms, her hips swaying temptingly. She has the most tantalizing curves, making me want her with every fiber of my being.

She strides into the restroom. A few moments pass before I enter, crouching to glance beneath each stall to make sure no one else is in here. I lock the main door shut, my heart racing hard and fast like thunder crackling between two clouds.

She steps out of her stall and her emerald eyes instantly flare wide in shock when she spots me standing by the door.

Panic appears on her face. "What are you doing in here?"

I smirk at her, "Not pleased to see me, princess?"

Her eyes narrow. "Certainly not."

"Why?" I ask, my voice low and gruff. "Because you haven't been able to stop thinking about me when you're engaged to another man?"

Her gaze drops to the floor, her eyes unable to meet mine. "I haven't thought of you at all," she whispers.

I walk toward her as if compelled by a supernatural force. My fingertips brush against her chin, coaxing her face to meet my gaze. "Liar," I shake my head. "You can deny it all you want, but I know it's true. I can see it in your eyes every time you look at me, you want me."

Gwen shakes her head. "You're delusional if you think I want you. It's clear that you're following me like an obsessed stalker."

I move closer to her, shortening the distance between us. "How often have you thought about our kiss last week?" I demand.

She sighs heavily. "Zero."

I laugh, because she's so adorable when she lies. "I bet you've played with yourself picturing me, haven't you?"

Her face turns red and her eyes betray her shame before she speaks.

"Let's save us both a waste of time and cut to the chase, princess."

"Don't call me that!" she snaps.

"Isn't it what you are? The Tesoro mafia princess?"

Gwen chews on her lip. "I'm just a girl."

"A fucking gorgeous one."

Her lips purse. "What is it you want from me?"

I close the gap between us so that there's merely a foot between our bodies, noticing the way her breathing labors and her eyes grow wider in anticipation. "What do I want from you, baby?" I ask, grabbing her hips and yanking her against me. "Isn't it obvious?"

Her eyes dilate even as she tries to fight the magnetic pull that we both feel, shaking her head. "No."

"I want you to admit the truth. Admit that you've played with your virgin cunt and thought about me."

She jerks away from me, her eyes wide as she spits out, "That's disgusting!

"Is it?" I ask, tilting my head to the side. "Or is it the plain and simple truth?"

"I'm engaged," she says.

I move my lips closer to hers, delighting in the way hers part. "And it means nothing, because your mind can't focus on anything but me ever since our kiss, can it?"

Her throat bobs as she swallows. "I'm marrying Piero in two weeks," she says, her voice a little hesitant. "Stop trying to get in the middle of that, whoever the fuck you are."

"That's right, you don't know my name." I move my hand to her throat, enjoying feeling her warm, soft skin against my calloused hand. "What do you call out when you come?"

Her nostrils flare. "I've told you—"

I squeeze tighter. "No more lies, Gwendolyne. Tell me the truth."

She's defiant as she holds my gaze, staring into my eyes with a fight that makes my balls tighten and my cock harder.

"Fine, I'll tell you what to shout out in the future." I move my lips to her ear, nibbling on her earlobe. "Captain."

Her brow furrows. "What?"

I lick her earlobe. "I said you can call me captain."

She frowns at me. "What are you? A pirate?"

I chuckle, as when Piero stole everything from me, I was homeless and had to rebuild everything from scratch. In a way, I was a pirate, stealing and bartering my way to the position I'm in now. It's why my outfit is called The Rogues. "Perhaps," I murmur, moving my hand across the front of her body, cupping her full breast in my hand.

"There's something wrong with you," she says.

"Does that mean there's something wrong with you for wanting me?" I ask.

Her nose wrinkles in disgust, but her eyes spark with desire. "I don't want you."

"Keep telling yourself that," I murmur, searching her eyes. And then I pull her against me, kissing her lips. "It's a lie, and we both know it."

Her cheeks are flushed as I pull back, and she tilts her head back slightly, as if willing me to kiss her again.

"You don't seem upset about being kissed by me again." I arch a brow. "I bet your pussy is soaking wet for me, isn't it?"

She pulls her bottom lip into her mouth. "Will you tell me your name?"

"I've told you already." I kiss her neck and drag the edge of my teeth down it to the juncture where it meets her shoulder. "I'm your captain, princess."

She shudders as I slide my teeth into her flesh, savoring everything about this moment.

Her scent.

Her taste.

There's a part of me that wants to tear into her right here, devour her and have her begging me for more over the countertop. There's another part of me that wants her to admit she wants me more than Piero willingly. Although, I doubt I'm going about it the right way.

She's a fucking treat.

"And don't forget it." I release her from my grasp, resisting the urge to give in to temptation. "Sweet dreams." I wink at her before turning away, leaving my beautiful little princess alone and needy in the restroom. It won't be long until I take her. I need a solid plan in place before I strike.

Piero won't know what hit him, and neither will sweet little Gwendolyne.

6

GWENDOLYNE

A sharp knock jolts me from my dazed thoughts. Piero isn't available for dinner tonight, like most nights that I've been here in Los Angeles, so I ordered room service. The point of me being here is to get to know him better, but he doesn't have time for me.

My heart sinks when I open the door and clash gazes with alluring chestnut eyes—my stalker from Macy's.

He's wearing a black suit and white shirt without a tie, the buttons done so far, displaying an impressive amount of ink scrawling across his chiseled chest.

The look on his face makes my insides twist and my heart race.

I push the door shut, but not fast enough.

He wedges his shoe into the gap and uses his powerful strength to force it open. "That's not nice, is it, Gwen?" he asks, stepping into my room without invitation.

This man is dangerous, and it's not his stalking tendencies that tell me that, it's the darkness in his eyes.

I stumble backward until I'm against the wall, desperation clawing its way through me like talons against flesh. "Stay away from me," I say, my voice quivering.

He doesn't scare me because he's unhinged. He scares me because of the way he makes me feel. I think that's why I haven't told Piero about him yet. If I had, I know Piero would have tripled my security.

Alejandro.

"What have you done with my bodyguard?" I ask.

A wicked smirk flashes across his beautiful face. "Don't worry, he'll live." He steps into the room, shutting the door behind him and trapping us together.

"I'm expecting room service," I warn.

"Is that supposed to be a threat?"

I narrow my eyes. "I'll beg them to help me."

He laughs and steps closer to me. "No, you won't, Gwendolyne, because you're intrigued."

"Intrigued?" I question.

He keeps moving closer, making butterflies erupt in the pit of my stomach. "Intrigued to learn what I want from you and what will happen between us tonight." He pauses and runs a hand through his dark hair. "If you're ordering room service, it means Piero doesn't have time for dinner with you tonight. Is that right?"

A pang of hurt clenches at my chest because he's right. What kind of man doesn't have time for dinner with his future wife? I fear it might be a preview of what I should expect when we're married. Loneliness.

"What's your point?" I ask.

"If you were mine, princess, I'd have dinner with you every fucking night." He tilts his head. "Or at least, I'd be eating you every night." His chestnut eyes are alight with desire and the way he's talking makes me hotter than I've ever been.

"Is there any point in me asking why you're here?"

His focus shifts from me as he glances around the room, an odd, haunted look in his eyes. He taps his foot rhythmically. "Is there a clock in here?" he asks.

"Yeah, there's one on the wall." I nod to it behind him. "Why?"

It's such an odd question.

His jaw clenches the moment he spots it. "I'm going to have to throw it out the window." He strides toward it before I can say a word.

"No!" I shout, trying to stop him but failing miserably as he shrugs my hand off. "You'll have to pay for damages if you do that."

"Screw the damage," he growls, pulling it from the wall and striding to the window. The window doesn't open wide enough for him to get it out. "Motherfucker!" He hurls the clock violently onto the floor.

I rush over and check it's still working. Thankfully it is. But when I look up, my stomach plummets. He's staring at me with an intensity that could freeze fire—his hatred palpable in the air between us.

"What the hell is wrong with you?" I ask, standing with the clock in my hands.

He moves closer until our faces are so close. "I can't stand clocks, princess," he says darkly. "Their ticking sends me spiraling off the edge…" He shudders. "Get it to fucking stop!"

My scalp prickles with dread at his words, and I feel an intense sensation stirring inside me—something greater than fear.

"There's a simple way to stop it that doesn't involve throwing it out of the window or smashing it." I turn it over and pull the batteries out. "See?"

"I prefer it when there's not one in the room I'm in, working or not."

This guy is fucking insane. I mean, I knew that already, considering he's stalking me, but the clock issue kind of cements the fact that he's batshit crazy.

I place the clock on a nearby chair and step away from him, crossing my arms over my chest. "I want you to leave."

He cocks his head and advances toward me. His intense gaze locks on mine as he backs me against the bed. He reaches out and grabs my hips, leaning in closer, making my heart flutter erratically. "I don't think so, princess," he whispers in a voice that sends chills down my spine. "Why are your cheeks flushed? And why are you breathing so heavily?"

"Because I'm scared," I stammer as his icy fingers graze my skin. "Scared of what you intend to do to me."

He grins. "This is the perfect place for you to explore other options, isn't it?" His gaze moves to the bed behind me. "How about we have some fun, princess?"

"No, this is inappropriate," I murmur, trying to remember why I'm refusing his advances.

Piero.

"I'm engaged to another man."

Thankfully a knock interrupts us, giving me the chance to get away from him and answer the door.

He grabs my arm and stops me. "I'll get it."

I swallow hard as he walks toward the door and opens it. "Thank you so much." He takes a silver tray from the staff at the door.

"No worries. Did you know that the man out here is passed-out?"

My stalker laughs. "Yeah, I think he went a bit heavy on the vodka."

I hear a laugh in return. "Fair enough." And then he shuts us back inside, holding my tray of food.

"I'm hungry," I say, glaring at him. "So if you don't mind, I think it's time for you to leave."

He purses his lips. "I'm hungry too, princess. Now go and lie on the bed so I can feast on you."

Heat prickles across my skin. "Feast on me?"

"Yes, I need to taste that pretty cunt between your legs."

I gasp, unable to believe the way he's speaking. My entire body sets on fire at his words.

"I bet you're so wet and ready for me, aren't you?"

I shake my head. "No. I'm engaged."

"Doesn't stop you from being a human with desires and needs. Let me make you come."

I search his eyes, trying to decipher what the hell I'm feeling right now. All I want is to agree and let this beast have his way with me. A sickening prospect, considering he's stalking me.

"Come on," he says. "Give in and let me make you feel good."

My body practically melts into submission, and I slide onto the bed.

He moves closer, his gaze intent upon me as he trails a finger down my arm. His touch is like fire, igniting something within me that I didn't know existed.

"Such a good girl," he purrs, pushing the hem of my nightgown to my waist. His hands cup my thighs as he parts them, his tongue traces a wet path down my stomach until he reaches my panties. With one tug, they're off and thrown away, leaving nothing between us.

For the first time in my life, I'm exposed, and it makes me hotter than I've ever felt in my life, even that time I was stuck out in the Saharan desert for two fucking days on a stupid desert life experience my dad booked for me.

His eyes dilate with desire. "So fucking beautiful." His tongue flicks against my clit, sending a shock through my body. And then he sucks it into his mouth and I'm lost.

My breathing becomes more frantic as he licks, sucks and teases until I'm panting with desire and pleasure combined into one powerful force of neediness. "Tell me your name," I gasp, wanting to scream it when I come undone.

He shakes his head, an evil glint in his eyes. "I told you, I'm captain to you, princess."

I grind my teeth as it's beyond ridiculous, and yet as

he sucks my clit into his mouth and slides two thick digits inside me, I'm lost.

"Fuck, captain!" I cry, my hips rising from the bed.

"That's right, princess. Such a good girl."

The pressure deep within me builds and I know in that moment I never want this to end.

He increases the rhythm of his tongue and his fingers, expertly teasing me closer and closer to the brink. I'm almost there, so close I can feel it as he slows and withdraws his fingers before covering my clit with his mouth again.

My body trembles in anticipation, focused on that one spot.

He smiles wickedly, his eyes alight with pleasure as I spasm around his fingers.

"Yes, captain!" I scream out, unable to hold back as wave after wave of pleasure takes over my body until I collapse in a blissful state.

He flips me over and starts massaging my back, his fingers working their magic as they knead the tight spots in my neck and shoulders. And yet, fear and anticipation overwhelm me as I'm naked. If he wanted, he could slam his cock inside me and tear away my virginity in an instant, and there's nothing I could do to stop it.

And when I'm sure he's about to, he kisses my spine. "You are such a good girl, Gwendolyne," he purrs into my ear. The bed shifts as he gets off, and I turn to face him, frowning.

"Where are you going?"

He smirks, tilting his head. "Why? Were you hoping I was going to fuck you?"

I swallow hard, realizing how insane that is. "No." I shake my head. "But you could have."

"Don't worry, princess." He winks at me. "I'll be making that pussy mine soon."

My brow furrows. "No way. I will make sure you can't get within fifty feet of me from now on."

He laughs. "I'm not the type to give up, so you better be ready to surrender, because I'm coming for you." He winks and turns away, slamming the hotel door behind him and leaving me to bask in the shame of what happened. Not to mention, it suggests that this isn't the last time I'm going to see him, and sickeningly enough, that ignites a flush of excitement in the pit of my stomach.

Why the hell did I let him do that? And more importantly, how am I going to face Piero?

I bury my head in my hands, clamping my eyes shut, but all I can see is the handsome stranger's face in my mind. My captain. I fear that's becoming a reality.

7

CILLIAN

S myth paces the entryway of my home. "This is dangerous," he says.

I roll my eyes. Smyth has always been pessimistic. "What's so dangerous about it?"

"It's Piero's restaurant, and while he's out of town, his men aren't."

"And your point is?" I ask, running my finger over the blade in my hand.

"My point is, you're running a high risk of getting caught."

I shake my head, fixing Smyth with a glare. "After all these years of working together, do you not know better than to question me?"

He gulps, the colour draining from his face when he realizes his mistake. At times, Smyth oversteps the mark. "Sorry... I think it's too dangerous to go into that viper's den."

I laugh without humor, a cold laugh full of venom

and hate. "Piero is a mouse compared to me. Do you understand?"

My loyal second-in-command has been with me since that start and he knows what Piero did to me. Everything he took from me and my family. Even so, I'm back in California now, corrupted beyond measure—and Piero won't stand a chance against me in a one-on-one fight if it comes to it. I'm going to take back what is mine.

Smyth looks at me, nodding in agreement. "I understand. When do you want to leave?"

I glance out the front door as my other men bring the van around. "Now. And I don't want to hear another word about this being a bad idea."

His brow furrows. "What do you intend to do with his fiancée?"

I'm not ready to tell Smyth that I'm going to marry her, so I shrug. "Haven't decided yet."

We both get into the back of the van as Tim is driving us to Los Angeles. It's a long and tedious journey, with Smyth sulking in one corner and my other two men fast asleep. I feel like I'm going insane until the van jerks to a sudden stop.

I glance at Tim. "Are we here?"

"Yes, sir," he says.

This is it.

"Okay, all of you stay in the van and listen listen via comms for anything going wrong. If something does happen, come in guns blazing. Got it?"

Smyth nods, and I glance at the other two men in

the back, Jeremy and Oliver. Each of them give me a silent nod in response.

Tim clears his throat up front. "Got it, sir."

"Good. Now make sure you don't fuck up this easy job," I say, keeping my gaze fixed on Smyth, daring him to challenge me again. He doesn't say a word, pursing his lips together.

I step out of the van and walk from the alleyway toward the main street before turning left toward Piero's restaurant, *Vincenzo's*.

It may have been ten years since I last had a conversation with Piero, but still, my hatred of him hasn't diminished. It has grown stronger as time passes. If he were at the restaurant, I couldn't say with certainty that I wouldn't do something fucking stupid if I came face to face with him. When I saw him at the engagement party, I felt my blood boil and the bloody visions race through my mind were desperate to become reality, but I need to buy my time.

According to my men, he's out of town. They'd better be right, as today isn't about him. It's about snatching the leverage I want to use against him, his beautiful fiancée Gwendolyne Tesoro: an innocent lamb caught between two ravenous wolves.

As I walk to the restaurant, the tension rises. The security here is heavy for a restaurant, but I straighten my back and climb the steps, giving the guard a confident glare.

He steps aside, and the tension eases. I slip inside, my heart pounding hard. This is my chance to make

Piero pay for what he's done. It's time to take back control.

The interior of Vincenzo's is what I'd expect from Piero. The marble floors are intricately designed and filled with stunning detail that one can appreciate in person, but must have cost an arm and a leg. Large glass chandeliers hang from above, illuminating each piece of expensive and original artwork with a soft glow that further heightens their beauty.

My attention shifts away from the decor and I scan the room for Gwendolyne. The treasure who has captivated my mind ever since we met two weeks ago. I haven't been able to stop replaying the kisses we've shared or the way she came apart so beautifully on my face in her hotel room.

As I enter the main dining hall, I scan the room and instantly my eyes snag on her. I move toward the bar, unable to tear my gaze away. I want her in a way I've never wanted a woman. She's pure and angelic and everything I'm not.

Gwendolyne Tesoro has the ability to shock me each time I see her beauty. She's dressed in a light pink dress that hugs her curves. Her cheeks are flushed and her emerald green eyes sparkle like gems. She looks angelic with the light from the chandeliers glinting off her luminous skin, casting a warm glow around her. And I'm as sure as I was when I first met her. She's a rare and precious gem worth stealing.

I can tell she's nervous; she's twisting a napkin between her fingers and tapping her foot on the floor beneath the table.

I can't stem the dark need to devour her whole and spit her out, devoid of all the light she emanates now. My cock is hard, as the memories of our meetings flash through my mind. Her spread on her hotel bed with her thighs wide apart while I devoured her pretty cunt.

I sit at the bar, watching her from afar and scanning the room, making sure Piero isn't here. My eyes snag on his second-in-command, Tino, disappearing into the back room.

Fuck.

He is a complication I didn't need, but if he stays out back, he shouldn't cause any problems. All I need is one moment when she's alone and unprotected to steal her away before anyone has time to realize what's happened.

As always, her bodyguard isn't doing his job. He's chatting up two women at the bar while Gwen sits alone. And despite the fact that her security has doubled since the night at the hotel, the second bodyguard isn't here. Perhaps she didn't want him here with Piero meeting her, as it would arouse his suspicion.

After a few minutes, her eyes snap in my direction and all the blood in my body rushes south. They meet mine, the emerald green even more intense when her gaze is directed at me. I swallow hard, clenching my fists by my side.

Her eyes flash with desire and recognition for a moment, but that's replaced with annoyance. She glances away from me in an attempt to hide the blush creeping up her neck and into her cheeks.

I bet she's soaking wet at the sight of me. It's

surprising she hasn't stood and approached me, but she thinks she's meeting Piero here. Which means she wouldn't want him running into the man who licked her to climax three nights ago.

Shaking my head, I clear the dirty thoughts from my mind. I need to focus. Not only does this form part of my revenge plan, if she were to marry Piero it would link the Los Angeles and San Diego Italian outfits, making life difficult for me. Jovani, her father, is my rival in the city and his power would increase exponentially.

How am I going to get her alone?

I can't take my eyes from her, even as she looks again to find me staring at her still. And I see desire and fear in her expression. She knows that I'm not like Piero, that I'm a different breed of danger altogether. She's right to be scared, because I'm going to steal her tonight and she's never going to escape.

The thought of dragging her away from here and taking her back to my home makes my veins hum with excitement. There's a sense of anticipation in her eyes as she watches me back, and I wonder what my little princess is thinking. I wonder how dirty her mind can be. I wink at her, and that forces her eyes away as she blushes a darker red and focuses on her drink.

Tino returns from the back and I notice his eyes zero in on Gwen, his brow furrowing.

Shit.

I think my plan is about to get foiled. If he reveals to her that Piero is out of town and there's no way he can be meeting her here, then her suspicion will land on me.

Tino speaks to her and takes a seat. I need to get

out of sight. When Gwendolyne realizes there's a plot afoot to draw her here, she'll point fingers at the man who has been stalking her the past couple of weeks; me.

I walk toward the bathroom at speed, keeping my eyes on her as I take a path around the outer side of the restaurant. Her eyes move to where I'd been standing and I realize that she's talking about me.

"How's it going, boss?" Smyth asks in my ear as I walk into the men's restroom.

"Not so well. Tino has spotted Gwen and is with her now."

"Fuck," he says through the earpiece. "What are you going to do?"

"She's been here awhile. The likelihood is she'll use the bathroom before she leaves."

"And if she doesn't?"

I clench my jaw, as I don't want to think of that eventuality. Piero is out of town until tomorrow, which means if she leaves, I have no choice but to try to get to her at The Ritz, where she's staying. It won't be easy, as she's got more security with her. "I'll think about it if we come to it."

Smyth clears his throat. "Yes, sir. Let me know if you need anything."

All I can do now is wait and see if Gwendolyne comes to the restroom. "Keep an eye out for her leaving the premises."

"Of course," he confirms.

I feel rage surge through my veins as I slam my fist into the countertop. Tino has to go and fuck everything up. As if the universe has made a decision to laugh at me, mock my efforts in a cruel joke.

I gaze at my reflection in the mirror, seeing the stranger staring back. Ten years ago, I was weak; someone played by those who knew how to manipulate me. Now, I'm hardened by the betrayal of my closest friend—a moment that sealed my fate.

"Get it together, Cillian," I grit out through clenched teeth, trying to focus on my main goal rather than allow myself to spiral into the darkness.

That's when I hear it: *Tick-Tock, Tick-Tock.* No wonder I'm going fucking insane. An annoying reminder of time slipping away from me and a sound that turns me into a monster.

In a fit of anger, I stalk over to the wall clock and smash it with one slam of my fist. Glass shatters and cuts open my skin in the process. But even though pain shoots through me, it's comforting knowing that I've stopped the relentless ticking.

I turn away and walk out of the men's restroom to go and check where Gwendolyne is, not caring that I'm bleeding.

As if like fucking magic, the sound of her heels against the hardwood floor echos as she walks my way. She's not looking where she's going. I stand in her path and she slams right into my chest. The unsuspecting little lamb has walked straight into the wolf's claws, and I'll be damned if I let her go.

8

GWENDOLYNE

"Gwen, what are you doing here?" Tino takes a seat by my side.

I don't understand why Piero isn't here. He left a message asking me to meet him here at eight o'clock. He's over an hour late now. And to add to it all, the stranger who's been stalking me is here. It makes the guilt I feel over wanting him deepen, as I'm supposed to be meeting Piero.

"Piero left me a message on my cell to meet him here."

His brow furrows. "That's not possible. Piero's out of town until tomorrow."

I pull my cell phone out. "Here, listen." I play the message and Tino listens, looking perplexed as it sounds like him.

"That must be a doctored message. It sounds real, but if you turn the sound up." He grabs my phone and increases the volume and I can hear the slight jarring, as if messages have been cut and pasted together.

"Oh, my God. Who would do that?" I ask, glancing at the bar. It's a silly question, as I know my stalker must be behind it. When I search for him, he's gone.

"I think someone is fucking with you." He purses his lips. "I'd be worried that someone drew you here on purpose, but how long have you been here?"

"Over an hour now." I pause, glancing toward the spot where my stalker was sitting. "Do you think I should call my father's security to collect me?"

Tino nods. "I think it is wise you return to the hotel. But don't worry about ringing your father's men. I'll get a couple of our guys as extra security to escort you back to the Ritz."

"Are you sure?" I ask.

"Of course. Piero would kill me if I didn't ensure your safety."

I swallow hard, wondering if he means that figuratively. Piero is a ruthless mobster, so it wouldn't surprise me if he means literally. "Okay, thank you."

"Sit tight and I'll go and get some guys together."

"Do you think it's safe for me to use the restroom?"

Tino laughs. "Yes, you'll be fine. This place has heavy security."

I smile, grateful that he came to my rescue. I might have sat here until closing. "Thanks. I'll be back in a minute." I stand and head toward the ladies' restroom, feeling tense and on edge. I know that Piero has enemies everywhere, and any of them could try to get to me, but it's not something I've considered before.

As I round the corner to the ladies' room, I slam into something hard. His scent is the first thing I detect;

masculine and woody. My breath hitches as I glance up to see those chestnut brown eyes staring at me with a hungry look in them that makes me want to run for the hills.

Who is this man and why is he here?

First, he appears at the engagement party, then Macy's and my hotel room. And now I get a weird request to meet Piero and he's here. I sense that this man is behind it all. "S-sorry, I didn't see you—"

"Quiet, princess," he murmurs, his voice as sinful as the rest of him. "You're who I wanted to bump into again. Have you been dreaming of our time together?"

Fear and excitement swirl in my stomach as the way this man makes me feel I don't understand. Piero is gorgeous, but there's something about this man that makes my body set on fire with one look. I haven't been able to stop thinking about him since the party, but I shake my head. "Certainly not," I say.

He smirks. "I'm not sure I believe you."

"Why is it you wanted to bump into me?"

"Because I invited you here."

I swallow hard, as I wasn't expecting him to confess. "You sent that message to my voicemail?"

He nods and grabs my hips, making me gasp the moment his hands are on me. And then he yanks me into the bathroom, slamming the door shut and turning the lock on the door. Fear fills me as he turns around, a wicked look in his eyes. "You're going to come with me. We can do it the easy way or the hard way. It's entirely up to you."

"And what is your exit strategy?" I ask.

His smirk is villainous as he advances toward me. "I hope that's not what you're pinning your hopes on, that I can't get you out of here." He tilts his head. "Why do you think I waited to approach you when you went to the bathroom?"

I glance around and notice two large frosted windows leading out to the back alley of the restaurant and all the blood drains from my body.

I need to stall and hope Tino comes looking for me. "So, what's the easy option?"

"You climb out of that window over there and go with me without question or putting up a fight."

I bite my inner cheek, knowing that whatever this man wants from me, it can't be good. "And the hard way?"

"A part of me hopes you choose it, so I get to carry your sweet ass out of the window." He licks his bottom lip. "I wouldn't mind getting my hands on you again, princess."

"Don't call me that." I hate that this man is assuming I'm a weak-willed woman who will roll over for him. "And I think I'll take option three."

He tilts his head in intrigue. "And what is option three?"

Grabbing a knife out of my pocket, I point it at him. "Fight you to the fucking death."

His eyes flash with appreciation. "You've got fire, I like it."

My dad taught me how to fight from a young age, even though it isn't feminine. It was more important that I remained safe if anything like this happened.

"Give it your best shot," I say, getting into a defensive stance.

"I'm not going to fight you."

"Why? Because I'm a woman?"

He smirks. "No, because I need you in one piece."

"For what?"

He sighs heavily. "You women and questions." He starts forward and I jab at him with the knife, slicing the skin on his right arm as he tries to grab me.

He hisses as blood pools at the wound, eyes narrowing to slits. "That wasn't nice, was it?"

"Did you think I was bluffing?" I shake my head. "I will stab you through the heart without hesitation."

His smile widens. "Oh, I don't doubt it, Gwendolyne." And then he moves forward again, but this time he reads my move before I make it and manages to disarm me, knocking the knife a few feet away by the door.

Shit.

"How about we go at this without weapons?"

I swallow hard and nod, putting my fists up in anticipation. The man circles me, the way a lion does its prey, until I have to turn around and back away, trying to keep him in my sight. Impatience unfurls within me as he has yet to make a move, so I dart forward and swing my fist toward him.

He catches it in his hand and pulls me closer, his flawless face inches from mine. "Try again." He pushes me away.

I swallow hard, realizing that he's toying with me. Although I know how to fight, I've never had to use my skills in a real-life situation. Something tells me that this man has countless times.

My heart races as we both step in circles around the room, eyes fixed on each other. You'd think by now, Tino would have gotten suspicious why I'm not back from the restroom yet, but there's no sign of a rescue party.

Darting forward, I fake swing and change direction, landing a punch to his abdomen.

Instead of doubling over as I expect, a smile stretches onto his face and he manages to capture my wrist, yanking me toward him so that my back is flush against his hard, muscular body. "Is that the best you can do, Gwen?" he whispers into my ear, his breath teasing my earlobe.

I'm fucked.

My heart stutters when I feel a hard bulge against my ass. "You know all this fighting has got me hard as fuck, baby," he murmurs into my ear.

I try to fight away, hating the way an illicit thrill spreads through my body at his touch. Even though he's about to take me captive, I can't deny the electric connection between us. "Please, don't."

He laughs in my ear as his hands slide around mine and immobilize them against my stomach. His lips brush against my earlobe as he speaks. "I could think of a better use of all that energy, such as riding my cock with your tight virgin cunt, for one."

I gasp at his dirty words. "I'll never sleep with you."

"Oh, Gwen, you will. Because you're mine now."

If this man knew what kind of power he had over

me. His words should scare me, but feeling his cock against my ass does something to me I can't explain.

"And I'm never letting you go," he adds.

The word *never* breaks the haze over my mind, making me panic and try to break his hold. He's too powerful.

And then I hear Tino's voice. "Gwen, are you okay? You've been in there a long time."

It's about fucking time.

My stalker covers my mouth with his hand before I can reply, dragging me backward toward the open window. I struggle against him, but he's too powerful.

"Quiet, baby," he breathes, pulling his hand off my mouth to maneuver me out the window.

"Tino!" I scream his name. "Help!"

"Fuck's sake," he growls, pushing me out onto the street first.

I get to my feet and run as fast as I can. A door to a van opens in front of me, blocking my path. A man stares at me from the back of it. "Alright, sweetheart?"

"No, please help! There's a man chasing me." I glance back to see my stalker smirking at me. He's not running.

The man in the back of the van smirks.

"Oh fuck," I say, as he lunges at me and yanks me inside.

"Got her, boss!"

"Start the engine. We need to get the fuck out of here now," my stalker says, jumping into the back of the van with me. "Little Gwen decided to scream, didn't you?"

I swallow hard as the doors shut and I'm trapped inside with these men.

"I'll have to punish you when we get to our destination." He has a wicked look in his eyes. "Come and sit on my lap, Gwen."

I shake my head. "I'm fine here, thanks."

He smirks. "It wasn't a request, it was an order."

The other men chuckle as they watch me.

Instead of obeying, I glare at him, crossing my arms over my chest. "You'll have to make me."

"Oh, I'm going to have so much fun breaking this one, Smyth," my stalker says, nodding toward me. "Bring her over here and put her on my lap," he orders.

"Yes, boss."

Smyth comes over and yanks me up, despite the fact the van is moving. We both stumble together, but he reaches his boss and ungracefully deposits me on his lap.

"Much more cozy like this, wouldn't you say?" he asks, his lips against my ear. "You have such a beautiful ass. Shame to have it sitting anywhere else." His powerful arms wrap around me, trapping me in a cage against his chest.

Fear overcomes me as I realize that there's no way out. I'm in the clutches of a monster and I get the sense he has no intention of letting me go. All I can do is hope that Piero comes to my rescue. Tino knows I've been snatched. The question is, does he know who this stranger is?

9

CILLIAN

We drive away from the city while I hold Gwen in my arms. Her warm body is pressed against my chest and her ass is firmly in my lap, making desire blaze through me like wildfire. Every nerve ending in my body is alive and begging to be fed.

She's so fucking perfect in every way. And soon, she'll be all mine.

I can feel the dampness of her arousal has soaked through her panties, leaving a wet patch on my pants. "Fuck," I breathe, only loud enough for her to hear. "You are making a mess of my pants, princess. Such a naughty girl."

A dark flush spread up her neck and face, painting her a deep red. She clears her throat. "I don't know what you're talking about."

I chuckle, my fingers tightening on her thighs.

She draws in a gasp. "Please stop," she breathes.

"Stop what, princess? I'm not doing anything."

Her lips purse together and she glares at me. "You know what."

The van rattles to a stop outside the old safe house I keep secret from everyone other than my top men.

"Do you need help, sir?" Smyth asks as he opens the door of the van.

I shake my head. "No, that'll be all for today, Smyth." Wrapping an arm around her waist, I drag her out of the van. Her feet barely touch the ground as I haul her toward the front door.

Her words are a raspy whisper as she fights against me. "Where are you taking me?"

"No questions, princess."

I force her into the old, dusty home. Her nose wrinkles as she looks around. Of course, this spoiled little brat would turn her nose up. This isn't where I live. It's an inconspicuous hideout and somewhere Piero will never find his pretty little fiancée.

She fights me at every step as I drag her up the stairs and into the bedroom where I want to keep her. It's the only room in the house we cleaned and decorated, especially for her.

Throwing her onto the bed, I lock the door behind me.

"Stay away from me!" she shrieks, jumping to her feet as she tries to search for an escape, but there isn't one.

"Calm down, princess." I tilt my head. "You won't find a way out, so it's best to conserve your energy."

Her emerald eyes are wide with fear as she glances at me, and that look makes my cock harden in my pants.

"What do you want from me?"

I bite my lip and step toward her. "What don't I want?" Moving closer to her, I revel in the way she trembles. This exquisite and innocent little thing is going to be my wife before long.

"Stay away from me," she warns, attempting to look tough. Her eyes give her away.

"That's the last thing I intend to do." I close the gap between us and curl my hands around her hips, yanking her body flush against mine. "You see, Gwendolyne, I intend to get close and personal with you," I murmur, moving one hand to her throat and squeezing gently, enjoying the way her pulse accelerates beneath my palm. "Such a delectable morsel and all for me."

"No! I'm Piero's fiancée. You can't touch me, he'll kill you."

I laugh, amused by the fact she thinks that I'm scared of Piero. "Exactly the reason I'm taking you. I intend to steal everything from that slimy son of a bitch, starting with you."

Her lip wobbles as she tries to take a step back, but I hold her firm. "What are you going to do with me?"

"Such a good question." I release her and she moves away. "I'm going to do so many dirty and wicked things to you."

Her face turns from flushed to beet red as she backs away from me. "You can't. I don't want you."

"I know that's a lie. When I'm through with you, you won't even remember your fiancé's name."

She shakes her head. "I highly doubt that. Piero and I have a connection."

Rage burns within me, and I grab her by the throat, only this time with force. "I don't care what you and Piero have. I'm going to fucking obliterate it."

She shakes and the fear in her eyes heightens as I block her airways. Those delicate fingers wrap around my wrist as she tries to pry my hand away.

"If you have any sense, you won't mention Piero or any connection you have with him ever again," I snarl. That man is the bane of my fucking existence, and I'll be damned if I'll stand here and listen to her gush about her connection with him. "In fact, how about I make you forget him right now?"

Grabbing her hips, I force her to turn around and push her toward the bed. I bend her over so that her face is in the covers.

"Please, stop!" she screams, trying to kick away from me. She's feisty and strong, but not strong enough to overpower me.

"It would be easier if you stayed still, but I like you fighting, princess," I say, hiking the hem of her pretty pink dress to her hips and groaning when I see she's wearing a thong, the string is sitting between her beautiful pussy lips and it's soaking wet with arousal as is the hem of her skirt. Grabbing it with my finger, I push it to the side. "For a woman who insists she's head over heels for Piero, you're fucking dripping wet for me." I spank her firm ass cheeks, knowing that I've never seen such a beautiful fucking cunt in all my life.

She gasps as I swat her ass four more times, her pussy getting visibly wetter at my rough treatment.

"Perhaps you like being manhandled." My fingers

dance over her soaking wet lips. "Every touch is making you wetter, princess," I say, shocking myself at the huskiness of my tone.

"Please," she murmurs, but it's not clear what she's begging for.

"Please, what, princess?" I ask, dropping to my knees behind her. I press my nose against her pussy and inhale. "Fucking hell, virgin pussy never smelled so damn good, Gwen."

She stiffens. "Why do you think I'm a virgin?"

"It's obvious. You're a mafia princess, kept under lock and key until marriage." I lick her, making her shudder. "And it tastes as fucking beautiful as I remember."

"Maybe I've had sex with Piero," she says, making my blood boil.

"Unlikely," I say, knowing that her father wouldn't have allowed that to happen. "You're a virgin princess, and don't try to deny it."

"This is wrong…"

I spank her ass. "No, it's right. Let's not try to pretend that this is the first time I've tasted you. The evidence you want it is here in front of me with your dripping wet pussy." I lick her again, groaning at how sweet she tastes. As sweet as I remember. "And I'm going to devour you again." Before she can say another word, my tongue is dancing in circles around her clit. I savor the taste, licking and sucking before I let out something between a moan and growl. "This pussy is mine."

"Please, I'm engaged," she protests weakly.

I continue until she's moaning. I run my tongue

through the length of her pussy, licking around her opening before diving in deep. I don't want to miss a single bit of her as I've craved this for three days, pushing further until I'm practically consuming her, loving the way she moans and begs me to stop as she pushes her hips back against my mouth.

My cock throbs in the confines of my pants, but I ignore it. Right now, I want her to forget all about that bastard Piero. It's all about her.

Once she's panting and gasping for oxygen, arching her back like she wants me to fuck that eager cunt, only then do I slide two fingers into her tight little hole.

"Oh, fuck, yes!" she cries.

I smirk, as this is going to be so much fun—forcing her to forget about the man I hate most in this world.

I continue to pleasure her. Using two digits, I thrust in and out of her, giving her what she needs, using my tongue to tease her clit.

Her moans are more desperate as I increase my pace and pressure, pushing both fingers deeper until I feel her muscles clamp around me like a vise. That urges me to curl my fingers forward, hitting the spot that has her shattering for me so beautifully. I keep going for a few moments before finally pulling my fingers out of her soaking wet pussy.

She's still shaking when I stand and yank her around to face me, groaning as my cock strains against the zipper of my pants, desperate to be free.

Her cheeks are flushed and she looks satisfied and fucking beautiful. "I-I…" She shakes her head. "I don't know your name."

I smile. "No, you don't."

Her eyes flash with anger. "Are you going to tell me?"

"Not sure. That all depends on how well you behave."

"Behave?" she says, shaking her head. "You're behaving disgustingly!"

I chuckle, finding her opinion amusing. "Strange, considering you came so beautifully, screaming 'yes' at the top of your lungs."

Gwen's jaw tightens in barely concealed fury. "You're infuriating."

I yank her closer, gripping her chin in one hand while my other moves between her legs again. "Admit to me that you enjoyed the way I behaved, princess," I murmur, stroking her tender and swollen flesh.

My touch elicits a shiver of pleasure and anticipation, causing her beautiful eyes to dilate. I force her hand onto my crotch and groan as she grips me tightly, stirring all kinds of delicious sensations. With a smirk that leaves little doubt about the evil thoughts lurking in my mind, I say, "You can feel how badly I want you." I need release, but I don't intend to get it from her, not yet.

"You're sick," Gwen seethes through gritted teeth, releasing her grasp on my throbbing dick.

I laugh, not denying it. "Yes, I am. But I don't care," I reply. "Because my hatred for Piero knows no bounds and I'll have him on his knees by the time I'm through with him."

Shaking her head slowly in disbelief, Gwen finally

breaks the heavy silence with a hushed whisper. "So what now?"

A smirk stretches across my face and I lean forward until our breath mingles together. "Now you wait for me to return and dream about sitting on my cock," I purr before letting go of her chin and sauntering away from her, locking her in the bedroom. My whistle echoes through the hallway as I revel in the knowledge that the most precious gem is soon to be mine. Claiming Gwendolyne Tesoro is going to be *almost* as enjoyable as watching Piero lose everything.

10

CILLIAN

"*P*iero has hit the fan. He's got men searching everywhere for Gwendolyne. And so has her father." Smyth paces the room. "Do you think he'll suspect us?"

Stupid Smyth, always underestimating me and my plans.

"No chance. He's too wrapped up in his own world to pay attention to me or what I've been doing the past ten years since he fucked me over." It's a fact. If he was threatened by me, he'd know that I've been living not that far from him, rebuilding an empire in San Diego. And I'm sure he would have come for me, but Piero has always been bad at focusing on details.

"I hope you're right," Smyth says, always the pessimist.

I roll my eyes and stand, walking over to the server who had hit on me the other day. "Hey."

Her eyes widen and she smiles. "Hey, how are you Cillian?"

I smirk at her. "Better now that I've seen you."

Her lips purse. "I'm surprised to hear that, considering the way you acted the other day."

I grab her hip, yanking her toward me and slipping a hand under her skirt. "I was in a bad mood, that's all."

Her eyes light up as she moves toward me. "Shall we go somewhere private?"

I lean toward her ear. "Lead the way."

The woman, whose name I still don't fucking remember, takes me into the main office. I shut the door behind us and move toward her, pressing my lips to hers.

Instantly, all I can think about is Gwendolyne fucking Tesoro. Her flushed cheeks and angelic fucking face are right there in my mind as my tongue thrusts into this woman's mouth. Feral need overcomes me as I lift her and place her on the desk, peppering kisses over her neck. "Fuck, Gwen, you are so delicious."

The woman before me stiffens. "Who's Gwen?"

Fuck.

I pull back, running a hand across the back of my neck. "I'm going to be honest. I don't remember your name."

Her eyes flash with fury. "Are you fucking serious? We've been sleeping together for weeks."

I clench my jaw. She's insane if she thought I was only fucking her. "Have we? I wouldn't know I fuck so many of the staff."

She slaps me, and I grab her wrist. "Careful, little girl," I warn, glaring at her. "It's not a good idea to prod a crocodile. You might lose something."

Her expression turns from rage to fear. "Fine, let me

go," she mutters, looking at the floor. "I've got work to do."

"Yes, you do, but not here."

Her eyes widen. "What?"

"You're fired. Do you think I'd keep paying your paycheck when you assaulted me?"

Her nostrils flare and I can tell she wants to bite back, but instead she nods and marches out of the office, slamming the door behind her.

I bend over the desk with my hands braced on the surface and shut my eyes, trying to calm the storm brewing within me. Fucking Gwendolyne Tesoro is cramping my style already.

She's all I can think about since I kidnapped her. The rage within heightens and I growl, swiping my hands across the desk and knocking documents onto the floor.

I glance at the floor and pause when I see a ledger on the top, a few key items circled in red. Bending, I pick it up.

What the fuck is this?

My heart races as I scan the paper, my eyes widening in shock. It's proof that someone in my organization is leaking details to my enemy. As in the past three months, all the circled shipments have been stolen.

As if I don't have enough on my plate right now, I need to work out who is fucking me over.

Smyth is surely too stupid, and yet I wouldn't put it past him. It means I'll have to investigate this myself without help from anyone if I want to ensure I catch the rat.

Whoever it is can't be smart, leaving this in here for anyone to find. Granted, I rarely come back here. The question is, who does?

I fold the ledger and place it in my pocket, walking out of the office. I need to find out who is responsible and put a stop to it. And when I find the rat, I'll make him squeal as I subject him to the worst torture imaginable.

Smyth gives me an odd look as I return to the table. "Why did Kirsty run out of the office crying and leave during her shift?"

"*Kirsty.* I thought that was her name." I run a hand through my hair. "She slapped me and I fired her."

Smyth shakes his head. "When are you going to listen and stop fucking the staff?"

"Do you know who you're talking to?" I snap, feeling on edge as that ledger feels like it's burning a hole in my pocket. Someone potentially in this club right now is a traitor.

"I apologize, I'm merely stating—"

"Don't," I say simply, grabbing my scotch and taking a long gulp. "I have no intention of continuing to fuck the staff, as I'm getting married."

Smyth's eyes widen. "You are?"

"Yes, to Gwendolyne Tesoro."

He spits out a gulp of beer, splattering me with it.

"What the fuck?" I say, wiping it off my face.

"I could say the same thing. Jovani Tesoro will murder you."

I know that Jovani will be an issue, but I'll come to that bridge later. "He can try."

"I thought you wanted her to piss Piero off and fuck her, not make her your God damn wife."

"Stealing her and marrying her, so that he can't have her, is the ultimate way to piss him off."

Smyth sighs, clearly realizing that he can't persuade me to reconsider. Once I've made a decision, there's no changing it. "When are your nuptials taking place?"

"Not decided yet, but it won't be too long."

His eyes narrow. "And what is your end game?"

"You know my end game. Take everything from Piero."

"Right, yeah, but marrying the girl?" His nose wrinkles in disgust.

"Have you seen her, Smyth? Or are you as blind as you are stupid?"

His jaw clenches. "Yes, I've seen her. She's beautiful, for sure, but—"

I grab his throat. "Have you been looking at what is mine?" I ask, feeling a possessive rage unfurling in my veins.

His eyes are so wide they look like they're going to pop out of the sockets. "No," he rasps out.

I release his throat. "Keep your eyes off her, do you understand? She's mine."

Smyth rubs his throat. "I'm definitely not interested in her, sir."

I always forget that Smyth prefers male company to female. "Fuck, sorry. Of course you aren't." I clap him on the shoulder. "I often forget."

There's an odd expression in his eyes that I can't

quite place. "No worries," he says, grabbing his scotch and knocking the entirety back.

"You'll be my best man, of course," I say.

He smiles, but it looks forced. "Of course." His eyes dart toward two of the staff who are gazing over here with doe eyes. "Does that mean you're going to leave the girls alone from now on?"

I nod. "Yes, I'm a one-woman man now." I pause. "At least until I get bored." I wink at him and hold my glass up in a toast. "To marriage."

I'VE CHECKED the CCTV at the bar, but there are too many men using that fucking office. It means I need to find someone to do covert digging who has no ties to my organization. Hence, the reason I'm standing outside of a fucking hillbilly shack in the hills. I didn't know there were shit holes like this here, but it's apparently the home of one of the best private detectives in the state.

"Hello?" I shout, noticing the door is ajar.

The door slowly creaks open, revealing a tall and slender figure wearing an ill-fitting suit standing in the doorway.

"Yes, can I help you?"

"We spoke on the phone," I say, rubbing a hand across the back of my neck. "Cillian."

"Ah, yes, of course." He opens the door wide. "Come on in."

I walk into the ramshackle of a place which consists of only two rooms.

"Mind the mess. I understand you need someone to work out who the traitor is in your organization. Is that right?"

"Yeah, I found this in my office." I pass him the ledger, feeling uneasy, handing over my ledgers to a stranger. However, my cousin Henderson vows that he's the best and won't fuck me over. "All the circled shipments are ones that got hit by the Tesoro mafia."

His lips press together. "I don't normally get involved in organized crime, but since Henderson sent you." He looks at me. "I'll make an exception."

"Thanks. Whatever the fee is, consider it paid."

He nods. "It might take a while, but I'll do my best to get this figured out for you. I assume you want it done in absolute secrecy?"

"Of course."

"Very well. It will be a covert operation and I'll have to tail possible suspects to rule them out. To ensure that the investigation is kept entirely under the radar, I'll need you to write a list of who you suspect may be guilty.

I nod in agreement. "That sounds like a plan."

"We'll also need to look into surveillance footage we can find at your club, the drop sights, and the docks. The footage may show something unusual or out of the ordinary happening, or provide insight into who is responsible."

I grind my teeth, as Smyth normally handles correspondence at the docks. "Fuck, okay, I'll get hold of it."

He tilts his head. "If you can't, I can."

"I'll let you know. It's not normally my style to visit the docks, so I don't want people to get suspicious."

He nods. "Makes sense. I can go and get a copy of the CCTV footage on those dates. Once I've got them, I'll let you know if I see anything suspicious."

I pause a moment, looking at the man whose name I don't know because he likes to remain elusive. "So you won't tell me your name?" I ask.

He shakes his head. "No, it's part of my policy."

I sigh heavily. "Fair enough. Let me know when you find anything. I'll text you a list of the possible suspects."

He nods and puts his hand forward. "It's good to meet you."

I take it and shake his hand, hating that I have to trust someone I don't know. I can't go poking around looking for a rat, as I'll send the bastard scurrying into hiding. A flood of anticipation races through me at the thought of finding who's working against me and slicing him to pieces.

11

GWENDOLYNE

I'm going insane, trapped in a cage like a bird. All I want is to be free and yet the stranger still hasn't returned.

My stomach rumbles. I'm not sure how long it's been since I ate, but it feels like days. Suddenly, I hear a jangle of keys on the other side of the door, forcing me to sit upright.

I expect to see the wicked stranger who kidnapped me, but instead an older woman walks in carrying a tray. "Hello, I'm bringing you your meals from now on, on request of my employer."

I stand and smile at her. "Thank you. What's your name?"

"Mary-Anne," she says simply, but doesn't return the smile.

Walking over, I take the tray. "I'm so hungry, thank you, Mary-Anne."

"You're welcome."

She turns to leave, but I'm so desperate to talk to someone. "Do you want to join me?"

Her brow furrows. "There's only enough for you."

"I don't mind sharing," I say.

"I'll sit with you if you want company, but I won't eat your food."

Nodding, I smile. "Thank you. I would like someone to talk to. How long have I been here?"

"Two days, I believe."

I sit on the sofa and place the tray on the coffee table, pulling the lid off. "It felt far longer. Why is there no clock in here?"

Her eye twitches a little. "The boss doesn't like them."

I purse my lips. "Who is the boss?"

Her jaw clenches. "I can't answer your questions."

Disappointment coils through me, as I only want to know who the hell I've been captured by. "Okay, do you like working for him?"

Her eyes narrow. "I'd rather not talk about him."

I grab a French fry, my mouth watering. "What do you want to talk about?" I ask, biting it and savoring the crispy deliciousness. It may have only been two days, but it feels like I haven't eaten in weeks.

She shrugs. "You're the one who wants the company."

I'm not sure why I want it. She's not exactly friendly. "Right, so what do you do when you're not working?"

Her expression hardens, staring at me for a few beats. "I like to travel," she says simply.

"Oh lovely, anywhere exotic?" I ask, grabbing my

cheeseburger and taking a bite, moaning at how good it tastes.

"I've been all over the world, visiting places most people wouldn't dream of going to. From the highest mountains to the deepest jungles, it's been quite a journey."

"Really?" I say, intrigued, as I've always wanted to travel, but Dad said it was too dangerous. I've only ever been to the Caribbean, and that was only once on a business trip with Dad. Other than that, I've rarely left San Diego.

It appears that my questioning set her off, as she talks about her travels after her husband died, telling me stories as I eat my food. This is what I needed, even if she was reluctant at first to give it. Company, as I'm so used to having someone around, even if it's my bodyguard.

Finally, Mary-Anne finishes, looking a little starry-eyed from recounting the places she's visited.

"Wow, it sounds amazing," I say wistfully. "The thought of leaving this place behind and exploring the world sounds so appealing right now."

Her entire countenance changes as she stiffens, glaring at me. "You can't leave."

"I'm well aware of that."

She shakes her head. "I shouldn't be in here talking to you. You're trying to manipulate me."

I stand, shaking my head. "No, that's not—"

"Quiet, I've had enough of your shenanigans." With that, she turns around and walks out, slamming the door so loud it makes me jump.

I slump into the chair, staring at the shut door as tears gather in my eyes. I don't let them fall. It's weak to cry and it won't get me anywhere, so I grab the basket of fries and continue to eat them, contemplating whether I could overpower Mary-Anne when she comes back next. It might be my only shot at freedom.

LATER ON THAT NIGHT, I hear the jangle of keys again, assuming Mary-Anne has returned with more food. The woman is crazy. All I said was I'd like to get away from here and she practically snapped my head off.

My heart skips a beat when I glance at the door and find my handsome captor leaning against the door-frame, arching a brow at me. "Did you miss me?"

I clench my fists. "Definitely not."

He walks inside and shuts the door. "Such a liar, Gwen."

"I'm not a liar." I hold my head high. "I wish you'd never come back."

His eyes narrow and he stalks toward me like an angry wolf. Once he's a foot from me, he stops, as if suddenly clawing himself back from the edge. "Be careful how you speak to me. I won't hesitate to punish you."

"What is this all about?"

"I told you already. I'm stealing everything from Piero."

I chew on my lip. "Yes, but what's my fate? Are you going to kill me?"

He starts laughing, a deep and wicked sound. "No, that would be counterproductive. I'm going to marry you."

My throat starts to close as I stare into his chestnut brown eyes. "There's no way I'm getting married to you. I don't know your name."

The man's hand wraps forcefully around my throat and he yanks me to my feet. "I've told you to call me captain, princess," he murmurs, his lips moving against the shell of my ear. "Because you'll answer to no one but me."

This man is infuriating, and while he's caught off guard, I manage to lift my knee and slam it into his balls.

"Motherfucker!" he growls as he doubles over.

I rush to the door, as I noticed he didn't lock it. The moment the door opens, I sprint left hoping beyond hope that I will make it outside.

"Run all you like, Gwen. There's nowhere for you to go," he calls. "If I have to restrain you and drag you to the altar, I'm going to do it."

I glance back toward the bedroom to find he's not running after me. Instead, he's walking casually. It terrifies me, as I'm sure it means he's right. He isn't worried about where I run, because I won't make it anywhere.

Even so, I keep running, only to slam into Mary-Anne, who glares at me. "Where do you think you're going?"

"Thanks, Ma," the guy says.

My eyes widen. "You're his mother?"

Mary-Anne smirks at me. "Of course, and you need to go back to your room." She turns me around, forcing me to face the monster who has captured me; the monster she brought into this world.

"You're as sick as him."

The woman sneers at me as Cillian grabs the back of my neck and drags me back into the bedroom, his eyes hot with rage. "You're going to have to learn to obey, and no one insults my ma." With that, he forces me over the bed and lifts the hem of my dress up, the same dress I've been wearing for over two days now.

His hand swats my ass, far more forcefully than the other day.

I yelp at the pain radiating from the spot of impact, unable to catch my breath as he does the same on the other side, repeating over and over until I'm panting in agony and yet throbbing between my thighs.

I can't deny that his dominance turns me on.

"Have you learned your lesson yet, naughty girl?" he purrs, his voice like velvet.

I remain silent, clenching my thighs together as the need for release heightens. But I don't respond. His fingers slip between my legs, causing me to gasp for air as he rubs circles around the wetness that has been building since he started spanking me.

Cillian groans when he feels it, his grip tightening around my waist as he pulls me up so that my back presses against his chest. His breath tickles my neck as he whispers in a voice filled with lust and danger. "Good girl."

Oh fuck.

I don't know what it is about him calling me that, but I'm about ready to beg him to fuck me.

No. I can't think like that.

This man has taken me captive, for God's sake. I'm losing my mind if I want anything from him.

One hand travels under me to cup my left breast, his fingers ripping at the fabric as he frees them, playing with my nipples one by one.

I moan, eyes clamping shut. The sensations he's making me feel are intense. Catching myself, I shake my head. "Stop this."

He licks my earlobe. "I told you to call me captain."

"What is with you and wanting to be called captain?" I ask, infusing my tone with sarcasm.

He chuckles. "If you don't like captain, how about sir?"

I shudder, as this man clearly has a superiority complex. "No thanks."

He growls and spanks my already red ass again. "Call me, sir."

I realized at that moment that I brought this upon myself. Breathing deeply, I mutter, "Sir."

He bites the lobe of my ear. "Like you mean it, Gwendolyne."

"Stop what you're doing, sir," I say, trying to keep the sarcasm from creeping into my tone.

"It'll do," he says, one hand sliding lower to part my thighs. And then he pushes two thick digits inside, making me moan again. "You don't sound like a woman who wants me to stop, though."

I grind my teeth together, trying not to moan again as he slides his fingers in and out, driving me closer to the edge with each movement.

"Time for a taste." He releases me, forcing me face first onto the bed, and drops to his knees behind me.

That's when I feel it, the warmth of his breath grazing my clit as he moves closer. His tongue flicks out, swirling around me in a tantalizing motion before pushing against me. His fingers join in, massaging me and pressing against the sensitive spot deep within. His tongue and lips teasing me and almost pushing me over the edge, only for him to stop abruptly and yank me upright.

I whimper in response, wanting to come so damn badly that I forget everything else. "Please, sir."

"Hmm, try, captain."

"Please, captain," I say, so far gone it's humiliating.

He shakes his head. "No, it's part of your punishment. No orgasm for you. But I intend to come down your pretty little throat."

I tense in fear as he yanks me upright and positions me on the edge of the bed, my eyes in line with his waist. He unbuckles his pants and pulls them down, revealing a huge bulge in a pair of tight briefs. My body heats as I notice the wetness where he's leaking.

"Take it out for me, princess."

I clench my fists and glare at him in defiance.

"Are you sure you want to be defiant right now? I do control whether you get to orgasm."

A part of me wavers as he's using my desperate need for release to manipulate me. Swallowing my pride, I slide my fingers into his briefs and wrap my hand around the velvety steel rod in his pants, pulling it out.

It's huge and veiny and the sight of it makes me want to lie back, spread my legs and beg him to fuck me. A ridiculous notion, considering I'm a virgin and have zero experience.

"Open wide," he orders.

I unhinge my jaw, my fingers still wrapped around the thick length of him. And then he slams his cock into my throat without warning, making me lose grip of him. I gag, thinking I'm going to puke on his cock, but he doesn't relent.

As I gaze at him, he's like an angry and tortured God, taking what he wants from me. His chestnut eyes flash with dangerous intent. "Fuck, Gwen. That throat feels like heaven," he breathes, his hips moving in and out at an unrelenting pace.

He fucks my throat hard and mercilessly, restricting the oxygen in my lungs and making me panic that he'll suffocate me with his dick. I'm sure I look ridiculous, gasping for air between each thrust, but he's barely giving me a chance to breathe. And that restricted oxygen coupled with his dominance gives me what I'd been craving.

I moan around his cock as wave after wave of pleasure crashes inside me, forcing me over the cliff edge.

He growls above me. "You dirty little girl, coming with my cock down your throat." His eyes are alight with such passion it makes my orgasm peak higher. He thrusts once more before spilling his cum down my throat, making me choke and gag as there's too much for me to swallow.

"Beautiful," he muses as he slips his cock from my lips, cum dripping off my chin.

I'm left panting on the bed, eyes wide with shock and disbelief at what transpired between us. It was rough and intense, yet beautiful as well, which is a sick thought.

"Well, your punishment was supposed to be no climax." He rubs his chin as if contemplating. "So, I think I'm going to have to ensure you can't have one while I'm not here instead."

My brow furrows as I'm unsure how he'd be able to ensure that. Walking over to a briefcase, he unlocks it and pulls it open, making my breath hitch at what's inside.

Proof of this man's utter depravity as it's filled with freaky looking sex toys; toys he clearly intends to use on me. He grabs one of the items and holds it. "Chastity belt," he says, smirking wickedly.

I stand and back away. "Please, don't—"

"Don't what? Are you saying you want to play with that pretty little pussy while I'm not here?" His eyes narrow.

I'm pretty sure this guy is insane, as the look in his eyes is borderline manic.

"No, I just—"

"You will wear this like a good girl as I control all of your orgasms from here on. Got it?"

This man is sadistic. The idea of wearing that thing,

which has a God damn dildo attached, is torturous. "Are you serious?"

"Deadly." He walks closer to me. "Now bend over for me like a good girl."

There's no use fighting, so I do as I'm told. I need to formulate an escape plan, but until then, this man controls me. "And you still won't tell me your name?" I ask, bending over with my pussy on display for him.

He affixes the belt, which has a hole no doubt for using the bathroom. The dildo presses deep, making me ache all over again. Once they are clasped together, he leans over my back and whispers in my ear, "Since you are so desperate to know, it's Cillian Hook."

Cillian.

With a quick nip of my earlobe, he stands and walks out of the room, leaving me bent over and filled with shame at what transpired between us. I've never felt such conflicting feelings for a person as Cillian Hook. He makes me hate him and want him all in the same breath.

12

CILLIAN

The old safe house looms before me. The lights are on in the kitchen. It's been a week since I kidnapped Gwendolyne and three days since I last visited her room and lost fucking control. She drives me insane with lust.

Stepping through the door, I find ma in the kitchen stirring a large pot of Irish stew. She hears me enter and turns, smiling widely.

"Ah, Jonathan," she says, her voice cheerful. "There you are, love."

I shake my head. "Ma, we've had this conversation. I'm Cillian, not Jonathan." Sadness unfurls deep in my gut as her condition has been worsening for a while now. She's seen the best specialists in the world and is on meds. It can't stop her dementia, only slow it.

Her expression turns confused for a moment, and she shakes her head. "Sorry, son. You look so like your da at times."

I purse my lips, as I know I resemble him, which

makes me angry. Looking at old photos, you'd think we were brothers other than the fact I'm missing a damn hand because of him. Most people wouldn't have a clue, considering my prosthetic is the best money can buy until I replace it with a hook when I want to intimidate. It's fun to torment my targets with it.

Walking over to her, I place an arm around her shoulders and squeeze. "Don't worry, Ma. It's okay." I sigh. "How is our guest?"

Her jaw clenches. "I'm sure she's trying to manipulate me."

"Manipulate you?"

"Yes, being all friendly, as if she's trying to get me on her side."

I laugh. "Perhaps she is. But you know best not to trust her, don't you?"

She nods. "Of course."

It was a risk putting my ma here with her to take care of her. As with her condition, Gwendolyne might be able to manipulate the situation. Which means I can't keep her here. "Don't worry, I intend to take her back to our home in San Diego tomorrow, and the staff can handle her."

"Oh, I was enjoying it here."

I shake my head. "Well, all good things must come to an end."

"Come and have a bowl of stew," she says, gesturing to the table.

My stomach rumbles as it smells delicious. "I'd never say no to your stew, but let me get a glass of whiskey first."

I notice the disappointment in her eyes as I know she thinks I drink too much, but I grab the bottle of scotch and tumbler off the countertop and take it to the table, sitting and pouring myself a large glass.

She grabs the pot off the stove and places it on a heatproof mat in the center, dishing me a large portion. "Eat up, little Cillian. You want to grow big and strong," she says.

I bite the inside of my cheek to stop myself from correcting her and pointing out that I'm now thirty years old and not ten.

I take a taste and it's as delicious as ever. "It's always so good, Ma."

Her throat bobs as she stares into space. "Your da and sister have been gone ten years now. It's hard to believe."

Pain slams into my chest hearing her talk about them. Well, Kira, since half the time she doesn't remember her, let alone that she's gone. It's rare that she speaks of her at all. "Yes, to the day," I mutter.

Her eyes shine with unshed tears. "I still miss them both every single day."

"So do I," I lie, as I miss Kira. Da can rot in hell for what he did to me. I cast my mind back to that hotel bar, where I saw the news on the television.

Smyth's eyes flick to the television screen on the back wall and the blood drains from his face.

"What's wrong?" I ask, brow furrowing. "You look like you've seen a ghost."

He points at the screen and I shift so that I can see it better. My entire world crumbles as I read the headline.

117

Jonathan and Kira Murphy are found dead at home.

I stare at the words for a long time, trying to make sense of them.

I've never felt more conflicted in a single moment. The relief and joy of seeing Da was dead, coupled with a deep and aching grief at seeing Kira's name there with his.

Why couldn't it have just been him?

Grabbing her hand, I squeeze. "Don't worry, the man responsible is going to be brought to his knees soon."

She nods. "I want you to make him pay dearly, Cillian. You hear me? It's been a long time coming, so do it right."

I arch a brow. "Of course I'll do it right."

"That girl. Who is she to him?"

I clench my jaw as I realize she's talking about Gwen. "His fiancée."

She tilts her head. "By arrangement or choice?"

"Arrangement."

"And what are you going to do to her?"

I drum my fingers on the table. "Marry her."

"What?"

"Yeah, I'm taking everything from Piero, including his fiancée."

"But what about your happiness, son? You don't love her."

I may not love her, but I don't believe I'm capable of love. After all, I'm a mobster and won't marry for love, but for convenience. Once I bring Piero to his knees and

118

destroy everything he owns, Jovani Tesoro will be thankful that I'm the man married to his daughter. At least, that's my hope. Otherwise, I might have to kill him too.

"I don't think I'm capable of love, Ma."

She makes a disapproving sound. "Don't be so ridiculous, Cillian. Everyone is capable of love."

"I'm marrying her and that's final."

She sighs heavily and grabs my hand, squeezing. "Okay, I want you to be happy."

Today my ma isn't too bad. There are days when she's difficult to have a conversation with. "I'll be happy when Piero is dead."

Ma nods. "I know you think that, but there's more to life than getting revenge. Once that's over, I fear you'll be empty, with nothing left to focus on."

My mind strays to the beauty upstairs locked away in her room, and I want to go to her. She has this draw on me that I can't resist, and yet I know I need to resist her for now. Until we're married, I won't take her virginity.

"You want to go to her, don't you?" Ma asks.

I swallow hard. "What?"

"Do you care for her?"

"I hardly know her."

"But you want her in that way?" Ma asks.

"I don't wish to discuss this with you."

She laughs. "Oh, Cillian. I'm not a nun. I know that human beings have needs and you're human."

I shuffle uncomfortably in my chair, not wishing to discuss my oddly primal desire for the woman I've taken captive with my ma, of all people. "I'm attracted to her," I say.

"She's a beautiful girl, and you two would make a lovely-looking couple, if that's what you want." Her eyes light up. "I hope there will be grandchildren."

My stomach churns at the thought of having a baby with Gwendolyne Tesoro, and I wonder if I'm rushing into this. "Are you trying to put me off?"

She laughs. "Not at all." Although there's a glint in her eyes that tells me that's not entirely true. She knows I'd freak out at the mention of children and doesn't want me rushing into this. Desperate to change the subject, I clear my throat. "Someone is working against me in the organization."

"What?"

I nod. "I found a ledger with all the shipments that have been hit in the last couple of months circled."

"Do you know who?"

I shake my head. "It could be anyone." My lips press together. "I'm worried it might be Smyth."

"Surely not. Smyth loves you."

"I don't treat him the best."

She sighs. "No, but I can't see him doing that."

I hope she's right, as all faith in humanity will be lost if I find out my second-in-command and closest thing to a friend is the one who has betrayed me.

"Are you staying here tonight?" she asks.

It's late and I've drunk more than I should to drive, but it opens the door to temptation. If I stay here tonight, there's no way in hell I can keep out of Gwendolyne's room.

"Perhaps," I mutter, not wanting to commit either way.

"With her?" Ma asks.

I grab my scotch and chug the rest of it. "Does it matter?"

Her lips purse together. "No, it's your choice what you do." She sighs heavily, pressing a hand to her forehead.

"Headaches again?" I ask.

"Yes, I get them so often, Cillian."

"Shall I get your pain meds?" I ask.

She shakes her head. "No, I don't like how they make me feel. I'll go and get some rest, I think. An early night."

She isn't kidding as it's eight o'clock.

"Okay, do you want help?"

"I MAY BE LOSING my mind, but my body is more than capable. Thank you very much."

I laugh. "Sorry, Ma."

She ruffles my hair like I'm a kid and leans down to kiss me on the cheek. "Goodnight."

"Goodnight," I say, watching as she walks toward her downstairs room.

Once she's gone, all I can think about is the tempting piece of ass locked away upstairs. My eyes move to the key hanging on the wall and I know there's zero chance of me staying away from her tonight.

I pour myself another large tumbler of scotch and knock it back before standing and grabbing the key. It burns in my hands, warning me that I'm playing with fire, as this girl has gotten under my skin already.

I ignore the warning, unlocking the door and stepping into her room. The floor is covered in a deep red carpet, which makes it easier to get closer without making a noise. I can make out Gwen sleeping peacefully on the bed ahead of me.

She's lying on her stomach in nothing but the chastity belt I fitted the other day, face pressed against the pillow, arms spread out to one side. I can feel my hard cock pressing against my pants as I stand there watching her sleep; imagining what it would be like to fuck her until she wakes with no protection, breeding her pretty little cunt.

The thought alone makes me want to slide into bed with her right now; feel my hands running over that soft skin and my mouth exploring every inch of her body.

That's what I intend to do, but first I need to remove the damned chastity belt and clean her up. I go into the bathroom and get a wet flannel and unscented soap before returning to the bedroom.

I take a deep breath and move closer, kneeling beside the bed. I can feel my heart pounding as I hold my breath, reaching up and putting the key into the lock and turning it before unlatching the belt around her waist. My hands are shaking slightly as I slide it off her hips, the insert sliding out of her slick pussy, as I try not to wake her.

Once it's off of her, my mouth waters as her pussy is soaking wet and her clit is swollen, begging to be sucked. I can tell she's climaxed multiple times without having access to her clit, as there's so much wetness there. I clean her as she's been wearing that thing for three days. Gwen stirs a little in her sleep but doesn't awaken. Once she's clean, I decide to indulge my desires.

My cock twitches at the thought of tasting her again; of being able to satisfy her after three days of this torture device fitted into her virgin cunt. And I release it from the confines of my pants through the zipper, stroking myself as I lower my head and begin to lick and suck her, savoring the taste of her sweet juices as I move my tongue around her swollen clit; exploring every inch of her body. I watch as her hips rock in pleasure with each touch. There's something so intimate about doing this to her while she sleeps; watching her body respond unconsciously as I touch and explore it.

My hands move to her breasts, cupping them in my palms before rolling the nipples between my finger tips until she's practically panting.

Before long, Gwen comes undone in pleasure, writhing on the bed sheets beneath me. "Cillian," she moans my name in her sleep, eyes still clamped shut.

And hearing her moan my name like that makes my cock harder than nails.

The sensation wakes her as I straighten, my cock still in my hands as I stroke it. She blinks blearily at me for a moment, looking confused.

"Such a good girl, coming for me and crying my name out in your sleep," I murmur, tightening my grasp on my cock. "Now, I'm going to come on your pussy," I growl, as I swell with pleasure, my cock throbbing as I explode all over her cunt, making a mess.

Gwen hasn't said a word, still looking dazed as she stares at me. Taking advantage of her stupor, I lean down and capture her lips, tasting them for the first time since I took her captive. I've craved her kiss since the restroom at Macy's.

My tongue forcefully enters her mouth as I kiss her deeply, and she kisses me back, despite everything.

"This is one vivid dream," she murmurs.

I smirk against her lips. "Does that mean you've been dreaming of me, baby?"

She stiffens, pushing back and searching the room. Her eyes snag on the chastity belt on the nightstand, realizing it has been removed. "What the fuck?" She scrambles to her feet and switches on the lamp. I see the instant regret on her face as she covers her beautiful tits from my view.

"No use hiding them. I've already seen them."

"What are you doing in here?" she asks.

"Well, I came to see Ma and decided I'd pay you a visit, too. That cunt was so eager for attention."

"Do you have to be so disgusting?" she spits.

I move toward her and grab her wrist, pulling her naked body against me. My cock is still semi-hard, pressing against her abdomen. "It's kind of my style, baby. Now get into bed, it's time to sleep."

Her body turns tense. "I'm not sleeping in bed with you."

"Oh, you are," I purr, yanking her toward the bed. I lift her into my arms and push her onto the bed.

"I need to wash," she says, looking at the mess I made.

"No, you're going to sleep with my cum on you. I don't want you washing it off."

Her slender throat bobs as she swallows. "You're evil."

"And proud of it." I unbutton my shirt and throw it to one side, noticing the way her eyes dilate with lust as they take in every tattoo on my chest.

When I move my fingers to my pants, I can see her breathing labor as I get naked for her.

She gets under the covers and wraps herself in them. I get on the other side and yank them away so that I can wrap my arm around her waist and pull her back against my chest, my still semi-hard cock settling against her ass. "Sweet dreams, princess," I murmur, pressing soft kisses to her neck. "Try not to get too horny and don't go begging for my cock in the night, as you're not getting it until we're married."

"Which will be never," she spits back.

I chuckle and shut my eyes, enjoying the warmth of her body against mine. Gwendolyne Tesoro already belongs to me. Hearing her cry out my name unconsciously is proof that her mind is no longer consumed with thoughts of Piero but me instead.

13

GWENDOLYNE

"G et up," a deep voice snaps at me.

I sit bolt upright, eyes wide. "Cillian?"

He smirks. "Oh, yes, I'm here, baby. It's not one of your fantasies, and neither was last night."

"You're too arrogant for your own good."

He smiles. "And you love it. Now get your sweet little ass out of bed. We've got somewhere to be."

At that moment, I notice he's wearing a navy tuxedo that appears to hug him like a second skin.

"Somewhere to be? I haven't left this room since you brought me here. Where could we possibly be going?"

"Things are changing as of today, baby." He's holding a garment bag over his arm and he puts it on the bed. Yanking the covers off me, he forces my thighs wide apart. He groans as he moves closer. "God, you're so damn wet," he says, moving his nose between my thighs and inhaling my scent like a feral animal. "I want to feast on you," he murmurs. "But we don't have time."

He stands, leaving my pussy throbbing and needy. "Shower and get dressed. I want you downstairs in half an hour at the most." He spins on his heels and marches out of the room, leaving me staring at the garment bag.

I push myself from the bed and walk toward it, opening it to reveal a beautiful blue dress with lace inserts. I run my fingers across the soft fabric, admiring the intricate detailing across the bodice and along the hemline. It's a long elegant dress that is intended to cascade to the floor with a waist that is cut inward. If it weren't for the fact I'm a captive of this man, it's the kind of dress you expect the princess to wear in a fairy-tale, but this is no fairytale.

Pursing my lips, I walk into the bathroom, running the shower and stepping under the calming spray.

Cillian Hook is clearly an insane narcissist, but if he's going to take me away from here today, it gives me hope of an escape. If I get the chance, I'm going to snatch it and run as if my life depends on it.

And yet, as I wash myself, I can't help my mind from wandering to dirty, fucked-up places. Ever since Cillian threw me into this room and licked me to climax, I've been having way too many sick fantasies of him, and it's all been made ten times worse by the fact that I couldn't touch myself. And yet, it hasn't stopped me from orgasming. The belt he had put on made me so sensitive that I've woken in the night sweating and coming apart from my imagination alone.

Then last night… God, I don't want to think about it.

The way he crept into my room and removed it while I slept. I'm a deep sleeper and didn't rouse. I thought I'd died and gone to heaven. And even now, the moment I touch my clit, I cry out, as it's still so sensitive.

It takes me a minute maximum to reach my release and I have to brace my hands against the wall to keep myself upright at the intensity of it. "Fuck, Cillian," I moan his name shamefully, hating that he's made me think of him whenever I come.

It should be Piero. He should be the only face I see and the only name I cry out.

Shame fills me as I grab the shampoo bottle and lather my hair, wondering where this monster is taking me.

I pull the shower door open and step out, wrapping a fluffy white towel around my body and walking back to the bedroom. I take the dress from off the bed and slip it over my head, feeling the silky fabric slide across my skin like a caress. It feels so good to have clean clothes on for the first time in a week, and I sigh as I look at myself in the mirror.

When I get downstairs, Cillian is waiting for me. He's tapping his foot on the ground, but when he sees me his eyes widen. "What a vision you are," he muses. "So damn tasty."

"What's this about?"

"No questions, princess. It's a surprise."

Normally, I love surprises, but I don't feel too keen on whatever this man has in store for me. He grabs my hip and yanks me against his side, guiding me out of the house and onto the driveway, where a sleek black sports car is parked. "You're a fucking vision," he murmurs into my ear. "I can't wait to get that dress off of you."

I pull away from him and glare at him. "Well, if I have anything to say about it, you won't get it off of me."

He chuckles. "Thankfully, you won't have a say."

I grind my teeth as this man has some nerve.

"Now, be a good girl and get in the car," he orders.

Despite wanting to turn around and sprint in the opposite direction, one quick glance around proves there are no houses nearby and a forest on one side. Although, I'd like to make him chase me for the hell of it.

"Stop thinking about running. It's a waste of our time."

I don't know if it's because he tells me not to, or what. But I make the snap decision to sprint off toward the forest, wondering if I could perhaps lose him in there and find a way to safety.

"Oh, Gwen. It is dangerous to run away from me, as I get turned on by the hunt," he calls after me, not running yet.

The man is crazy, and perhaps I'm as crazy for running from him. I use all of my energy to sprint as fast as I've ever gone. Something tells me he's still going to catch me. My lungs burn as I twist and turn around the trees, searching for a way out. I trip over a fallen tree branch, my body tumbling to the floor.

Before I can register what's happening, Cillian catches me. He grabs my arm and pulls me into his chest. His breathing is heavy, but not from the run; it's from desire. "You can't escape me," he whispers in my ear. And without warning, he yanks me around so I face him.

The intensity of his gaze makes me gasp out loud. It's like he's looking straight through me—into every hidden corner of my soul that I've tried to protect for so long now—and there's nothing I can do about it.

"I think you wanted me to chase you. The idea of being caught excited you, didn't it?"

I hate that he's right, that a part of me was excited by the idea of being chased by him. Ever since this twisted game started, he has managed to get under my skin. I long for him as much as I dislike him.

"No," I reply.

He smirks and his fingers dance between my inner thighs. "I think you wanted me to fuck you out here, Gwen, didn't you?" His breathing labors as he brushes his fingers against my pussy. "You wanted me to fuck you like an animal in the forest. Breed that pretty little cunt on the forest floor. And while the idea is highly appealing," he murmurs, his fingers barely skating over my pussy, which is shamefully wet. "We have somewhere to be." With that, he stops touching me and yanks me over his shoulder, carrying my back toward the car.

I beat my fists against his back. "Put me down. I can walk, you know?"

"I know, but you don't want to do as you're told and walk in the correct direction, so I'll take matters into my own hands."

I continue to fight him every step he takes until he places me in front of his car.

"In. Now," he orders, and for the first time, there's a lethal and dangerous edge to his voice.

Deciding it's best not to push him, I get into the car

and squeeze my legs together. Cillian gets in to the driver's side and turns on the engine, making it purr beneath us.

We drive for what feels like hours but is properly only twenty minutes before Cillian parks in front of an enormous mansion.

"Out now," he orders.

I get out of the car and look around. "Where are we?"

"You're new home, princess."

"What?" I ask.

He smirks. "When we're married, this is where we're going to live together."

"You're insane if you think I'm going to marry you."

He chuckles. "You're fucking insane if you think you have a choice."

I set my hands on my hips. "How exactly do you intend to force me?"

Cillian gets closer, closing the gap between us. "The minister is already paid off to marry us if you're dragged kicking and screaming down that fucking aisle, so you may as well have some dignity on the most important day of your life." He grabs me by the throat, his eyes swirling with danger. "Because believe me, it'll be until death do us part."

"Hopefully yours, and swiftly at the hand of Piero," I growl.

His grasp tightens so much it feels like he's trying to kill me, forcing me to claw at his fingers. "What did I tell you about saying that filthy bastard's name?"

It's not like I can reply, not when he's strangling me.

My eyes are wide as panic coils through my body, and finally it's as if the realization of what he's doing kicks in and he relents.

"You need to stop pushing, Gwendolyne. Or you'll wind up hurt."

I place my fingers over the sore skin where he'd had me in a hold, wondering why I push him when he's dangerous.

He clears his throat. "Now, let me give you a tour," he says, as if he didn't assault me.

I shudder as he places a hand on my shoulder and guides me toward the grand entrance of the huge house. Every room we enter is bigger than the last; vast living spaces furnished with antiques and paintings, opulent bathrooms complete with luxurious marble bathtubs and shower rooms fit for royalty. It's too much to take in. My dad is wealthy, but if he has this kind of money, he doesn't splash it on our house.

"What do you think?" he asks, his chestnut eyes intense and searching.

"I think this place is exactly what I'd expect from you."

His jaw clenches. "And what exactly is that, princess?"

"Over indulgent."

"And there's nothing wrong with indulging in pleasures," he murmurs, dropping his hand to my hip and pulling me closer to him. "I could indulge in you all fucking day."

I shiver, hating that his words have an effect on me. It's as if he's untouchable. Any insult I throw his way, he twists it around, except when I mention Piero, then he goes crazy. Which makes me wonder what the hell happened between them to make him hate him so badly.

"How about I show you the bedroom?" he murmurs.

"The bedroom?" I ask, looking at him. "I assume this place has about twenty."

He chuckles. "Fine, our bedroom."

"Our bedroom?" I ask, panic coiling through me.

"Yes, princess, ours. You're going to be my wife, and husbands and wives share bedrooms."

I grind my teeth together. "We're not married yet."

"Do I strike you as the kind of guy that gives a shit about that?"

I swallow hard as he strikes me as the kind of man that doesn't give a shit about anything but himself, so I shake my head.

"Exactly, now be a good girl and come with me." He grabs my hand and yanks me the way we came in and climbs the sweeping staircase to a grand landing with doors leading off it. "Here is our room," he says, taking the furthest door on the left.

He opens it to reveal a huge room with a giant four-posted bed in the center. The bed is big enough to fit three people and is adorned with soft blankets and plump pillows in all shades of blue, green, and gold.

"Wow," I breathe, forgetting for a second who I'm with. "It's absolutely gorgeous."

"Only the best for my princess," he says, and that comment snaps me out of it as I shake my head.

"You're crazy."

He ignores my comment as I walk further into the room, my feet sinking into the plush beige rug that covers the entire floor as I wander around, taking in the details. A grand chandelier hangs from the ceiling, and there's intricate wallpaper adorning the walls. It's fit for royalty.

"I can tell you love it, and it's fit for a princess, isn't it?"

I glare at him and don't comment.

"Let me show you the bathroom," he says, signaling to one of the doors on the right.

I follow him into the adjoining bathroom where one of the walls is made of mirrors, and a gigantic Jacuzzi tub sits in the middle, surrounded by marble counters and illuminated light fixtures. A large vanity table with an array of makeup drawers stands against one wall. Instantly, I heat at the thought of him having his way with me in that Jacuzzi, as we'd be able to watch ourselves.

"This is ridiculous."

"Ridiculous in a good way?" he asks, eyes fixed on me.

I shake my head. "You know I don't want to be here."

"And yet your cheeks turned red the moment you saw that wall," he muses, moving closer to me and placing his hands on my hips from behind, his lips moving against my neck. "You were thinking about watching while I fuck you, weren't you?"

I grind my teeth because I hate that he's so percep-tive of my thoughts. "No," I lie.

"Filthy lies, princess, filthy fucking lies. Almost as fucking filthy as your thoughts."

I shudder as he suddenly releases my hips and grabs my hand. "I've got to show you your closet."

He drags me back into the bedroom and takes the door next to it, leading me into a huge walk-in closet filled to the brim with clothes, shoes, jewelry and more accessories than I could need. And while I've never wanted for anything, this is completely over the top. It's too much.

"Why the hell would I need this much stuff?"

"Because you're my princess," he murmurs.

I roll my eyes. "Reluctant princess," I reply.

He smirks and leads me back into the bedroom, signaling at a door on the left. "That's my closet."

My eyes shift to the only door left that he hasn't mentioned. "And behind that one?"

His eyes twinkle before he gives me another smirk and chuckles. "Wouldn't you like to know? That is the best room of all." He yanks me toward it and opens the door, and my heart drops into my stomach. Behind the door is a sex room with all kinds of toys and apparatus. My whole body heats and I realize that I've literally fallen into hell with the devil. This man is evil fucking incarnate for showing me this.

The walls are covered in velvet wallpaper with an assortment of paddles, restraints, and other BDSM items hanging on them. On one wall is a full-length mirror, while the opposite wall has several hooks and chains mounted on it that I can only imagine would be used to restrain his lover. In the middle of the room stands a large round, red bed with four posters that are attached to the ceiling, adorned with black silken ropes and chains.

I'm shaking at what I'm seeing - it's like nothing I've ever imagined and yet my thighs are wet with the thought of this evil man using me here.

Maybe I'm unhinged too.

He moves my hair out of the way and grazes his teeth down the back of my neck. "I thought you'd appreciate this, princess," he says softly in my ear before kissing my neck. "I'm going to make you come so many times in here."

My breath catches as I realize how much pleasure we could experience together in this room if only I allowed myself to let go... A ridiculous notion, considering the man stole me from the man I'm meant to marry. Even so, I can't help the thoughts that run wild in my mind.

14

CILLIAN

*R*age infects my blood because the rat has struck again. Tonight, I've got my hook on instead of my prosthetic. A sign I'm ready to claim blood. Smyth is pacing the bar area of my club, Neverland.

"How the fuck did this happen?" I growl.

Smyth spins to face me. "Honestly, sir. I don't know."

I march toward him and slide the end of my hook through the fabric of his collar, dragging him toward me. "You don't know?" My nostrils flare. "It's not fucking good enough." I release him and swing my hook across a nearby table, sending the bottle scattering to the floor with an almighty crash. "Everyone out!" I shout, my heart pounding erratically in my chest. "We're fucking shut."

Despite the fact patrons in the club are still drinking, no one ignores me. Every single asshole in this part of the club gets to their feet and rushes out of the door, because they know better than to ignore the owner.

Smyth stands before me with his arms crossed over his chest. "Sir, I apologize that it happened, but I wasn't there. Why are you taking your anger out on me?"

"Why?!" I march toward him. "Because you." I point my hook in his direction. "Are my second in command, which means anything that goes fucking wrong is your fault? Got it?"

His jaw clenches in response, and I know that I give him too much flack. Especially when he's been loyal to me all these years, even when I had to rebuild everything. I pace the floor in an attempt to divert my anger. Otherwise, I might lose my cool and interrogate all of my men, making the rat scarper before the detective I've employed does his magic.

"Someone is fucking with us," I say. "This many shipments getting hit isn't a coincidence. There's someone on the inside feeding information to the Tesoro mafia." I stop and glare at Smyth. "I'm sure of it."

Smyth's brow furrows. "It's possible. I didn't want to think it, but you're right. It can't be a coincidence."

I glare at him, wondering if he's agreeing to shift suspicion away from him or if he isn't the one betraying me. My ma doesn't believe it's him, but I trust no one.

"And who do you think could be behind it?"

He shrugs. "Your guess is as good as mine, but..." He trails off, and I can tell he wants to say more, but is unsure.

"But what?"

Smyth sighs. "Tim has been a little shifty."

"In what way?" I ask, as Tim isn't on my list of possible rats that I sent to the detective.

"He hangs around the office a lot, and a couple of times I've gone in there and he's acted off."

"Off?" I ask.

"A bit shifty is all."

I bite the inside of my cheek, unsure whether to believe Smyth or not. "I'll look into it."

"If you need help, I can—"

"No." I shake my head. "This is something I have to do myself."

There's a flash of hurt in his eyes, no doubt because I think he might be the rat. "You don't think I'd—"

"I don't know what to think, Smyth, but I can only trust myself."

His Adam's apple bobs as he swallows, and he nods. "Fair enough."

"Where are we on the deal with the cartel? I want a new contract brokered at a better value since we've increased our numbers year on year."

Smyth sighs. "They aren't playing ball."

"Motherfuckers. Okay, set up a meeting with their leader as soon as possible." I run my hand across the back of my neck. "If I want something done right." I glare at him. "It appears I've got to do it myself."

He looks hurt by my remark, but I don't give a shit about his feelings. Smyth has always been too fucking touchy. "Do you want me to accompany you?"

I shake my head. "No. Arrange the meeting."

"When for?"

"As soon as possible." I turn toward the door. "I've got somewhere to be."

Smyth doesn't say a word as I march toward it and open the door.

"Oh, and Smyth." I glance at him.

"Sir?"

"Make sure you watch Tim for me. Let me know if he does anything else suspicious," I say, wanting him to believe that I don't suspect him. As this could be a test either way. If he tells me bullshit about Tim, I'll know he's covering his own tracks.

"Yes, sir, I will."

I walk toward the bar, pouring myself a tumbler of scotch. Three of the servers are standing there, watching me. "Evening," I say to them.

They all glare at me, and I wonder if it's because I let Kirsty go.

I take a sip of my drink and slam the glass on the counter. "Evening, Cillian, is what I expect to hear from my employees. Or do you want to go looking for a new fucking job?" I ask, pointing my hook in their direction.

Two of the girls panic and straighten, eyes wide when they notice the hook. "Evening, Cillian," they say in chorus. The other girl, continues to glare at me.

"And what's your problem?"

"Why did you get rid of Kirsty? She was one of the best servers in this place."

"It had nothing to do with her work ethic, but she slapped me. I won't be assaulted by my staff."

The girl rolls her eyes. "You insulted her first."

My nostrils flare and I clench my fist, feeling the

ache where my other hand used to be. Challenging me is a bad idea when I'm like this. It's as if this girl has a death wish, but I take a deep breath, trying to stay calm. "Look," I say, in a low voice. "If you want to keep fucking breathing, you'd better stop questioning me. As by the time I'm through with you, you'll wish I'd fired you instead."

The girl pales, her throat bobbing as she nods. "Fine," she mumbles under her breath.

I look at the other two girls, who both look terrified now. "Good," I reply before turning on my heel and stalking away without another word.

My anger fades as soon as I'm out of sight of the staff members, but I remember what an important lesson this was for everybody involved: no one challenges Cillian Hook—or else they'll be gone like Kirsty was gone in an instant, or buried six-feet under if they're not careful the way my rage is getting the better of me.

And I know part of the reason why. It's because my pretty new fiancée still belongs to Piero, which is disgusting. I need to obliterate him from her mind and heart. A feat I fear will be easier said than done, but I'm nothing if not persistent.

I MARCH to the dockmaster's office, still angry from the incident with the girls at the club. He looks at me when I enter and his face pales. Most likely because I look ready to murder someone. His eyes drop to my clenched fist as if he knows he's in trouble, but he isn't. I'm angry at everything else going on.

"Hook," he says, his voice shaky. "What can I do for you?" I notice the way his eyes linger on the hook, as I don't often wear it.

I take a deep breath and unclench my hand before balling it into a fist again. "The shipments that got hit a few weeks ago," I say in a cold voice. "I need access to your CCTV footage from those nights."

He nods, understanding what I'm implying. "Yes, sir." He taps away at the computer. "Let me access it for you."

I walk over to stand behind his desk, making him infinitely more nervous, while he brings up the footage of the dates we had shipments hit.

"This is weird," he says, shaking his head. "It appears someone has deleted the footage."

"What?" I snap. Someone had access to the computer system and must have known what they were doing—erasing evidence that could lead back to them.

Not only did this person betray me, but they had enough skill and knowledge to cover their tracks as well.

"Do you know which of my men has access to your computer systems?" I ask, my voice tight with anger.

The dock-master swallows hard and gives me a list of five names: Salazar Johnson, Tim O'Malley, Alex Carter, Tom Delaney and Oliver Wilcox. I don't miss the fact that Tim is on the list, and Smyth mentioned that he's been acting off. And I'm thankful that Smyth's name isn't on the list, as it means I can rule him out as a potential suspect.

Even so, it means one of these fuckers is involved in selling me out and stealing for the organization, and that fucking detective better find out who is it sharp. Or I'll murder all five of these idiots and be done with it.

"I want you to keep an eye out for anything out of the ordinary with my next shipments, and as soon as another one gets stolen, make a copy of the CCTV footage."

The dockmaster nods. "Yes, sir. I'll be vigilant about that."

"Good. Because if those fuckers keep stealing my shipments, there's going to be hell to pay."

His eyes dilate with fear. I don't have boundaries when it comes to torture. Most would say I delight in it.

I know that I can't entirely attribute that part of me to Piero's betrayal. I've been unhinged for longer than that, ever since I was a child, and lost my fucking hand. There's been this violence inside me that has a life of its own. An inherent part of me that will never be erased.

I point my hook in his direction, struggling to contain the glee as he shudders. "You don't want to be on the wrong end of my hook, do you?"

He shakes his head. "Certainly not."

A tense silence fills the air as I watch him shudder in fear. "How is she?" I ask.

The dockmaster's brow furrows before he realizes I'm talking about my boat.

Poison.

It's been three months since the engine blew on it,

and since I've been confined to land for that time, it's driving me more crazy than normal.

"The mechanic thinks he can get her up and running in a week or two."

I slam my hand on the nearby cabinet. "That's what you said three weeks ago."

His throat bobs as he swallows. "I apologize, but there's been trouble sourcing the parts for it."

"I told you to get it done. Fuck the cost. Do you understand?" I move closer to the desk and slam my hook on it. "If you have to pay a million fucking dollars for the part, so be it. I need that boat in one week or there will be hell to pay."

His entire body quivers. "Yes, understood. I'll get it sorted within a week, I promise."

The guy is a sniveling excuse of a man, but if he does get me my boat, I don't give a shit. I need to get back on the water.

"Good. Questions?"

He shakes his head.

"I didn't think so." I turn and walk out of his office, leaving him shivering in terror as he considers what I'd do to him if he doesn't get my boat ready. I'll gut him with my hook and make him watch while I feed his guts to the crocodiles at the zoo as he dies a slow and painful death.

15

GWENDOLYNE

I step out of the bedroom, my heart racing and my mind tortured by the fear of bumping into my captor.

As I walk down the staircase and into the entrance hall, I feel a strange sense of admiration for the crafts-manship of his home. If I were here under different circumstances, I'd be happy to be living in a place like this.

It's like something out of a fairytale, but I'm caught in anything but a fairytale.

Since Cillian brought me here, I feel like a bird in a beautiful cage. It's clear he's insane the way he smirked and told me this was my new home.

The only thing holding me together is that I know Piero or my father won't sit by while someone steals me from him. They're both powerful mob bosses, and this guy is insane to take them on.

I have no intention of marrying him, yet here I am, entrapped in his home with no clear way out.

As I walk toward the garden room, which has a stunning view of the ocean, I slam into a woman coming the other way. My heart pounds as she stares at me with wide eyes, and I wonder who she is.

"Don't look so scared, Gwendolyne. I work here."

I nod. "Okay, I thought you were a prisoner too."

Her lips press together. "No, but I might as well be."

"Don't you like your employer?"

She shakes her head. "Not too fond, no."

"What is it you do here?" I ask.

"I'm Cillian's personal assistant," the woman replies, her voice a combination of resignation and disdain. "Trust me, I don't like him any more than you do."

My heart skips a beat and I feel a wave of relief wash over me. Someone I can relate to. "What's it like, working for him?"

"Tough work. He's not a friendly boss, and he makes us work ridiculous hours."

I can imagine that he'd be a terrible boss. "Count yourself lucky. At least you don't have to marry him."

There's a look of pity in her eyes. "I feel for you. How about we grab lunch?" She glances at her watch. "It's midday."

I smile. "That sounds good. As long as you don't get in trouble?"

"No, because he's not here, he's dealing with business for The Rogues."

I'm relieved to hear he's not here, but that name piques my interest. "The Rogues?"

She nods. "Yes, Cillian is the leader of the Irish mob in San Diego."

I draw in a deep breath, realizing he's not so insane to take on my dad and Piero. He's a ruthless and powerful mob boss, too. The Rogues have been causing problems for my father for about five years now, encroaching on the territory he controls. I had no idea who the leader was. "Shit, that makes this all ten times worse."

Her brow arches. "Why?"

"Because that means Cillian is my dad's competition."

She nods. "Yeah, I don't think that's why he stole you, though. He's more interested in bringing down Piero Panarello."

My brow furrows. "Do you know why?"

"No idea."

We head into the kitchen, where an older lady is whistling to herself as she kneads the dough. "Hey Rosa, we're going to grab lunch together," the girl says, and it's at that point I don't know her name.

"I'm so rude. I don't know your name."

She smiles. "It's Tilly." She glances at the cook. "And this is Rosa."

Rosa gives her a disapproving look. "You know the boss would be pissed to hear you're befriending his fiancée," she warns.

Tilly crosses her arms over her chest. "Are you saying you intend to tell him?"

"Of course not," Rosa says, placing a hand on her chest. "But I can't say the same for the rest of the staff here, especially Jensen. You know he's in the boss's pocket."

"If he says anything, I'll merely say she was hungry and asked me to get her some food, no harm, no foul."

"And I'll back that up," I add.

Rosa nods. "Fine, it's your funeral." She goes to the stove and lifts a heavy pot. "Stew?"

Tilly licks her lips. "Sounds good. Have you got some bread?"

She rolls her eyes and fetches a freshly baked loaf. "Don't eat it all."

"Can't make promises." Tilly chuckles.

"How long have you worked for Cillian?" I ask as Rosa dishes two bowls of stew.

"Too long," she says, pinching the bridge of her nose. "I think it's been about five years now."

"That doesn't sound that long."

Rosa chuckles. "No it's not. I've worked for Cillian for eight years. And I don't think he's that bad. He can be an asshole when he's angry, though."

Tilly shakes her head. "Careful, someone might report you," she quips. "The last time Cillian heard someone call him an asshole, he gutted the guy."

"Gutted him?" I ask, choking on a mouthful of delicious stew.

"Yep, it's as disgusting as it sounds. He did it in front of the entire staff to teach people a lesson."

I swallow hard and nod as my appetite vanishes. Glancing around, I search for a clock. "What's the time? Are there no clocks in this house?"

Tilly and Rosa exchange an odd glance. "Thought you would know about his problem with clocks as his fiancée," Rosa says.

Despite knowing he does have an issue with clocks, I wonder if they realize I'm a prisoner here, not his fiancee by choice. "Do you realize I'm here as a captive and never agreed to marry Cillian?"

Rosa's eyes widen. "No, I didn't." She shakes her head. "That sucks."

"So I know nothing about him."

"Cillian has a problem with clocks. The ticking gets to him," Tilly says, pursing her lips together. "It's scary actually seeing what happens when he's in a room with one. He turns into a monster."

I remember the way he freaked out about the clock in the hotel.

"Isn't he already a monster?"

Someone clears their throat at the doorway, and when I see Cillian, I jump out of my skin.

"May I ask who you're talking about, princess?" His eyes fix on me with an intensity that makes me shudder.

Both Tilly and Rosa turn pale the moment they see him.

"No one," I say quickly.

"Rosa and Tilly, will you excuse us for a moment?"

I swallow hard as the two of them rush out of the kitchen as if their lives depend on it.

"Now, princess, I want you to tell me the truth. Who is already a monster?"

"It's not important," I murmur, hating the fact that he scares me.

"If you were saying I'm already a monster, it means Rosa or Tilly called me a monster. Who said it?" he asks, eyes narrowing.

"We weren't talking about you."

He shakes his head. "Shall I torture them both to find out?"

I swallow hard. "Don't touch them. It's not their fault."

Cillian takes a step closer, and for the first time I'm scared of him, because I know what he could do to them. "Tell me what you were talking about or else I'll hurt them." My heart is pounding in my chest as I realize that he's serious. "I asked where all the clocks are in the house, and—"

"And they mentioned that I turn into a monster when there's one around?" he finishes for me.

I nod in response. "And I said you're always a monster."

He smirks, and I'm not sure whether to be relieved or not. "Well, I can't punish them for telling the truth. I'm a monster when there's a clock around."

"Why?" I ask, remembering the way he tried to throw the clock out of the hotel window.

His jaw clenches. "I'd rather not speak about it."

"Fine." I stand. "I'm going back to my room."

He steps into my path. "You mean our room? And I want your company, so you're not going anywhere."

My heart accelerates as his fingers move beneath the hem of my dress. "You're going to leave Rosa and Tilly alone, right?"

He shakes his head. "No, I'll punish them for speaking to you." His jaw works. "But they'll live, at least."

"You are a monster."

His fingers move beneath the string of my thong, thrusting inside me. "And proud of it," he murmurs, thrusting deeper and making my knees buckle. "I think you love my monstrous side."

This man is insane if he thinks I love any part of him. "I hate you," I spit. "There's nothing about you that I love."

"We'll see about that when we're married."

"I'm not marrying you."

He chuckles. "Princess, you're marrying me, and there's nothing you can do about it." He curls his fingers in a way that hits the spot deep inside me.

I crumble, moaning at the sensation as I clasp onto his jacket for support, trying to stop myself from dropping to my knees—not a position I want to be in when he's like this.

"That's what I thought, moan for me," he purrs, dark eyes watching my every move. "I can't wait to be inside you, fucking you so hard that you can't remember your own name." His fingers delve deeper inside of me. "Breeding this pretty pussy and making you big and round with my baby." That thought should make me feel sick, but instead it drives me crazy with need. "And believe me, I'm going to fuck you, Gwendolyne, before you tell me it's never going to happen."

I hate that he drives me crazy with desire. "I hate you," I say, knowing that I hate myself for feeling the way I do around him.

He slams his fingers deeper inside me, and it feels like I'm going to explode. The sensation is too intense to control my reactions as I moan, pulling him toward me

as I try to use him as a crutch. "Such a dirty little liar."
He kisses me, our tongues tangling together in a
passionate kiss. And then, he breaks away and drags his
thumb over my clit, the pleasure so intense I know I
won't last much longer. "Come for me like a good girl,"
he breathes.

What I hate the most is the way my body responds
to his command.

I can feel it. My body tensing up, the pleasure
bubbling inside me and threatening to overflow. I claw at
his back, trying to keep it down but unable to resist the
warmth and heat that washes over me in waves. The
orgasm builds to a crescendo within me and soon I'm
screaming, "Oh God!" my voice echoing as I come
harder than I ever have before, pleasure radiating
through my body.

"That's right, princess, I'm your God now. Pray to
me and me alone," he growls.

My breathing is ragged, every nerve ending in my
body alive and firing with pure pleasure and energy.

He kisses me with a tenderness that surprises me.
"Good girl," he whispers against my lips. "Open your
mouth."

Still drunk from my climax, I open my mouth and
he slips the fingers that had been inside me into my
mouth. The taste of my own arousal coating my tongue
and making me ache.

"Suck them clean for me," he instructs.

I do as I'm told, sucking my own juice from his
fingers like a dirty little whore. "Such a good girl when
you're turned on, aren't you, princess?"

The question breaks the lust-filled haze from my mind, and I shake my head. "I don't know what came over me…"

He chuckles. "I do. You want me and I want you. It's cruel to deny your own basic instincts, don't you think?"

I ball my fists. "They aren't instincts. I don't want you."

He turns away from me and walks toward the door, pausing at the doorframe. "Tomorrow we have a date at the altar. I can't wait to make you mine for real." He walks away, whistling to himself like a maniac.

I've barely got time to plan my escape from here before he makes this irreversible. No matter how good he makes me feel when he touches me, he's nothing more than a monster.

Standing and heading out of the kitchen, I turn right and venture into another part of his mansion. I open a door on my left and it feels like my prayers are answered when I spot a landline on the desk.

I glance down the corridor to make sure no one is around. And then I rush into the office and shut the door, dialing my dad's cell fast.

It rings five times before my dad picks up. "Hello?"

"Dad! It's me, Gwendolyne."

"Oh, thank God. Are you okay?"

I swallow hard, tears prickling at my eyes, but I can't break now. "No, Cillian Hook has me captive."

"Cillian Hook?" he asks, his voice full of dangerous rage. "Are you sure?"

"Certain. He says he's going to marry me tomorrow."

"That motherfucker! Did he say where you're getting married?" he asks, his voice panicked. "And where are you now?"

I purse my lips together, realizing I have no information on our location. "I have no answer to either of those questions. All I know is I'm in a large house by the sea."

Dad growls on the other end. "That could be anywhere. Hold on, I'll get my guy in here to trace your call and get the location. Can you stay on the line?"

I swallow hard, glancing around the little room. "Hopefully. There's no one around at the moment."

"Okay, sweetheart, hold tight. We're going to save you."

The tears flood down my cheeks, and I feel so much relief at hearing his voice. But then the line goes dead, making my entire world sink. The door flies open to reveal Cillian standing there, rage burning in his eyes.

"Who has been a naughty girl?" he asks.

I swallow hard and face my fate, knowing that it wasn't long enough for Dad to trace me. All hope is lost.

16

CILLIAN

Gwendolyne looks a vision as she stands at the entrance of the church, her expression fearful.

Her wedding dress is a simple white dress with a delicate lace bodice and a long, flowing skirt. The entire gown is fitted snugly against her figure until it sweeps out at the bottom, brushing the floor. Thin straps wrap around Gwendolyne's shoulders, emphasizing her delicate frame, and there are more detailed embellishments along the neckline and back. The waist is accented by a thin ivory ribbon tied in a bow to bring attention to her hourglass shape. Its simple elegance makes her look more beautiful. I prefer it to a huge, over-the-top gown that you see most brides wear nowadays.

The Tesoro mafia was out for blood after my darling fiancée called her father. I had hoped to avoid war with the Tesoro family, but it's inevitable now. When I told Gwendolyne last night we were marrying today, I was bluffing, and yet here we are.

I enjoyed punishing her, though. She's such a

naughty girl who loves getting spanked, which I know will be fun incorporating into our sex life. Approaching her, my heart races as I take her hand in mine.

She tries to pull away, her skin cool and clammy.

"Cillian, don't do this, please," she begs.

I clench my jaw as she looks at me with fear in her eyes, but I can also see the determination that lies beneath. There's no way we're getting through this without a fight.

"It's already done, princess." I pull Gwendolyne into the church, my grip on her hand tightening with every step I take.

We walk down the aisle where members of The Rogues are gathered, their guns trained on my pretty little fiancée. None of the guns are loaded, but I want her to believe she's in danger. "Remember, one false move and my men sink a bullet into your perfect skin." I'd rather claw my own eyes out with my hook than harm her.

She shudders and a few tears roll down her cheeks. "You're a monster," she mutters.

I don't acknowledge her assessment. Once we get to the altar, I face her and feel a pang of guilt in my chest at the tear stains on her cheeks. Her eyes dart around as if searching for an escape or someway to stop this wedding. There's no stopping it.

The priest we paid stands before us, looking a little nervous as he glances between me and my reluctant bride. "Shall we begin?" he asks.

I nod. "Yeah, and make it snappy."

He nods. "Of course."

The priest begins his chanting, but all I can focus on is my princess's beautiful face. She's a fucking angel, and I'm the devil. It's clear we're perfect for each other. Her light is as bright as the sun, while my darkness is as dark as the deepest ocean on earth. I can't wait to corrupt and infect her, turn her into my queen.

Soon enough it's time for me to say "I do". I take Gwendolyne's hands in mine and squeeze them, gazing deeply into those fear-filled eyes. I speak those two little words that seal our fates together: "I do".

Her lips purse together, and I wonder if she's going to refuse to say them in return. If she does, it doesn't matter.

The priest turns to her and asks her, "Do you take this man to be your lawfully wedded husband? To have and to hold until death do you part."

Her nostrils flare and eyes flash with irritation. "No, but apparently it doesn't matter what I say."

"Of course it doesn't."

The priest looks uneasy as he nods. "By the power vested in me, I now pronounce you husband and wife. You may kiss the bride."

"With pleasure," I say, wrapping an arm around her waist and yanking her against me. "You're mine now, Gwendolyne... Or should I say, Mrs. Hook?"

Her eyes narrow to slits. "I'll never be yours."

I press my lips to hers, kissing her passionately. My tongue delving into her mouth as I dominate her entirely, making her melt for me despite the tension racking her muscles. And once I break away from her breathless, I murmur in her ear, "I can't wait to claim that pretty virgin cunt tonight."

She stiffens, and I'm certain the priest hears me as he clears his throat, looking shocked by my dirty language.

"Sorry, Father, I'm no saint." I wink at him, which makes his embarrassment deepen. "Now, time to get to the party." I walk Gwendolyne toward the exit of the church.

"What party?" Gwen asks.

"I couldn't marry you and not celebrate, could I?"

Her jaw works in frustration. "There's nothing to celebrate."

"Our marriage is something to celebrate, as it means tonight I get to fuck your eager cunt for the first time." I press my nose against her neck and inhale. "I have been wanting to fuck you since the day I saw you at your engagement party to another man," I say.

"Well I haven't. I can't think of anything worse."

I grab the back of her neck forcefully as we step out of the church and onto the steps. "Such a liar. I can practically smell your arousal from thinking about it, princess."

"You don't know what you're talking about. I don't want to have sex with you." Her throat bobs as she swallows, as if scared to ask her next question. "What if I say no? What if I scream and shout for you to stop?"

I move my lips to her ear and murmur. "The more you scream and shout for me to stop, the harder I'll fuck you. I will fuck the fight right out of you if I have to, Gwendolyne, so best to be a good girl and open your legs for your husband. After all, you were pretty willing when you had my cock thrust down your throat, weren't you?" I let my breath tease her against her skin. "Not only then, let's not forget the two times I've made you come by feasting on you, and once with my fingers. Think how good it will be when I'm deep inside you."

She shudders, a visible sign that the thought of it drives her wild with need. No matter how much she tries to deny her desire for me, it's there and it's not going anywhere. "You're sick in the head if you think it's okay to fuck someone when they tell you no."

I smirk. "I never professed to be anything but sick in the head. It's best to embrace it."

"We're ready to take you and your wife to the party, sir." One of my men interrupts our conversation.

I clench my jaw and yank Gwendolyne over to the car. "Get in, princess."

She gives me an irritated glare but slides into the back of the limousine. I follow and sit close to her, my hand firmly planted on her thigh.

"This limo has so much room, so can you give me space?" She asks, nostrils flaring.

I shake my head. "No. There's no reason to give you space now that you're my wife. I want to be close to you as often as possible."

She tries to move away, but I keep her held down. I won't allow her to escape. We commence the short journey back to our home in heated silence. Once we're there, she gets out of the car and glances around at the hundreds of cars parked outside. "What did you do? Invite the entire City of San Diego?"

"Not quite, as that would include your dad."

Her eyes darken. "Yes, and my dad wasn't invited to his own daughter's wedding."

"As if that would have worked. Your dad would have stopped it." I pull her toward the house. "Now, no dilly dallying, we've got guests to greet." I press my lips to her cheek as we get to the steps into the house. "Pretend to be happy."

"This is the worst day of my life. There's nothing for me to be happy about."

I inhale her sweet scent, knowing that I'm already dangerously hooked on her. "Well, you better be a good actress." I pull her up the steps and into our home, where the party is in full swing without us. The house is filled with people, laughing and talking over the sound of jazz music coming from the speakers. My guests are dressed in their finest party attire, sipping champagne and enjoying delicious finger food. Servers circulate with trays of hors d'oeuvres, as well as waiters carrying flutes of champagne.

"This is over the top," Gwendolyne says, glaring at me. "Especially to celebrate a forced marriage."

I yank her against my side and bite her earlobe in warning. "Don't say that word again. Do you understand?"

"Which one?"

"You know which one."

She tries to loosen my grip, but I hold firm. I won't have her make a mockery of our marriage. The guests don't notice our entrance at first, but after a minute or two, one of the politicians who supports my organization comes to congratulate us.

"Cillian, congratulations on the sudden marriage. I didn't realize you were engaged," Carson says.

"No, it was sudden. A whirlwind romance."

He arches a brow. "That's not what I heard." Carson's attention moves to Gwen. "I hear you weren't thrilled by this match?"

Gwen is about to open her mouth when I pinch her backside hard, making her jump. "Not thrilled, no."

I laugh. "Gwen doesn't know what she's talking about. She's happily married." My hand move back to the small of her back. "We must make the rounds. "Thanks for coming today."

He nods his head. "Of course, enjoy."

I guide Gwendolyne away, and once we walk out of earshot, I lean toward her ear. "What did I say?"

She glares at me. "You said don't mention the word forced, but I didn't. He said he heard I wasn't thrilled, and I wasn't about to lie to his face." I notice the way her nose wrinkles when she gets angry. "It's pretty obvious everyone here knows the wedding is a farce."

I squeeze her backside again. "And yet you react so well to my touch. I bet you're soaking wet right now."

"You wish," she hisses, glaring at me.

I slide my hand under my jacket and press the tip of my gun to her rib cage beneath it. "Are you going to make me shoot you right here in front of everyone?"

She looks at me and searches my eyes. "You wouldn't."

I arch a brow. "Try me. You're the one who believes

I'm crazy. Why not put the theory to the test?" The fact is, killing her isn't an option, and the gun isn't loaded. All I want is to protect her and make her mine.

If she believes it an option, it might make her easier to control tonight. I don't need her causing a scene in front of politicians I want to win over, not when her father is ready to declare war on me.

Desperate times call for desperate measures, even if I'd take a bullet for her before I shoot her. My obsession with taking down Piero has warped into a deeper and darker obsession with the woman. Step one of my plan is complete, but I fear it has cost me more than I ever imagined.

17

GWENDOLYNE

*T*he music is loud and overwhelming. A cacophony of sounds that fill the entire room. Perhaps I'm finding it too loud because of what transpired beforehand.

Mrs. Hook.

That's what he called me, and I wanted to punch him. Cillian's hand remains on the small of my back, making me wish I could melt into the floor and disappear. His touch is the most conflicting thing I've ever experienced. It makes me angry and yet it makes me burn for him. It doesn't make sense.

There's an overwhelming sense of dread building in my stomach. Everywhere I look, I see people laughing and dancing, celebrating the evening. All while I can feel his gun shoved against my ribs as Cillian has instructed me not to make a scene.

He leans toward me and murmurs, "Are you going to be a good girl?"

I glare at him, wanting nothing more than to wipe the smug look off his face. "I don't have a choice, do I?"

His eyes twinkle with an evil spark. "What I'm saying is, do I need to keep the gun on you, or can I trust you to be a good girl?"

I swallow hard, as I'm not entirely sure he can trust me. "I won't do anything."

His eyes narrow. "I'm not sure I'm convinced, but I have to hope you'll be good, as I've got a people I need to speak with." He pulls the gun from my ribs and he kisses me on the cheek. "Know that if you try anything, I won't hesitate to use this gun on you, but not in the way you think."

My brow furrows as I wonder what other use there could be for a gun other than shooting someone with it.

He chuckles. "Intrigued, aren't you? Maybe I'll show you later, princess."

"I won't try anything," I confirm.

He marches away from me and heads toward a group of men at the far end of the room. As he moves away, I can feel the security guards watching me like hawks. He undoubtedly instructed them to watchme.

Sighing, I move around the room, searching for something to distract my mind. And then I spot Tilly sitting at a table.

Perfect.

"Hey Tilly," I say, approaching her.

She gives me a sad smile. "Hey, I'm so sorry."

I slide into the chair next to her and smile. "Don't be. It's not your fault."

There's an odd look in her eyes. "You should have married Piero."

"I'm surprised to hear Cillian's employee say that."

Her jaw clenches. "Can you keep a secret?"

"Of course," I say, as she glances around.

"I'm on Piero's side, and he's trying to find a way to get you back."

My eyes widen and hope bursts to life in my chest. "But you said you've been working for Cillian for—"

"Five years, yes. Piero stationed me with him when he learned Hook's true identity, knowing he'd come at him in the end. I didn't find out about the plot to snatch you until it was too late."

I sit in stunned silence, trying to process the news. "Before we were getting married, Piero knew Cillian was a threat?"

"Yes, he's had me keep tabs on him." Her expression turns serious. "On this occasion, I well and truly failed him." Her shoulders slump.

"Wow, so Piero knew he'd make a move against him?"

Tilly nods. "Suspected, yes."

"Why? Do they have history?" I ask.

Tilly sighs. "I don't know all the details, but yes, I believe so. Piero hasn't revealed that to me."

I sit back and contemplate what she's saying, knowing that if Piero is looking for a way to get me out, all hope isn't lost. Although, it might be now that I'm married. "But it's too late, isn't it? I'm married to Cillian."

"Not by choice," Tilly says, shaking her head.

"Which means we can still get you out." Her brow furrows. "Hook's security is tight."

I sigh heavily. "I wish I could escape."

"Escape?"

That voice makes me tense. I glance over my shoulder to see him glaring at Tilly. "What kind of ideas are you putting in my wife's head, Tilly?"

I stand. "She wasn't putting ideas in my head," I say, glaring at him. "She congratulated me and I told her there was nothing to congratulate, and that I want to escape, rather than be married to you."

Cillian's expression darkens. "Is that so? Well, if you try to escape, don't think I won't come after you, Gwendolyne." He steps toward me and yanks me against him. "I'll find you wherever you are and bring you back home to me, understand?"

I try to pull away, feeling my heart pound in my chest as he tightens his grasp.

"Yes," I whisper.

"Good," he says, nodding, before turning his attention back to Tilly. "I suggest you keep your mouth shut and do your job like a good little employee." His eyes narrow. "Scurry off somewhere else, Tilly."

I'm thankful that he didn't hear the other part of our conversation. Tilly works for Piero.

"You are rather close to that girl," he says, watching me through narrowed eyes. "What could you two possibly have in common?"

I shrug. "She's friendly to me, that's all." If Cillian found out the truth, Tilly wouldn't survive the night.

I can tell he doesn't believe me, but he shakes his

head. "Fine, come on." He grabs my wrist and yanks me toward the dance floor. "Let's dance."

I try to resist, but I can't break his grip. He leads me onto the dance floor and we stand face-to-face. Cillian's dark eyes are intense, and for a moment I'm afraid he can sense both my fear and my desire. He takes my hands in his and starts to move, guiding me in an effortless waltz.

My heart pounds as I allow him to take control, twirling us around the room faster and faster. I can feel the heat radiating from his body, and I can smell his cologne. It's an addictive scent.

"Why is it that the moment we started dancing, your eyes sparkle with desire? Is it because you can't help but think about getting me into bed later tonight?"

I was thinking about how good he is at dancing, and he spoils the moment by opening his mouth. Although we danced before, it was briefly in a small confined space, not like this. "Definitely not."

His strong hands guide me through each step effortlessly, as if he's danced this dance thousands of times before.

He yanks me closer to him. "I don't believe that for a second, princess," he murmurs into my ear as the music fades away. "I can't wait to do the tango between the sheets, as you'll be screaming my name all night long." He pulls away and when he meets my gaze, his lips curl into a smirk.

That's when I realize all eyes are on us, and no one else is dancing. Heat floods through my entire body as I break away from him, reclaiming my hands.

His eyes flash with anger as he places his hand on the small of my back and leads me away from the dance floor. "Don't pull away from me like that in front of people again, do you understand?" There's a lethal edge to his voice.

I nod once. "Fine."

He sighs heavily. "Come on, we need to make the rounds. Start acting like a bride who is happy on her wedding day."

Tilly's words repeat in my mind.

Not by choice, which means we can still get you out.

She believes that I can escape, which gives me hope. Hope that this fight isn't over.

"Andrea," Cillian says, walking over to a middle-aged woman on the arm of an older, graying-haired man. "It's been a long time."

She turns around and gives him a tight smile. "Cillian. Yes, I was surprised to receive an invitation."

I wonder who this woman is, as she isn't thrilled to be here.

"I think it's time to rekindle our business relationship."

Her eyes narrow. "To what end?"

"I'm married now and The Rogues are doing better than ever. Why not reconsider the offer I made you two years ago?"

"What offer?" the man asks, taking the question I was too afraid to ask right out of my mouth.

His wife glares at him. "It's not important." She returns her gaze to Cillian and passes him her card. "Call me and we'll schedule a meeting."

Cillian takes the card, and I catch a glimpse of it. She's the police commissioner of the San Diego PD. Whatever faith I had in law enforcement is eradicated then and there. This woman should be bringing the cavalry in to shut this man's operations down, but she's considering offers from him.

My dad has always kept me blind to the way his business operates, but I'm sure it's same way Cillian operates. He probably bribes police officers, too.

"Perfect, I'll be in touch," Cillian says.

"Nice to meet you," I give them a false smile.

The man nods. "Nice to meet you, too."

Cillian guides me away.

"How corrupt is this city? The police commissioner is considering making a deal with you?"

He smirks. "Don't pretend like you didn't already know. Your father has more cops in his pocket than I do."

"If that's the case, why's the police commissioner attending a forced wedding involving his daughter?"

"Because he hasn't got her on his side yet, and I want to get her first."

"Does she know this wedding was forced?" I ask.

He tilts his head. "What's your obsession with the police commissioner?"

"Nothing. I'm trying to work out how corrupt this city is."

"It runs deep. Let's leave it at that." He leans toward my ear. "And I think it's common knowledge that this wasn't a consensual match."

"If that's true, why does it matter if I cause a scene

or not?"

"Appearances, Gwendolyne. They're important and if you made a scene, it would appear like I can't control my woman. And if I can't control my woman, how can I control a hoard of criminals?"

I sigh heavily as his logic makes sense. "What now?"

"Now, we are having fun in each other's company. And don't pretend that's so hard." He winks. "I know you want me."

My jaw drops at his arrogance. "No, I don't. You may think you're irresistible, but all you are is arrogant and irritating."

He steps closer and grabs my chin with his hand. It amazes me how much force he can put on my jaw with his fingers every time, as I feel like he's going to break it. "Every time things are pleasant, you have to go and spoil it, don't you?"

"Pleasant? None of this will ever be pleasant for me. I'm here against my will and no flirting or brushing it under the carpet will ever change that."

"We will see, princess. Now shut that pretty mouth." He releases my chin. "And smile like you mean it." He takes my arm and leads me around the room, greeting politicians and other corrupt individuals.

Despite everything this man has put me through, I hate the nagging voice in my mind. A part of me that is secretly happy that Cillian took me and saved me from marrying Piero. The connection that was there when we first met hasn't gone. It's there pulling me into his darkness. I fear that this is the start of an incredibly volatile relationship that will get me hurt if I'm not careful.

18

CILLIAN

I'm so thankful it's the end of the night and every idiot I invited to my home has gone, meaning it's time for me to claim what's mine.

She stands to one side, her arms wrapped around her waist in defense, but nothing can save her now. I intend to devour her, turn her world upside down, and make sure the name Piero is obliterated from her mind.

The look she gives me is one of passionate anger and desire, and I feel it right to my balls.

"Bedtime, princess," I say, winking at her.

"I'm not tired."

I tilt my head. "Good, because we aren't going to be sleeping." I reduce the distance between us and grab her hips, yanking her toward me. "I'm going to show you what it's like to go to heaven."

"Hell, more like," she replies.

"Well, hell can be as fun, princess." I press my lips to hers before murmuring, "Let me show you."

"Do I have a choice?" she asks, her voice sounding resigned to her fate.

"No, you don't." I tilt my head. "But that doesn't stop you fighting me, baby. I like it when you fight. It makes me harder." I grab my crotch and squeeze.

"You are being disgusting."

"I'm the only one here not resisting my desires," I grab her hand, forcing it over my crotch. "Do you feel what you do to me, princess?"

Her eyes dilate and she squeezes slightly, her lip trembling. As if she snaps out of it, she grabs my balls, squeezing hard enough to hurt.

I grab her wrist before she can do damage.

"I think you want me to punish you, Gwendolyne. Fighting me only makes sense if you want me to hoist you over my shoulder and carry you into my sex room so I can paddle that beautiful ass of yours."

Her nostrils flare, but her beautiful emerald eyes betray her as desire overwhelms anger.

Fuck this.

Grabbing her arm, I lift her over my shoulder and head toward the stairs.

"Put me down," she protests.

"No, princess, you're mine now. I'm taking you to the sex room to consummate our marriage."

She turns stiff as I carry her up the stairs, gripping her with one hand as she half-heartedly tries to fight.

Reaching the top of the staircase, I turn into our bedroom and push through the door nearest the bed frame that leads into the sex room.

I throw her onto the bed so that she's propped

against pillows and proceed to clamp the chains on each post of the bed onto her wrists and ankles so that her arms are dangling in the air and thighs are spread wide.

This is what she needs right now—to be at my mercy and let go of everything else that ties her down in life, including Piero.

Once I'm done securing her arms and legs, I stand back admiring how perfect she looks on that bed like a gift waiting for me to unwrap in that pretty, elegant white dress.

"You look delightful." I walk over to the bed, unable to take my eyes away from hers. "True perfection."

"Stay away from me!"

"We both know that's not what you want." I tilt my head to the side. "Tell the truth, princess, or I'll be forced to punish you for lying."

Her lips tighten into a straight line as she glares at me in defiance.

I pull my tie off and throw my jacket aside, unbuttoning my shirt as I watch her.

Gwen can't help but look at my chest, tracking the tattoos across it.

I notice the desire written on her face, but I don't say anything. Instead, I move my hands to my belt and pull it off before dropping my pants to the floor.

Her face flushes deep red the moment she sees the outline of my cock as she takes her eyes off me, trying to look anywhere else. She can't resist as her gaze drifts back to my throbbing erection.

I smile before moving toward her, bringing my hand

to her face to swipe a lock of hair behind her ear. "You're mine now."

Moving away from her, I grab a blindfold off the nightstand. I return and fix it on Gwen. The sensation of being unable to see heightens all other senses.

"P-Please," she quivers.

I run my hand along her body, feeling the way she trembles beneath me.

"Please, what?" I ask, enjoying the way her breathing grows shallow and rapid as I brush my finger-tips across her skin, moving from her neck to her legs and back again until she's shaking.

"Don't do this," she grits out.

"It's already done, princess. You're my wife now. I'm going to show you what that means tonight." I remove my prosthetic hand, grabbing the blunt hook out of the nightstand drawer to put on. She has no idea that I have a prosthetic. It cost me millions of dollars because no one can tell the fucking difference. It's that good.

I climb between her spread thighs, lifting the hem of her dress to her ribcage to reveal a pair of lacy white panties that barely cover her cunt.

"So damn perfect," I growl, moving my face to her pussy and inhaling her scent. "You're so fucking sweet, Gwendolyne."

"You're insane."

I smirk, as her insults are meager at best. "I can take you places you never dreamed of. I know that you want to go there with me."

She fights against the restraints as I use the tip of my

hook to draw soft circles on her skin. She turns as stiff as stone. "I—Is that a knife?"

"No, relax," I murmur, dragging it lower toward her panties. "Give in to the way it feels."

I drag the tip lower and stop above her clit, making her gasp. "Cillian, what are—"

"Quiet," I interrupt, drawing patterns in her skin with the tip of my hook. "Be a good girl and listen to what I say."

She exhales a long breath as her body relaxes into the soft mattress.

I use my good hand to pull her panties down and I circle her clit with the tip of my hook, enjoying the way she shudders. It's sexy seeing her at my mercy, bound and blindfolded, while I play with her.

A strangled moan escapes her lips as she tries to fight it, and it's the single most beautiful sound I've ever heard. Gwendolyne Hook is divine and I don't deserve her, but that's not going to stop me from claiming her and keeping hold of her so damn hard someone would have to burn me alive to win her off me.

"You make me hard, Gwen," I breathe, allowing my breath to tease against her clit and soaking wet folds. "The smell of you." I inhale again. "So fucking divine."

I suck her clit into my mouth, watching as her face contorts with pleasure. The only bad thing about the blindfold is I can't see those emerald eyes as they dilate for me.

I dip between her lips, dragging my tongue through them. She tastes as good as I remember, like fucking honey. I want to devour her, inside and out.

"Once I'm through with you, princess, there won't be a part of you that doesn't crave me. I'm going to ensure you're ruined for all other men, so that you can never be without me. All thoughts of escape will be eradicated."

"That's not going to happen," she replies, but she doesn't sound certain.

I slide two fingers inside her, watching the way her back arches. "I wouldn't be so sure."

Her slender throat bobs as she swallows, and her answer is hesitant. "It's not possible," she breathes.

I use the tip of the hook to slide it through her pussy, coating it in her arousal. "Moan for me," I demand, before sucking on her clit.

Her hips buck and she does moan. It's music to my ears as I devour her. Pushing the hook further into her, she groans.

"What the hell is that?"

"Don't think, feel."

Her hips buck wildly and my cock leaks all over my hand as I pleasure myself, wanting nothing more than to feel her hot little mouth around me. Once I'm sure she's on the edge of oblivion, I stop.

"No," she cries out, her hips rising.

"Don't be so greedy. What about me?"

She tenses, turning as stiff as stone. "What about you?"

"I think it's about time you had another taste."

She shudders. "I'd rather not."

"Greedy Gwendolyne, only wants her own pleasure." I unhook her wrist chains and link them together before yanking her forward. She rests on her knees at the edge of the bed, her ankles still chained. "Now be a good girl, and open wide for your captain."

She spits at me, which has the opposite effect of what she intends.

"Dirty Gwen, spitting on my cock. You're making me harder."

"You are disgusting," she snarls.

"Open. Your. Mouth," I demand.

Her breathing labors as I release the chains and grab her hair instead, forcing her head backward. "Please, Cillian."

"Shut it, princess. It's all a different story when I'm eating your cunt, but the moment I want to use you, you go all stiff. Open."

Her lip wobbles before she opens her mouth, barely enough to fit the tip in. But I take advantage of the moment and press forward, savoring the sensation of her slick tongue as it slides around my flesh. "That's it, suck it like a good girl."

She moans around me, proving she's enjoying this as much as I am. The urge to dominate her bubbles through the need flooding through my veins. The thought of pushing forward until she gags on my cock sets my skin on fire, making me crave it.

All I want is to take hold of her hair and fuck her throat so hard she chokes on me. I'm not one for resisting my urges. Grabbing a handful of her hair I shove my cock into her throat without warning.

She tenses as she chokes on me, trying to pull away. The sadistic side of me takes over and I press deeper, forcing her to submit to me. After a few thrusts, she works out how to breathe through her nose, relaxing a little as her lungs fill with oxygen.

I want to see into her eyes. So I use my hook to pull away the blindfold, keeping it out of her view.

"Keep going, baby, breathe through your nose like that," I order.

Tears spring to her eyes as she frantically begs me with them to end this torment. Yet her wrists are hand-cuffed together and her ankles are still shackled to the bed, so there's no chance of escape. I love having her like this, completely at my mercy. As I move faster and faster, all I can do is groan, loving how good it feels to be taken so deeply into her throat.

Once I'm sure I can't last longer, I stop. Determined to make this pretty little treasure mine forever. Once I've had her, I know there's nothing in this world, other than death, that will stop me from keeping her.

19

GWENDOLYNE

I pant for oxygen, sure he was about to suffocate me with his dick. Death by oral sex surely isn't common, but that's what it will say on my post-mortem.

Cillian moves back and the flash of something shiny catches my eye. I scream as I notice the hook in place of his hand.

How did I not notice until this point he's missing a fucking hand?!

His jaw clenches. "I guess you didn't realize I only have one hand?"

I shake my head. "No."

He rolls his eyes. "I think the guy I commissioned to make my prosthetic did too good a job." Cillian comes closer. "Why do you think they call me Hook?"

"Because it's your surname," I say.

He laughs. "Not originally. I changed my name."

"Why?" I ask.

"Too many questions. And that's not why we're here, is it?"

I swallow hard, wondering if he can actually have sex with that thing without tearing me apart. "Can you put your hand back on?"

A flash of something in his eyes, I think might be hurt, ignites, but just as quickly a wall of steel shuts it down. "You know, sex with the hook can be fun."

I swallow hard. "I'm scared you'll gut me with it."

He laughs, bringing it closer to my face. "It's blunt, feel it."

I reach out and place a finger on the tip of the hook, thankful to find the end is blunt. "It still looks lethal."

He smirks. "And don't you know lethal is exciting?" He brushes the tip of the hook down my neck, moving lower, circling my already hard nipples with the tip.

Need pulses between my thighs as I watch him, wondering what happened to his hand. He's so unhinged and tortured, and I'm intrigued about what made him that way. The last thing I should feel toward Cillian is intrigue.

"Lie down for me, princess," he says, nodding toward the bed.

A part of me is hesitant about doing what he says and another part longs to obey him. It's so fucked. So I flop inelegantly onto my back, unable to control my movements with my ankles still chained to the bed and my hands bound together. And that's when my attention moves from the hook to his hand, which is stroking his dick.

My entire body blazes with heat as I stare at the

erection between his legs. He's huge, not only long, but thick. The thought of that inside me makes me shudder.

"I'm going to claim you," he purrs, eyes fixated on mine. "And you're going to love it. That, I guarantee."

His words make the ache inside me deepen. It's hard to believe how badly I want him after everything. My mind is blank as I watch him crawl between my thighs, a predatory look in his eyes. It's like I'm a wounded antelope in front of a lion, waiting for him to pounce with no way of escape. He wraps his hand around my throat and settles his cock against my pussy.

I'm completely at odds with myself—my body begging for him, despite the disgust coursing through my veins. His touch is cold and forceful, but it sets my skin on fire. And the sickest part is, the mere thought of him fucking me makes my pussy ache more.

He rubs the swollen head of his cock over my clit, coating my pussy in pre-cum. "I've been waiting too damn long for this."

My brow furrows. "Two weeks isn't long."

He moves his lips to mine and murmurs, "No, I've been waiting my entire fucking life to find my home and I've found it. In your tight little cunt. You're my home, Gwendolyne. And I will fight to keep hold of you so long as my heart is still beating in my chest."

The intensity of his words steals the oxygen from my lungs and makes goosebumps erupt on my skin. Conflict over loving the way he speaks to me and hating the way he's gone about this rage a war in my head.

I close my eyes tight, wishing he'd do it and get it over with. I'm sure I'm going to die from anticipation, but then he slams into me. His cock breaking me apart as I scream in pain.

"Breathe," he coaches, his lips lingering over mine. "It'll get better if you relax."

Relax?

This man is insane if he thinks I can relax. He's breaking me apart with his giant dick. "I can't relax. It hurts."

"You can relax, princess." He moves his lips to my ear and murmurs. "I know you don't think I'm capable of winning your heart, mind and soul, but I'm going to prove to you that I am."

His words send a shiver down my spine. He thinks he can win my heart, and that scares me. Because what he's done should make that impossible.

Why do his words send butterflies fluttering to life in the pit of my stomach?

And yet I feel myself succumb to the pleasure that consumes my body. Every thrust is better than the last, as Cillian takes me without mercy. His cock pummels a spot deep within that makes me moan.

"Cillian," I breathe, wanting him to look me in the eye.

He looks at me; eyes wild with a fire I can hardly describe. "It's captain to you, princess."

I swallow hard and nod, wrapping my hands around the back of his neck. "Yes, captain."

He groans, clamping his eyes shut as he murmurs, "Good girl." His hand has a firm girp on my hip, while his hook rests at my side, and he thrusts himself deeper, pushing me toward the edge with no sign of letting up.

"Oh fuck, captain!" I cry, knowing that any minute I'll come.

And he stops, leaving me panting and wanting.

"No!" I squeal. "Why did you stop?"

He kisses me, his tongue gently swiping against my lips until I grant him entry. After a torturously slow kiss, he says, "Because when you come with me inside you, I want it to be the single most explosive orgasm you've ever experienced. I want you to see stars and pass out from the intensity so that nothing on this earth could ever erase that memory from your mind." He bites my earlobe, sending a thrilling pain through my body. "And the only way to guarantee that is to delay it." He bites my bottom lip before sucking on it. "Now, on your hands and knees for me." He pulls his cock out of me, leaving me empty and desperate for more.

"Cillian, this is—"

"Be a good girl and do as your captain tells you."

I grind my teeth together, but the need to climax wins over as I have to twist the chains on my ankles to get onto all fours for him, glancing over my shoulder to watch him.

He stands there with his hook gleaming, his cock in his other hand as he strokes it. And I hate how badly I want him.

I shouldn't want anything from him. He took me captive and I'm on the brink of begging him to fuck me.

"Tell me what you want."

I swallow my pride. "You. I want you."

The smirk on his lips is pure fucking sin. It's evil. The kind of smirk I'd expect to see on the devil's face if

I were to meet him. There's a darkness in this man that scares me and excites me all at the same time.

"Good girl, Gwendolyne." I don't know why him using my full name gives me shivers. "Now, face forward."

I do as he says, looking forward at the headboard as my heart hammers erratically. When I finally feel his cock nudge against my dripping wet entrance, I sigh in relief. The need for him is all-consuming. He shoves into me, one hand clawing at my hip and the tip of his hook pressing hard into my other hip, drawing me closer to him as he fucks me with force. The hook, although blunt, adds an exquisite pain that I can't believe I enjoy.

All I can do is succumb to his touch, his demand, and allow him to take me.

"That's it, you are doing so well taking my cock like that," he praises, his voice sinfully deep and laced with desire. "You are such a good fucking girl and all mine."

"Fuck me harder, captain," I say, glancing at him over my shoulder.

His lips curve and he spanks my ass, the impact making me gasp in surprise. "You have a foul mouth for a princess."

I arch my back more, knowing that I've never been this turned on.

"Please," I beg.

He removes the hook from my hip and drags it down my spine as he shoves his cock into me with such force that I can hardly catch my breath. "I get the sense you enjoy pain. And I can't wait to inflict more on you."

I bite my lip, as I think he's right. The pain only amplifies the pleasure, which is confusing.

"Tell me what you want," he demands.

"I want you to make me come."

His cruel laugh slices through my thoughts, making me desperate to get away from the reality of this situation.

"Such a needy girl, but it's not time yet. Tell me that you're my whore," he demands.

My body turns stiff at the thought of saying that. "What?"

He grabs my neck from behind, pulling me at an odd angle so that his lips are against my ear. "Tell me that you're a whore only for me. And that this pussy is mine to fuck and breed, forever and fucking always. Then, perhaps I'll let you come."

The desperation for release wins out. "I'm your whore," I murmur, grinding my hips backward as he viciously drives his cock deeper.

"More," he demands. "Make me believe you."

I swallow hard, staring forward as the shame heightens at the words I'm about to say. "I'm a whore only for you, captain. My pussy is yours. It belongs to you."

He growls against my ear and then bites at it, sending a thrill through my veins. His grip on my throat tightens, forcing me to arch my back further with each thrust. "Good girl," he purrs. "Take my cock and moan for me. Moan for me, like a dirty little whore who can't get enough of her captain's cock."

He digs the hook into my hip so hard it brings tears

to my eyes. I want him to keep going until all of my inhibitions are obliterated and I can no longer stand on two feet. Nothing compares to this sweet torture. Cillian takes ownership of every part of me until all that's left is a submissive slut panting in need and screaming in pleasure. I'm going to die if I don't come soon.

And then he stops and pulls out, making me scream in frustration.

"Don't worry. It's almost time, but when I breed you, I want to see your face." He flips me back onto my back and slides his hand around my throat, his hook still clawing into my hip. "Tell me who owns you," he orders.

"You do."

He arches a brow.

"Captain," I breathe, knowing I've never been more desperate for anything in my life.

"Good girl," he praises, sliding inside me. His cock drilling me deep and hard as I rest my head back against the pillow, his hand still wrapped around my throat like a collar. "I want to feel this tight little cunt come all over my cock," he grunts, eyes filled with a determination that makes me wetter. "And when you come, I want you to make a fucking mess of the bed with your juices so I can lap it all up afterward. I'll taste both of our essences mixed together and I'm going to keep devouring you all fucking night. I won't stop until you're well and truly bred with cum and pass out."

The mere idea makes me shudder, my muscles clamping around the thick girth of him.

"Do you understand?"

"Oh, fuck! Yes, captain!" I shout as my climax hits me with an intensity so extreme it feels like I've died and gone to heaven. Every part of my body spasms as my nerve endings set on fire. Cillian sends me off a cliff edge, spiraling into an abyss of pure pleasure. "Oh my God."

"That's right, princess. Call your God. That's me now," he growls, the thickness of his cock swelling before he explodes inside me. "I'm your God and don't ever fucking forget it."

As we both recover from our mutual highs, reality hits me. Cillian took my virginity. A part of me which was meant to be reserved for Piero. The sickest part is that I loved it. Hell I begged for it.

Shame plagues me as Cillian rolls off of me and then climbs between my thighs. And before I can question him, he's lapping up my arousal and his, tasting our mixed essence. And the fire reignites within me. "Delicious. Once I've finished eating you," he murmurs, eyes burning with wicked intent. "I'm going to fuck you again. By morning you will be so full of my cum it will be dripping from you all day tomorrow."

God save me, as I'm not sure I'm going to survive this night, let alone the rest of my life married to Cillian Hook.

CILLIAN

"The dockmaster is involved." I pace the detective's living room. "Why else would all five of the guys he told me have access to his system be clean?"

This detective has got no answers for me and all the while the rat remains in my organization, plotting against me. And there's nothing I hate more than a fucking traitor. I rub my prosthetic across the back of my neck.

The detective shrugs, which angers me. "I couldn't say, but it's whoever betrayed you is good at keeping the trail clean. I'll keep digging."

This is terrible fucking news. This means that all bets are off, and Smyth could be behind the stolen shipments. If he is, I'll cut his fucking balls off and feed them to the sharks at the Goddamn aquarium. Hell, I'll break in and feed the entirety of him to them.

"Where have you gone?" The detective asks.

"What?"

He shrugs. "I've noticed when we've met that you get this far off look in your eyes. And you look a little insane each time it happens."

I narrow my eyes, glaring at him. "I am fucking insane. What's your point?"

He clears his throat. "No point, just an observation."

"Well, observe who the fuck is messing with me, or I'll be out for blood."

"I'm not one of your thugs in your outfit." His eyes narrow. "And I don't expect to be threatened."

Motherfucker.

I clench my fists. "Is that right?"

He stands taller and looks me dead in the eye. "Don't threaten me again, understood?"

The desire to claw his eyes out for speaking to me like that is strong, but he's right. He's not in my outfit and I need him, so pissing him off isn't an option. If he doesn't find out who is behind the stolen shipments, it's costing us too much money. I'll be left to try to find out who the fuck is behind it by myself, which wouldn't be easy.

"You've got that look again."

"Do the job I pay you for and then we've got no problem. Okay?"

He nods, but it's unconvincing. "Fine, I'll ramp up my efforts."

"Thank you," I say, trying to keep things cordial between us.

"Congratulations, by the way."

"For what?"

He arches a brow. "Getting married."

The mention of getting married draws my mind back to my obsession with Gwendolyne. "How did you know about that?"

He laughs. "I wouldn't be a good detective if I didn't know about the most talked about mafia marriage in Californian history, would I?"

He has a point, but I can feel my suspicious side taking over. I fear that soon enough I'll fire this idiot and go it alone, because I don't trust anyone.

Never have and never will—okay, that's a lie. Stupidly, I trusted Piero, who fucked me over. But I vowed from that moment the only person I would trust was myself and Ma.

"I want answers, okay? And I don't care how you get them or how much it costs me."

He arches a brow. "Surely you care how much it costs?"

"I won't have you ripping me off, but within reason. I'll pay whatever is necessary to find the bastard double-crossing me."

He nods in response. "Fair enough. As I said, I'll get you results as fast as I can."

I narrow my eyes. "Good. And no more investigating me, got it?"

He chuckles. "Wouldn't dream of it."

I sigh heavily, hating that I have to rely on this guy to get my answers. He's a douchebag with no allegiance to me, which is risky. "I'll wait for your call," I say, before turning and heading out of his rundown shack of a house.

All I can think about is my wife and the fact she's

waiting at home for me. My cock pulses to life and I know that I need to have her now before I go insane. It's a two-hour drive home which will be excruciating. Swallowing hard, I push away my rage and get into my car with one destination in mind. Gwendolyne's perfect little

I STORM INTO MY HOUSE, still pumped and angry about learning that the detective has no answers. Not to mention, if I don't get back out to sea soon, I'm going to lose my shit, and yet I don't trust hiring a boat. It's too risky, as I have many enemies in the city. For now, my wife is going to have to be my salvation.

"Where's Gwendolyne?" I ask one of my staff, whose name I can't remember.

He pales. "I-I'm sorry, sir. I haven't seen her."

"At all?" I snap.

He shakes his head. "Not since this morning."

My eyes narrow, a sense of foreboding skating across the back of my mind. If Gwendolyne escaped, I'd kill every member of my security team. Heading for the kitchen, I'm sure Rosa, my cook, would have seen her during the day.

As I turn the corner toward it, I hear her voice echoing down the corridor. It's a sweet and beautiful sound that I'll never get tired of hearing.

"I'm going to go out of my mind trapped in here," she says.

I creep closer to the doorway, eavesdropping on the conversation she's having.

Someone sighs. "Is it much different from when you lived at home?"

Tilly.

I don't know what's with that girl, but she's hanging around Gwendolyne like a bad smell.

"At least I was allowed to go out when I was at home. Albeit with a bodyguard, but still..."

"Maybe you can go outside for a bit to the beach? I'm sure one of the guards would be alright with it if I'm with you."

I've heard enough of this shit.

I storm into the room. "Gwendolyne is forbidden from leaving this house, do you understand?" I glare at Tilly.

Her eyes widen. "Certainly, sir. I apologize."

"You work for me, which means you follow my rules." I glance at Rosa, who's busying herself with cooking. "That goes for everyone who works for me. I don't want anyone taking my wife outside of these fucking walls, understood?"

Gwendolyne stands. "Do you realize I'm right here?" Her nostrils flare. "Are you going to keep me a prisoner in this house forever?"

I tilt my head. "Not forever, just until I'm sure I can trust you not to run away."

Her eyes narrow to slits. "Which will be never."

I shake my head. "You and I both know you don't want to go back to your old life."

Tilly clears her throat and stands, drawing my attention to her. "I will continue my work, sir. Again, I apologize for suggesting I take Gwen outside. It won't happen again."

I clench my jaw and nod.

She leaves and I notice Gwen watching her go with an odd expression. I don't know what is going on with those two, but I intend to find out.

"Come on." I grab her wrist. "You want to go out? We'll go out together."

"I don't want to go anywhere with you. I'd rather stay locked in a room!" she growls, sounding hysterical.

"You're being unreasonable."

She yanks her hand out of my grasp. "Unreasonable? I'm the one person in this marriage being reasonable."

I sigh heavily. "Shut up and come for a walk to the beach. If you want to get out of these walls, you can go out with me only."

Gwendolyne searches my eyes for a moment before realizing that if she wants some fresh air, she has no choice. "Fine."

I lace my fingers with hers and pull her toward the back door to the garden, which leads to my private beach. The garden is well manicured since I have two full-time employees working on it. I haven't been to the beach where Poison is usually moored ever since it's been out of action.

I can sense she wants to pull her hand away, as it's stiff against mine, but I persevere and keep my hand wrapped around hers.

"Do you like the sea?" I ask, trying to make small talk with my wife.

Her jaw clenches. "Yes, when I'm not being held captive."

"You're such a liar. I think your favorite part of this is being held captive." I wink at her.

She rolls her eyes. "Shut up and let me enjoy my time out in the fresh air."

I clench my jaw, as I rarely allow anyone to speak to me like that. Gwendolyne appears to be the one exception to my rules. Instead of responding, I allow her the peace she requested as we make our way toward the beach. I hate seeing the slip without Poison there. It doesn't feel right.

Once we get onto the beach, I release her hand and allow her to wander freely, keeping a watchful eye.

She glances at me, looking a little surprised that I let go, but she doesn't question me. Instead, she walks toward the calm water and once she's close to the edge, removes her shoes and sits, dipping her feet into the soft waves.

I watch her, wondering how the hell this happened. Rage and my desire for revenge are what have fueled me for so long that I can't understand why that's being overshadowed by my obsession and desire for Gwendolyne.

She glances back at me, a crease forming between her brows as she notices me staring at her. And I can't help but feel in awe of how beautiful she looks with her dark hair blowing in the gentle breeze.

"Why are you standing there staring at me? It's kind of creepy."

I tilt my head. "Because I'm admiring the view."

She shakes her head and returns her attention to the sea, but doesn't invite me to sit with her.

I close the gap between us and take off my shoes and socks before sitting on the sand beside her. Other than the soft sound of the waves lapping against the shore and the birds in the sky, silence falls between us.

My wife breaks it, sighing heavily before turning toward me. "Do I have to locked in the house?"

"It's for your own safety."

Her jaw clenches. "My own safety? This place is like Fort Knox."

"Yes, it is, but that doesn't mean you won't try to escape."

Those emerald eyes are full of fire as she looks into mine. "Then make sure I have a security guard with me or something. I'm going insane locked in that fucking house."

"It's a beautiful house with lovely views, and you're going insane? I'd hate to see how you'd do in a real prison."

"At least in a real prison, I'd have time outside. Do you realize that prisoners are allowed outdoors?"

"Fine. "I'll allow you outside with a security guard escorting you." I pause, rubbing a hand across the back of my neck. "Actually, make it two."

She laughs. "Why? Because you think I could take one on and escape?"

"Possibly. You're strong for a lass."

A hint of a smile curves her luscious lips. "I'll take that as a compliment."

"You should." I force my gaze away from her and out toward the sea.

"I'm surprised you don't own a boat." She gazes at the empty pier.

"I do, but it's in the shop." I run a hand through my hair. "The engine failed."

"Oh." She glances at me. "Is it a big boat?"

"Big enough." Talking about it adds to my irritation at not being able to get out of the water. If the dock-master doesn't deliver on his promise, there will be hell to pay.

She relaxes slightly, placing her head on my shoulder and leaning into my embrace.

I squeeze her more, finding this moment a little at odds with all the other time we've spent together. Mainly because she's not trying to rip my head off. All that rage I'd felt not ten minutes ago has dissipated as I stare at the calming movement of the waves before us.

I could get used to spending time with her, not just with my cock deep inside her. And while that thought alarms me, it's what I expected from the moment I set eyes on her at her engagement party. Gwendolyne is a treasure that I would risk my life to keep for eternity.

GWENDOLYNE

"I've got to get away from him no matter what it takes," I say, shaking my head as I sit in the library with Tilly. We're going over possible escape options. I'm getting desperate to get away before I fall deeper into this warped trap he's constructed for me.

Piero can pick us up, so we need to get out of the house and gates undetected by Cillian's security.

The best option is for me to get into the trunk of Tilly's car and hope they don't check it. She said it's a fifty percent chance they won't, but they're not the best odds.

All other options are too risky, like trying to bribe a guard. If the guard is loyal to Cillian, it would reveal Tilly as a mole within his household staff.

"This is it then? Do we try to go today?"

She nods. "I think it's our only option. The quicker we get you out, the better. Piero is desperate to see you."

My stomach churns at the mention of Piero. While I want to get away from here for my own sanity, I know for certain I don't want Piero anymore. The idea of him touching me makes me feel a little queasy. It makes no sense, considering it's all I wanted before.

"I might throw up," I say.

Tilly purses her lips. "Try not to throw up. I'm not good at dealing with sick people."

"Don't worry, I'm not actually going to throw up." I stand, bracing myself against the bookshelf next to me. "I don't think..."

"I'll have to get out of here if you are going to be sick. Otherwise, we'll both be throwing up."

"No, I think I'm fine." I sit again. "It's the anxiety about trying to pull this off."

"It's going to be dangerous," Tilly admits.

"You don't think we could try a disguise? Like as one of the other staff?" I suggest.

Her eyes narrow and she rubs her chin. "Not sure it would work, but then if they check my trunk tonight, we're screwed, too."

Cillian pushes open the door and strides into the library, making me freeze. He looks furious, and my stomach drops as I realize he's caught us plotting my escape. This is it; our plan is over.

"What are you two doing in here?" he asks, his voice cold.

I can't help but exchange a nervous glance with Tilly, as I've got to work out what to say.

"We were talking. I don't have anyone to talk to. Sometimes, Tilly keeps me company."

"Talking," he repeats the word as if it's a curse word,

his tone suggesting he's suspicious. "What is it you two talk about?"

I hesitate a moment, glancing at the book I'd been reading. "We were discussing my favorite wildlife photographer and how I'd love to be as good as him one day." I pick up the book and wave it in the air.

I didn't believe his eyes could narrow further, but they do. "You," he says, glaring at Tilly. "Leave. Now."

A look of concern enters Tilly's eyes, but she doesn't have a choice. "Of course, sir."

I sense in that moment from the look she gives me that this is the last time I'll see her. It's too hot with Cillian catching us scheming together to attempt a breakout. If he suspects she's not loyal to him, then he'll kill her.

It makes my heart sink; without Tilly's help, I'll never escape. I fear in time I'll learn to like being here a little too much, considering the way he makes me feel when he touches me.

Tilly gives me a sad smile before turning and walking out the door. I watch her leave, feeling more alone than ever.

"Why do you have to be so rude to your staff?" I ask, glaring at him.

"Shut it!" he barks, walking over to me and grabbing a piece of paper that Tilly left on the seat. I realize that it's my escape plan and panic overrides everything else.

"Cillian, I need you," I murmur, drawing his eyes away from the paper he's about to unfold. "It's why I'm hanging out with Tilly. I'm going crazy on my own, thinking about you."

There's a flash of hope in his eyes, but then they narrow. "Are you messing with me, princess?"

I shake my head. "Of course not. I've been fantasizing about you fucking me against the bookcase since I found this place."

He licks his lips like an angry wolf and stalks toward me, placing the piece of paper in his jacket pocket. At least it gives Tilly enough time to get away. I tell myself that's the reason I suggested sex because I wouldn't be able to live with myself if Tilly gets captured by him and murdered. However, I know there's a dark part of me that wants this—wants him.

Cillian lifts me, his prosthetic hand more forceful than the other. Ever since I learned it's bionic, I've noticed subtle differences. He carries me to the bookcase and slams me against it, books falling off it from the force. "I'm going to make that fantasy a reality," he murmurs against my lips, making my stomach fill with butterflies. "Every single one, so tell me your wildest fucking dreams and I'll make them come true."

I swallow hard, wishing that he wasn't so good with words. He makes it sound so tempting, although I'm here against my will. His lips capture mine in a passionate and all-consuming kiss, stealing my breath away.

One arm remains around my back while the other slips between us as he slides the string of my thong out of the way. His finger dips into my soaking wet pussy.

"Fuck, princess," he growls, sounding feral. "I love how wet you are for me."

I hear the zipper of his pants as he pulls it down,

feeling him fumble between us as if he's desperate to get inside me. And then, I feel the hot and heavy press of his cock against my entrance.

"Look at me," he demands.

I look into those chestnut eyes and the moment I do, he drives every inch inside.

A scream catches in the back of my throat because two weeks of constant sex with him hasn't gotten me used to his size. Every time it feels like I'm being torn apart.

He rests his face against my neck and kisses me. "I can't get enough of you, Gwendolyne. I'll never get enough of you."

He moves back enough to look into my eyes as he lifts me up and down his cock, fucking me against the bookcase as if I weigh nothing. I'm sure he'll bruise my back as it slams against the wood of the shelves behind, but it feels so good.

I can feel the books shifting behind me as he fucks me, each thrust more forceful than the last. I cry out in pleasure, clinging onto him and wrapping my legs around his waist like a vise as we continue moving together in a frenzied rhythm of lust.

Although I may have been lying about this being my fantasy, I can't deny how hot it is. I claw my fingers through his hair, not wanting this moment to end, because once it does, I will remember how much I hate what he's done to me.

"You're such a good girl, taking my cock so well." His arms strain as he increases the force of his upward strokes, fucking me so hard I can hardly breathe. "As if you were made to fit me, princess."

The suggestion we're made to fit each other should terrify me, but it doesn't.

"Tell me what I like to hear." His eyes blaze with fire as they hold mine.

"I'm a whore for you, captain," I murmur, my body reacting to the words in kind. The word whore is so degrading, but the way he puts it heightens my arousal.

"That's right, my good little whore taking her captain's cock like a pro," he purrs, moving away from the bookcase and lowering me onto the sofa I'd been sitting on before. Still inside me, he shrugs off his jacket and tosses it aside before fucking me in this new position. Every thrust hits a spot deep within me that sets my world ablaze.

"Fuck," I breathe.

"You like it deep, don't you?" he asks, watching me.

I swallow hard. "Yes, it feels so good."

"Good," he growls, fucking me harder. "Because I'm going to fuck you so hard you can't breathe."

I cry out, the pain and pleasure excruciatingly good. "Oh fuck!"

Cillian pulls my bottom lip between his teeth and nibbles before releasing it. "Such a dirty mouth," he breathes.

I groan, the intensity of this moment is almost too much for me. It's impossible to hate the way he makes me feel when he's like this. He's taking me to heights I never dreamed of.

"I'm going to fill you so full with my cum it will drip

out of your pussy for hours." His thrusts become erratic, all control slipping away as primal desire takes over. "And you're going to fucking come on my cock when I tell you to and make a nice mess of this sofa, like the good girl you are."

I moan. "Yes, captain, please make me come."

His jaw works as he fucks me harder than I believed possible, forcing me to claw onto the sides of the sofa to ground myself. "Tell me you want my cum, Gwendolyne. Tell me how much of a whore you are for it."

I swallow hard, all inhibitions no longer present. "I want your cum so bad, please give me it," I beg, running a hand over my nipples.

His eyes snap to them, narrowing. "And how badly do you want to be bred?"

I stiffen, as he keeps throwing that word around. "What?"

"You heard me, princess. I'm going to get you pregnant," he growls, sounding a little feral. "Breed your pretty little pussy until you're growing big and round with my baby."

I shudder, as the thought is terrifying. However, his comment can't fight off the violent need to come apart. "You're crazy," I murmur.

He wraps his fingers around my throat. "Crazy for you, princess. Now come for me."

He restricts my airway, making stars filter into my vision. And then I'm hit by the most intense and delicious sensation I've ever felt as my orgasm comes. I feel the pleasure rush through me like a storm, taking over my body until I am shaking and quivering, unable to do anything else but surrender to his will. Cillian doesn't stop fucking me until I'm spent from the pleasure, spilling his cum deep within me.

The intensity of the moment is overwhelming and fills me with a strange combination of terror and euphoria as reality rushes back to me. But before I have time to think it through, Cillian's lips are on mine in a passionate kiss.

He rolls off me, breathing heavily. And then he tucks his cock back into his pants and clears his throat, glancing at the carnage of books we left in our wake. "That was fucking beautiful, but we need to tidy this up."

I swallow hard as I sit up, feeling shame as his cum drips from me. He's had me countless times since our wedding night, but this was the first time I instigated it.

His eyes dilate as they fall on my pussy. "You're a fucking vision filled with my cum," he murmurs.

Heat coils through me. Even though we just had sex, I feel oddly vulnerable. I pull my panties back into place and yank my dress from my hips, jumping to my feet.

Cillian's expression is conflicted as he turns to clear up the books, putting them back. While he's distracted, I take advantage to retrieve the piece of paper that he took from Tilly from his jacket pocket, stuffing it into the cup of my bra.

Cillian turns around then, eyes narrowing as if he suspects something. "Aren't you going to help, princess? This was your fault."

Thankfully, he didn't notice me take the paper from his pocket. I walk over to help him put the books back.

"Is there a particular order?" I ask, as I pick the first one up.

He shakes his head. "No, put them back wherever."

As I gather a handful of books and place them back onto the bookcase, I glance at him. "Do you like reading, then?"

Cillian's chestnut eyes snap to me and there's a haunted look in them. "No, not much of a reader."

"Why so many books then?"

He tilts his head. "Why so many questions?"

The fact he dodges my questions increases my intrigue about Cillian. Ever since I learned he's missing a hand, it made me wonder how he lost it? I don't buy the crocodile story.

What is his story?

I shouldn't want to know it, because he's a psychopath who has stolen me from my fiancé, forced me into marriage, and acts like we're a normal married couple.

Then why the hell do I want to find out what makes Cillian Hook tick?

CILLIAN

"*W*here are you taking me?" Gwendolyne asks, her arms folded across her waist.

"I told you, it's a surprise."

Her eyes narrow. "I'm not fond of your surprises, Cillian."

"You'll like this one, trust me."

She laughs. "I'm pretty sure you're the last man on this earth I'll ever trust."

I ignore the pang in my chest. She will come over to the dark side and it doesn't matter whether I have to drag her into it. Once she accepts that we're meant to be, everything will fall into place.

The rest of the drive to the docks is silent and tense. We pull up to the docks, and Gwendolyne's eyes widen as she takes in the sight before her.

My yacht sits majestically in the water, the sun glinting off its black hull and the round windows shining like stars against a dark night sky. I climb out of the car and walk around, opening her door and offering her my hand.

She doesn't take it, opting to get out herself.

"Is this yours?" she asks.

I nod. "Yes, it's my yacht. Poison."

"Apt name," she says, glaring at me.

"Come on," I say, ignoring the dig and placing a hand on the small of her back. "Let me give you a tour. Then we'll take it for a spin." It's a sleek black vessel that glistens in the sunlight like polished obsidian stone. Poison is the only thing, other than my ma, that I love in this world. Poison has been my refuge for so long, I can't imagine life without it.

By the look of awe on Gwen's face, I can tell that she likes the boat, even if she wouldn't admit it. An excited energy radiates from her as we explore each part of the boat from the luxurious open plan living room and kitchen to the hot tub on the top deck, and then the luxurious bedrooms. I notice the way her lips part when I show her the sex room, her thighs subtly squeezing together.

It looks like my wife craves sex with me as much as I crave it with her. I've never wanted a woman the way I want Gwendolyne. She's pure fucking fire in bed.

"Would you like to take it out on the water?"

She nods. "Yes, I've never been out on a boat before."

I arch a brow. "You've lived in San Diego all your life and never been on a boat?" I find it impossible to believe.

"Never," she confirms.

It's odd because her father will have been on yachts, but then he has kept her sheltered. Until recently, I had no idea how beautiful my rival's daughter was, otherwise I may have kidnapped her years ago.

I steer Gwen toward the captain's deck and stand behind the wheel.

Her eyes widen. "Don't you have someone to drive it?"

I shake my head. "Why the fuck would I get someone else to drive this beauty when I can do it myself?"

"You have a license?" she confirms.

I yank her against my side. "Of course, that's why you call me captain." I wink.

She rolls her eyes. "I thought you liked it because you're a narcissist."

"That too," I say, trying not to get offended by her judgment.

The engine of the boat roars to life. A sound that is music to my ears. Over three months it's been out of action, and finally I can take to the ocean.

I sit in the driver's seat, pulling Gwen onto my lap. "Where would you like to go?"

She looks at me and I see a flicker of annoyance in those emerald eyes mixed with desire. "I don't know. You're the one that knows the ocean."

"Santa Catalina is beautiful," I say, squeezing her hip. "Although it may take a couple of hours to get there."

"Isn't there somewhere closer? I don't want to spend that much time with you."

"Liar," I say, holding her tighter. "You know two hours will speed by once I have you chained to the bed in my sex room."

Her thighs clench together, proving me right.

"How far have you been on this thing?" She clutches onto the counter in front of us, trying to change the subject.

"I've been to the Caribbean in it. I was at sea for about seventy days in total to get there."

Gwen looks shocked. "That's a long time. Did you have a crew with you?"

I nod. "Of course, I couldn't handle this thing on my own for that kind of trip."

"How come you sailed there? Isn't it easier to fly?"

I sigh heavily, as that trip was part of me running away from it all. Ma came with me while we regrouped and tried to work out how we could recover everything Piero stole from us. "I needed to get away," I say.

I don't speak about that time to anyone, not even Ma. Kira's loss haunts me to this day. I'll never be able to come to terms with the fact she died, and I survived. Kira was always good and pure. She didn't deserve to die so young.

Eighteen years old.

"Cillian?" Gwen is looking at me in an odd way. "Where did you go?"

I try to push away the dark memories infecting my mind. "Nowhere, princess." I tighten my grip on her hip. "How shall we spend the next two hours?"

"Surely you need to steer the boat," she says.

I smirk at her. "No, it has autopilot." I type our

course on the computer to Santa Catalina and ensure it's plotted correctly, and make sure the radar is on. "I don't have to focus at all."

She crosses her arms over her chest. "Can we enjoy the scenery?"

"Are you saying you don't want to scream my name the entire way?"

"I'm saying I'm sore and wouldn't mind a break." There's a vulnerability in her eyes because she's being honest with me.

I nod in response. "Of course, princess. Whatever you want." Saying that, I'm not thrilled. It means we need to talk, something I'm not good at. "Let's go onto the deck."

I allow her to jump off my lap and she leads the way out of the helm and onto the main deck, where there's a jacuzzi. "How about a dip?" I ask.

She shakes her head. "I didn't bring a swimsuit."

I chuckle. "Do you think you need one, considering I've seen you naked enough times?"

Her cheeks flush dark red. "But that will result in sex, which I don't want."

I grab her hip, pulling her back against my chest. "Are you suggesting that I have no control over my urges?"

She shrugs. "Isn't it inevitable?"

"I'll prove you wrong, princess. Strip." I may want to fuck her, but I won't. She's taken my cock night after night without complaint about being sore. I can grant her a day off from fucking.

She pulls her blouse from her waistband and then

unbuttons it, throwing it to one side. And then she unfastens her pants and pushes them down her hips, revealing her beautiful fucking ass and her white string thong.

My cock pulses in response, but I ignore it.

Gwen glances at me as she unhooks her bra and adds that to the pile of clothes before dropping her thong to the ground. Once she's naked, she's quick to hop into the bubbling hot tub, groaning the moment the water encases her. "It's nice in here," she murmurs, eyes clamped shut.

I don't waste time getting undressed and slipping into the tub with her, my cock as hard as stone.

Her eyes snap open, watching me with a mix of desire and caution. "It's peaceful at sea." She glances across the expanse of ocean as the boat navigates toward Santa Catalina.

"That's what I like about it, that it's so close to nature," I watch her. "No hustle and bustle of life on land. All you hear here is the sound of the waves and the wind. It reconnects me with the natural world and makes me feel as if I'm part of something bigger than myself." I know that she's shocked by my response as her eyes widen slightly.

"I agree. It's like you're connected to a vastness that can't be comprehended from land? A connection with every creature that shares this space."

I hate the way she looks at me, as if she can see into my soul and all the dark and deranged parts of me that battle with the minuscule part of me that has goodness within. "Yes," I breathe, moving closer to her. "I'm going to touch you, princess, but don't worry." I set my hand on her thigh, delighting in the way she trembles. "I'm not going to fuck you. I'm going to give you a massage."

She raises a brow. "That's unlikely."

"I'm going to prove you wrong. Turn your back to me."

She's hesitant, but does as she's told. I clamp my eyes shut and fight the part of me longing to impale her on my cock, grabbing her shoulders and kneading the tight muscles.

A soft moan escapes her lips as I work at the knots.

"Careful, princess. I have restraint, but if you keep moaning like that..."

"Sorry," she says, shaking her head. "You're good at this."

"Of course I am."

"Do you always have to be so cocky?"

"I thought it was one of my charming qualities," I tease.

"There are a lot of words I would use to describe you, Cillian, but charming isn't one of them."

I work on a difficult knot in her shoulder and she groans in response, head dropping forward. "I think I'm being charming. Here you are naked and ripe for fucking, and I'm helping you relax instead. You have a lot of tension, Gwen," I murmur.

"Can you blame me?" She glances over her shoulder at me. "You kidnapped me, for God's sake. What do you expect?"

I open my mouth to respond when she gasps, moving forward to look at the sea. "Oh my God!"

"What?" I ask.

Then I see what caught her attention as dolphins leap above the surface to the side of the yacht.

"They're majestic, aren't they?" I say, watching them, unable to help the pang of jealousy that they're forever at sea.

"Yes, I've never seen anything so beautiful," Gwen says, her face turned to the side. I watch her eyes sparkle with an innocent curiosity and it makes my chest tight, seeing her like that.

While she's focused on how beautiful the creatures are swimming beside the yacht, I can't take my eyes off the true beauty. Gwendolyne is like an angel who has fallen from heaven. More beautiful than anything I've ever seen.

For the first time in a long time, I feel a twinge of regret about the way I've handled everything with her. The stalking and kidnapping. How am I going to make her realize we belong together after that? The moment we first met, there was this connection between us. I know she feels too.

She glances at me. "Why aren't you watching the dolphins?"

"I've seen them a million times before. I find you far more fascinating."

Her cheeks flush red and she shakes her head. "That's ridiculous."

"It's ridiculously attractive how unaware of your beauty you are."

She glances away from me.

"Don't worry, I'm going to tell you how goddamn beautiful you are every day for the rest of our lives."

Her throat bobs as she swallows. "I hope that isn't long."

"Are you saying you'd rather be dead than married to me?" Her words have the power to wound me because I'm hooked on this woman. She has me in a chokehold, even if she doesn't know it. I would fall at her fucking feet and give her the world—the only thing I won't give her is her freedom.

A crease forms between her brows as she looks at me oddly. "Surely you don't intend for this to go on forever."

"This? Meaning you and I?"

She nods.

"I don't believe in divorce. And I've told you already, you're mine."

Her expression hardens. "When I think you aren't so bad, you go and ruin it all by being unreasonable. You're acting like a monster."

I chuckle, but can't deny that her words cut me. "A monster? I think you're a bad judge of character, considering the man you wanted to marry is the monster."

"What did Piero do to you?"

A steel wall shutters around my heart at the question. Kira's death is something I never talk about. I don't care what he did to Da, because he deserved everything he got, but Kira didn't. She was sweet and innocent and untouched by the darkness. And that bastard took her from me. The things he and her men put her through are unspeakable before they ended her life.

"Cillian?" Gwen's voice cuts through the violence, stirring like a storm in my mind.

"It's not important." I clench both of my fists. "He's not the man you think he is."

There's a glimmer of intrigue in her eyes. There's no way I can tell her what he did, not right now—I'm not ready. I want my princess to choose me because she wants me, not because she knows what kind of man Piero is.

I rarely regret my actions, but my skin crawls with the memory of how I forced her to the altar and into my bed. It was unavoidable. Ever since the moment I set eyes on Gwendolyne Tesoro, something inside me shifted. I knew I had to have her. She became my obsession, consuming every waking thought.

Even so, I'm not a fool. I know it was the worst way to win her heart, but I'll win it in the end, one way or another.

23

GWENDOLYNE

The sun dips in the sky, casting a beautiful golden hue across Santa Catalina. Cillian was right. This place is beautiful. I wish I had my camera, as the wildlife here is phenomenal.

This trip has mixed my feelings up more. It's made me view him as a human being rather than the ruthless and cold kidnapper that stole me from my fiancé.

There's a comfortable silence between us as we stroll along the beach.

"What do you think of this place?" Cillian asks, glancing toward me.

I smile, unable to help myself. "It's stunning. Do you bring the boat here often?"

He shakes his head. "I rarely have time. And for over three months, Poison has been out of action." His lips purse together. "This was the first time I've taken her out since."

"You seem attached to your boat."

"She's not just a boat." His eyes search mine. "I feel at home when I'm at sea."

I frown. "Then why don't you live on it?"

His jaw works. "It's not as convenient and difficult to keep guarded in my line of work." He rubs his hand across the back of his neck. "Boats are easy to blow up, and my enemies wouldn't think twice."

"But you would like to live on it?" I confirm.

His eyes narrow. "Why do you ask?"

"I'm curious, is all." It's a little worrying that I'm curious about Cillian.

What made him the way he is?

Why does he hate Piero so much?

"I love the sea." His eyes narrow as he gazes out over the blue expanse. "It's freeing. No barriers."

After my first experience out at sea, I admit I see the charm. There's a sense of freedom you can't get anywhere else. "I did enjoy my first boating experience."

Cillian chuckles. "Of course you did. Because I gave you the best massage ever, right?"

I roll my eyes at his arrogance. And while he did give me the best massage, I can't believe it didn't end in sex. A part of me was a disappointed that it didn't, despite being sore. "Do you always have to be so arrogant?"

He shrugs. "It's who I am, don't like it? Tough."

I give him a small nod as we continue toward the speed boat moored at the dock. We couldn't bring Poison in as she's too big, so Cillian anchored her at sea.

"I'm not ready to leave this place," I admit.

"Good," he says, nodding toward the busy harbor. "As I've booked us a table at a restaurant."

I swallow hard, as it will be dark soon. "Won't it be too late?"

He tilts his head. "We can stay on the boat tonight, if you'd like?"

I don't want to go back to my gilded cage. "Sure."

We pause on the way to the main harbor and watch a pelican swoop to snatch a fish from the ocean before soaring skyward again.

"I wish I had my camera," I say.

Cillian looks at me. "Camera?"

"Yes, I like photography and bird watching, actually." I can't understand why telling him that makes me feel so self-conscious.

"You should have told me sooner. I would have taken one from the boat. We have cameras on there."

I swallow hard and shake my head. "It's fine. I enjoyed my time without taking photos."

"But it's what you love to do?"

I don't know why I'm telling him this, but I nod in response.

"Then I'll ensure you have a camera at home to take photographs in the garden and on the beach."

"Don't think that means I'll be happy about being held hostage there."

He rolls his eyes. "You're hardly a hostage."

I struggle to understand how he believes that statement. "I think being kidnapped, forced to marry you, and then locked away in a house makes me a hostage. What do you call it?"

Cillian yanks me to face him. "I call it you being stubborn, not wanting to admit that ever since we met, you've wanted me. That we belong together, and once you admit that, you're free to come and go as you please, as my equal." His eyes dip to my lips. "Until you admit it, I'll keep chipping away at the bullshit notion that we're not meant for each other."

I hate that I want him to kiss me. "It's not bullshit," I say, half-heartedly. I'd have to be thrown in the looney-bin if I think I'm meant for Cillian. He has no idea what a healthy relationship should look like. For a start, it should never begin with stalking or be followed by kidnapping.

Cillian yanks me against him. His lips press against mine in a frantic kiss. One that I can't help but give in to, allowing his tongue access as he plunders it. It's getting harder and harder to resist the pull between us, despite everything he's put me through. I fear his declaration we're meant for each other may be true.

Cillian releases me from the kiss and smiles a wickedly handsome smile that makes my insides flutter. "Come on, or we'll be late for our reservation." He grabs my hand, his fingers entwining with mine as he leads me across the sand.

There's a comfortable silence between us as dusk falls across the island, giving the place a peaceful atmosphere as the sound of music drifting from the harbor mixes with the soft sound of the waves meeting the shore.

After about a twenty-minute walk, we come to a small fish restaurant right on the seafront. We enter the elegant little restaurant which has walls of glass that look out onto the sea.

"Good evening, Mr. Hook." The host greets us. "Let me show you to your table." He leads us out onto a patio and past other diners until we get to a private courtyard with breathtaking views. The soft sound of waves caressing the shore echoes up the cliff the restaurant sits upon.

The air smells of salt and freshly cooked seafood. Soft music plays in the background while a waiter moves toward our table with a silver platter of appetizers.

Cillian pulls out my chair. "My lady."

He's trying to act charming, and I can't fall for it. I sit and watch him as he takes his seat.

"Some champagne?" the host asks, holding a ridiculously expensive bottle of Bollinger.

"Yes, thank you."

The host smiles and pours me a glass before pouring Cillian one. And then he leaves us alone.

I can't help but draw similarities to the way Piero wined and dined me before I was kidnapped.

Cillian's eyes look majestic as they appear to glow in the candlelight. "What are you thinking?" he asks.

I shake my head. "I think this is crazy. I should try to kill you rather than have dinner with you."

"I'd love to see you to try." He smiles wider. "Any tousle between us would probably end in my cock in your sweet little cunt." He lifts his glass of champagne. "To us."

The crass comment goes over my head. I pick my glass up. "To my escape."

He chuckles. "If you wanted to escape, you would have tried it by now."

"Perhaps I'm biding my time for the opportune moment." I reach forward and grab some calamari off the platter, putting it on my plate.

"And when would that be?"

"I'm not going to tell you, am I?" I bite into one of the delicious calamari. "That would screw up my plan."

"Keep pretending you have one." He winks and takes a sip of his champagne before serving himself shrimp.

Little does he know he had an enemy on the inside with Tilly, who hasn't been back for the last three days since the near miss in the library. She's given me ideas, and I'll bide my time for the perfect opportunity to escape. It's foolish to mention it to Cillian, but perhaps it'll make him believe that I wouldn't mention it if I was going to try.

"I hope you like lobster, as I've ordered it for us."

My brow furrows. "Why didn't you let me order for myself?"

"Because the lobster is the best I've ever had here. You have to try it." He tilts his head. "But if there's something else you'd like, you can order it as well."

"No, lobster is fine, but I'd appreciate a choice in the future."

He chuckles. "Oh, I didn't think there would be a future, since you're intending to break out of prison."

I clench my jaw. "The place is fucking impenetrable."

"So you've given it thorough consideration, then?"

"Anyone in my shoes would, don't you think?"

He shrugs. "I guess I'm biased. I can't see why you wouldn't want to be married to me."

"As always, your arrogance knows no bounds."

He smiles over the rim of his glass before taking a sip. "Let's talk about something else."

"Such as?" I ask.

He rubs his hand across the back of his neck. "What's your favorite food?"

I purse my lips as he's trying to get to know me better. If it weren't for the fact we're already married, people would think we're on a date. "I love Caribbean food. There's a place in San Diego that has the best Jerk chicken ever."

He smirks. "Creole Kitchen?"

"How did you…" I shake my head. "I forget that we live in the same city."

"I love it there too," he admits. "Although my favorite food is my ma's stew."

It doesn't sound as exciting as Jerk chicken. His ma freaks me out. She acted odd while holding me captive.

"Your ma was suspicious of me."

His jaw works. "She's not well."

"Oh, what's wrong with her?"

"She has dementia, and it's severe. She's on medication, but it can only slow it down. Some days are better than others."

I feel guilty for thinking she was crazy. "I'm sorry to hear that."

"Our time has to be up at some point. For my ma, her time is numbered according to the doctors."

I feel an odd sadness for him, as I sense his mum is all he's got. "Do you have any siblings?"

The flicker of hurt that enters his eyes is visible for a second before they shutter. As if he's closing off. "No." The tone of his voice is cold, which results in an awkward silence.

Thankfully, the server comes with our lobster, breaking the ice that has encased the entire table.

Cillian hasn't mentioned his dad either, but considering the way he reacted when I asked if he had siblings, I think it's best to steer clear of talking about his family at all.

"Can I ask you a question?" There's something I've been wanting to ask him ever since I found out about his hand.

"Depends what question."

I swallow hard as his tone returns to playful. "How did you lose your hand?"

"A crocodile," he says.

My eyes widen. "Really? Where did that happen?"

"I don't like to talk about it. It's a bit of a sore subject."

I narrow my eyes, wondering if he's messing around. There aren't crocodiles in California, at least not wild ones. "Are you lying to me about the croc?"

"How about you stop asking me questions?"

My husband has a lot of things to hide, and annoyingly, that intrigues me.

"Fine," I say, digging into my lobster as an uncomfortable silence falls between us. What has been a nice day exploring the island is turning awkward.

Cillian makes me feel conflicting feelings. One minute he makes me want to murder him, then he makes me want to find out more about him, and when he kisses me... I've never felt more wanted in my life.

And I have to remind myself who he is.

My father's enemy. My fiancé's enemy.

A man who stalked me, stole me, and then forced me down the aisle.

How is it that all of those terrible things fade into the background the moment his lips are on mine?

24

CILLIAN

*A*n alarm rings, breaking me out of a hazy sleep. I sit straight, realizing it's the radar alert on the boat. Jumping to my feet, I rush out of the bedroom toward the helm. The damn thing shouldn't be going off, not when we're anchored so close to shore, unless some idiot is heading straight for us.

Once I get to the helm, I find another yacht heading straight toward us.

"Fuck," I mutter, running a hand through my hair. I turn over the engine and rush out onto the deck to get the electric winch to haul the anchor off the seabed, tapping my foot.

Too many idiots drive boats out here, so it was stupid to leave Poison anchored where someone could hit us.

"What's going on?"

I turn to see Gwen standing in a sheer nightgown, her nipples rock hard and peaked through the fabric. I almost forget the urgency of the situation. My cock instantly turns hard. Shaking my head, I nod toward the lights of the boat in the distance. "Someone is on a collision course with us. We need to move. Come on."

I walk back to the helm of the yacht and steer her away, heading toward San Diego.

Gwen follows me inside. She stands with her arms across her stomach as if they're a defense. I pull her toward me and place her between me and the steering wheel, pressing my lips to her neck. "Don't worry, princess. I'll get us home safe."

I don't miss the way she shudders, her body reacting to my touch. As I force the yacht to speed toward San Diego, I find it odd that the yacht behind us has also sped up and is closing the distance between us. It's smaller and faster than Poison.

"What the fuck?" I murmur.

Gwen leans back against me. "What's wrong?"

"The yacht is gaining on us."

Gwen tenses. "It couldn't be one of your enemies, could it?"

I pause, wondering if someone has sold me out. The dockmaster would have seen me take the boat, and what if... I move Gwen away from the helm and rummage under the GPS location system. When my fingers snag on the small device fitted to the bottom, rage bursts to life inside me. I yank it out and throw it on the floor, stamping on it.

A tracker.

"Motherfuckers." I ramp the engine of the boat to the highest speed, truly testing the work they did on it. "Gwen, hold on," I say, as the yacht jerks to life in an attempt to escape the pursuing boat.

I've been so fucking distracted by the woman before me that I didn't check the boat for tampering. Something I would do normally.

"What's that?" she asks, looking at the little broken device.

"A tracker. Someone must have planted it when the work was being done on the boat." I run a hand across the back of my neck, wondering why I didn't do a sweep before taking her out. "I should have checked."

Gwen's expression turns curious as she glances behind at the boat in pursuit. "Who do you think it is?" There's hope in her voice.

"I don't know and I don't give a shit." Grabbing her wrist, I pull her close. "Stay close to me."

"It could be my dad." Her throat bobs. "Or it could be Piero."

I grab her throat and squeeze. "What have I told you about saying that bastard's name?"

It's possible to could be Piero. The man I want to destroy in pursuit of me. It means the rat in my outfit is not only selling me out to the Tesoro mob, but to Piero, too. When I get my hands on the piece of shit betraying me, they'll wish they'd never been born.

She glares at me as I keep my hand around her throat. "If it's him, I'll jump from the boat and swim to it."

I squeeze tighter. "Careful, Gwendolyne. You're playing a dangerous game, speaking to me like that."

"Speaking to you like what? Like a sane person who wants to escape her captor and return to her fiancé?"

I can't help my rage as I drag her closer, searching

those alluring emerald eyes. "Piero is a snake. No sane person would ever want to go near the man."

She tilts her head. "How can I believe that when you won't tell me why you hate him so much?"

"It doesn't matter why I hate him." I glance away. "He doesn't deserve you."

The boat in pursuit is smaller and faster, and it's getting dangerously close now. I feel my heart thud against my chest as I try to outrun my pursuers. The engine roars in protest as it pushes us further, but the boat behind us keeps gaining ground.

Soon enough, the yacht pulls by our side, so close it grazes ours. I have to put the brakes on and face Piero head on. I know it's him before I see him.

"Fucking Piero." I pull my gun from under the steering wheel and walk onto the deck to find him standing with a gun aimed at me.

"Let Gwendolyne go and I might not shoot you in the head," he orders.

Gwen rushes out onto the deck behind me. "Piero!"

"Don't worry, Gwen. You'll be safe soon," Piero says, his eyes roaming her body in a predatory way, making me want to gouge them from his skull. I add that to the mental list of things I'm going to do to him.

All she's wearing is her skimpy, sheer night gown and her hair is ruffled from sleep. She's a fucking vision. I'd rather take a bullet to the head than give her over to Piero.

"Piero," she calls his name and my stomach sinks. "I'll jump over." Gwen tries to rush past me, but I grab her wrist and yank her against my chest.

"Not so fast, princess," I murmur into her ear, keeping her in front of me. "Are you sure you have a good enough aim not to hit Gwendolyne?" I ask Piero.

Piero's eyes narrow, as we both know he was never a great shot. "It's clear she doesn't want to remain with you, so let her go and we can fight this out like men."

I arch a brow. "Fight it out like men? You aren't a man, you're a fucking weasel. And weasels never fight fair."

"Cillian," she breathes, I can feel her heart beating at a hundred miles an hour. "Let me go."

"Never, princess," I murmur into her ear.

She tenses as I think fast. "What's it going to be, then?" I press.

Piero glares at me. "I have backup. We can fucking take your boat and Gwen and leave you dead at the bottom of the ocean."

Gwen tenses at the tone of his voice, no doubt witnessing his violent side for the first time.

I arch a brow. "Then you'll feel the wrath of the Hook outfit in full fucking force. I've already sent word for backup the moment I realized I was being followed." I bluff, as I didn't think to call them. They can't help me out here. "You won't make it back into dock alive."

Piero glares at me for a moment, his eyes moving between me and Gwendolyne. "I'm sorry, Gwen." He turns away.

"No, Piero!"

I pinch her ass, making her jump. "I don't want to hear that filthy son of bitch's name leave your lips ever again. Understood?"

Piero looks at Gwendolyne with an odd expression in his gaze. "Sorry. We'll have to try to find another way." And then he turns his back on her.

Piero's boat turns away, and he watches us both as he sails the yacht in the opposite direction, toward Los Angeles. My old home turf, which I intend to take back.

"I think someone needs punishing." I tighten my grasp on her wrist.

"Cillian, I..." Her throat bobs as I force her around to face me.

"You what? I bring you out here and give you a day of freedom, and you repay me by offering to throw yourself over the edge of my boat to be with a man who is a complete sociopath."

She scoffs. "Are you listening to yourself? You act like you're better than him when you kidnapped me and forced me to marry you. You need to get a grip."

I snap, grabbing her by the hips and hoisting her over my shoulder.

She beats her fists against my back. "Put me down."

"Not until I teach you a lesson." I storm into my sex room on the boat and throw her onto the bed face down, and then I proceed to lock her in the restraints.

"What are you doing?" she asks, trying to fight.

"Punishing you," I say, my voice as cold as ice.

She glances over her shoulder at the tone, a flicker of fear in the depths of her emerald eyes that fuels my lust for domination. Her actions have unleashed the full force of my darkness. I long for her to break beneath my touch. Leaving her there locked to the bed, I return to the helm and charter the course on the navigation system back home. And then once I'm sure we're on course and Piero's yacht is out of range, I return.

Gwendolyne made a big mistake messing with me like that. She has awakened the monster that lies within. I march back into the room to the vision of her bent over the bed for me.

I grab the back of her neck and yank her into an awkward position, forcing her back to arch. "There's nothing better than painting a woman's ass red and making her scream in pain and then fucking her until she screams in pleasure."

"You're sick," she spits. And then I feel something hard against my chest as I didn't secure her left arm. She managed to find a gun. Although the safety is still on. Before she can try to pull the trigger, I grab it off her.

"Naughty girl." I shake my head. "You thought you could shoot me, did you?"

She trembles as I move the muzzle of the gun down her spine. "Cillian," she gasps, her fear heightening.

I move my hand so it's cupping her throat and squeeze, blocking her airway a little.

She gags, but refuses to look away from my reflection in the mirror. She's determined despite the fear that oozes from her pores.

"Keep trying to offend me, princess. I don't fucking care." With that, I release her throat and chain her free wrist to the bed. And then I step back and admire how beautiful she looks at my mercy. The gun is still firmly in my hand.

"Cillian, please."

"Silence," I growl, no longer accepting disobedience.

Without warning, I spank her ass hard enough to make it hurt, pulling her nightgown higher so she's exposed to me fully. I move the muzzle of the gun through her soaking wet lips. "Such a naughty princess trying to shoot me."

She shudders. "Are you going to kill me?"

"Never." I bring the muzzle to her clit and circle it. "You're so naughty aiming this at me. And that's not your only crime tonight."

I throw the gun onto the nightstand and place my hands on her hips; my voice comes out low, like a purr. "I'm going to make you regret ever saying his name," I whisper in her ear. And then I release her to retrieve a riding crop from the rack of implements on the wall.

Gwendolyne's eyes go wide. "What are you going to do with that?"

I move the tip of it over her flesh, to the base of her spine. I've no intention of answering that question.

I think my little princess doesn't understand how wicked I can be. I've been too lenient with her, but that changes now.

Rage has been a constant companion for years, but now it's burning a hole inside me so deep I can't see a way out. And Gwendolyne is at the wrong end of it.

"Please, Cillian," she begs.

I won't show her mercy, not this time. I bring the riding crop down on her ass in a heavy swat.

She cries out, jolting forward at the shock.

I do it on her other ass cheek, which results in an equally satisfying cry from her lips. After a few heavy swats, I notice her pussy is wet. It looks like my wife enjoys the pain.

I move forward and slip three fingers into her.

She groans in pleasure, hips pushing backward in an attempt to find friction from me.

"My dirty little whore enjoys being spanked." I make a disapproving sound. "Such a naughty girl. This is a punishment, not a reward." Her thighs quiver the moment I hit the spot deep inside her, making me wish my cock was inside her. But she hasn't been punished enough.

I pull my fingers out of her and give her ass a soft slap with my hand, loving how her skin is already tinged red from the riding crop.

She groans in protest the moment my fingers leave her. I take a step back, allowing her time to prepare herself before I strike again. "Don't ever say that man's name again." I swat her ass harder with the riding crop.

It elicits a scream from her lips that'll stay with me longer after we're done here. A sound so achingly beautiful it makes my cock pulse with need. Every time she screams out in pain, it heightens my desire for her.

My fist tightens around the handle of the crop and I spank her skin until both of her ass cheeks are bright red.

Her cries are music to my ear. When I finish, a faint hint of bruising is visible. It's a mark of my ownership over her and it makes me want her more.

"Have you learned your lesson?" I ask her.

Gwendolyne throws me a look of heated anger mixed with desire. "Never."

I love her resolve not to yield mentally while her body is responding. "That'll change, princess." I run my hand lightly over the curve of her ass before punishing her with a slap to her cunt. "Your pussy is so wet your juices have made a mess of the sheets."

My finger slides inside her and she lets out a gasp as she wriggles her hips, making my cock leak in anticipation.

"I think it's time for you to take my cock," I announce.

Gwen glances at me and says, "Not after—"

I spank her again. "You don't tell me what to do." I unzip my pants and free my hard cock from my briefs.

My arm slides around Gwen's waist as I pull her as close to me as the restraints allow, pushing the tip against her pussy. "You can try to resist all you want, but I know you're my dirty little whore," I say.

She doesn't deny it, shuddering as the head of my cock grazes her clit.

"You're shaking with need, princess." I tease her as I allow my cock to rock back and forth against her clit. It gives her pleasure, but not what she wants.

"Stop this," she gasps.

"Okay," I say, removing my cock from her pussy and stepping back. "I'll watch you dripping for me all damn night and stroke my cock instead of filling you with it."

Her head snaps around to glance at me, eyes narrowing to slits. "Don't be an asshole."

I arch a brow, as the word draws my attention to the tempting ring of muscles between her bright red ass cheeks. "I'd love to fuck your asshole."

Her face pales and she tenses. "No," she mutters.

"It wasn't a question."

All the color drains from her face as she thrashes in the restraints.

"Don't worry, princess, I'll save that for another time." I wink, as there's no way I have the patience right now to stretch her ass out.

"Tell me you want my cock in your pussy, and I'll give it to you." I drag my fingers across the red flesh of her ass.

"Are you serious?"

"As serious as I've ever been."

She sighs. "Fine, I want it."

"How badly?" I push, gripping her hips so hard I'm sure I'll leave bruises.

"I want it so badly. Fuck me, captain."

I snarl and sink my teeth into her shoulder, making her gasp. "Good girl," I whisper against her skin. I move the head of my straining cock to her center and push inside, filling her to the brim.

She shudders, her body coming apart.

"I take it back." I spank her ass. "You're a naughty girl for coming that damn quick," I growl, taking hold of her hair and jerking it back hard. "You belong to me, Gwen, which means I control your orgasms. You don't come unless I say you can, understood?"

She arches her back, making me groan as my cock slides deeper.

"Understood?" I repeat.

She nods. "Yes, captain."

I drive into her with all my strength, our bodies

coming together in a violent clash of skin against skin. My rage, aggression and desire mege, as I claim her.

"Tell me who owns you."

She moans, throwing her head back as I reach around to caress her clit.

"Now," I demand.

"You do, Cillian."

I spank her ass. "That's not what I want you to call me."

"You do, captain." Her pussy tightens around my shaft.

I lean forward and encircle her throat with my good arm, squeezing. "Fuck, you're tight, baby. Are you about to come before I've given you permission?"

Her hips buck back against me as she tries to get me to move in and out again, but I hold firm.

"Answer me."

"No," she lies.

I release her throat and give her ass a hard slap. "Don't lie to me."

She shudders. "I'm so close, please."

"What did I tell you?"

She glances over her shoulder at me, her bottom lip caught between her teeth. Fuck me, she's the most angelic thing I've ever seen. "I can only come when you tell me."

"That's right. Now hold on until I say."

Her eyes roll back in her head as she nods, facing forward again. "Yes, captain."

"Good girl." I grab a fistful of her hair and thrust into her with slow and teasing movements, building again to the violence of earlier. I'm barely holding on as I fuck her into oblivion. My balls tighten and while I want to keep going, I know I won't last long.

She drives me to the edge and I'm about to explode inside her. Grinding my teeth, I force myself to hold on and fuck her with all my strength.

"Cillian," she breathes my name.

"That's right, say my name," I murmur, keeping her hair wrapped around my fist as I shove into her over and over. It's impossible to stop my climax, so I give the order.

"Let go, princess. Let me feel your tight little cunt milking my cock while you orgasm." I yank her hair harder. "I'm going to fill that pretty little cunt with cum and make sure everyone knows it belongs to me."

She moans. "Oh God, yes!" she screams, shaking with pleasure as she comes apart. Her muscles milk me as I shove into her once more, growling as my release comes. I don't stop until I'm spent, and she's slumped in a heap on the bed before me, exhausted and full of cum.

I pull my cock from her and stare at her well fucked pussy, tucking myself back into my pants. "You'll remain like that until we get back to San Diego, feeling my cum drip out of your soaking wet cunt the entire time." I spank her red ass. "Reflect on what it means to be owned by me, princess."

I turn away from her and walk out of the room, leaving her restrained and hunched over on the bed. Gwen made a big mistake tonight, and I won't rest until she learns her lesson.

She's mine.

25

GWENDOLYNE

I shift on the sofa, my ass sore from Cillian's constant spankings.

Three days it's been since I tried to throw myself overboard to get to Piero. Cillian insists he'll keep punishing me until I write him an apology. He can forget it. I won't apologize for doing something most sane humans would do—try to escape captivity.

Someone clears their throat and I look up, those chestnut eyes fixed on me. "Morning, princess."

I clench my jaw. "Morning."

He walks closer, something behind his back. "I've got something for you."

"What is it? A new riding crop for you to spank me with?"

"You wish," he murmurs.

I swallow hard as I know why I haven't written that letter. Deep down, I enjoy every spanking he doles out. My messed-up body loves the pain, perhaps as much as the pleasure. I fear I need to see a shrink.

"No, I promised you I'd get you a camera. Here it is." He reveals the Nikon D850, which is one of the best cameras for wildlife photography. It beats the one I have at home since my dad refuses to buy me one and I had to use a small amount of savings I had in my account since he won't let me get a job either.

I hesitate, wondering why he'd give me this when he's punishing me. "What about punishing me?"

He tilts his head. "I've been doing that in the bedroom." He thrusts it into my hand. "Why don't we go to the beach and you can try it out?"

It's been a while since I last took photos and I'm dying to get back into it. Nodding, I stand. "Sounds good."

He smiles and leads the way out of the library toward the garden. "Sometimes I see the dolphins here. You might get lucky."

The idea of capturing those beautiful creatures in a photo spurs me on and I quicken my pace, desperate to get to the beach.

"Slow it down, princess," Cillian says, grabbing my hip and yanking me against him.

I shake my head. "Sorry, I'm excited."

He smiles, and it's the most beautiful smile he's given me. "Good, I enjoy seeing you happy."

"That's strange. I thought you lived to torment me."

His jaw works. "Nothing makes me happier than seeing you smile, princess."

Heat radiates through my entire body as I turn my attention to the garden, not wanting him to see how much his words affect me.

When we get to the beach, I notice a Brandt's Cormorant perched on the wood post of Cillian's slip. "Quiet," I whisper, grabbing the camera and creeping close enough to get a good shot. I snap quite a few angles before the bird startles and flies away. I snap a few of it in flight.

"Did you get any good ones?" Cillian asks, glancing over my shoulder.

I move my camera screen out of his view. "I don't know yet."

He chuckles. "Are you embarrassed, princess?"

I shrug. "I'm not used to people taking an interest in my hobby."

"Well, get used to it, as my only interest is you."

Butterflies erupt in my stomach. The longer I'm with this man, the more difficult resisting him becomes when he says things like that.

I sit on the sand and he does too, sitting close to me.

We sit on the beach in silence, watching the wildlife. I snap a load of great shots, thankful to the man sitting next to me for supporting this. It's more than my dad ever did.

"Do you want a career in photography?" Cillian asks after a while.

I nod in response. "Yes, but my dad says it's stupid."

"Tell him he's fucking stupid. There's nothing stupid about following your passion." His lips purse together. "I don't want you to listen to anyone who tries to shoot you down like that, princess. Understood?"

God damn it. Why is he making it so difficult to hate him?

"I understand," I murmur, flipping through the

photos I took. The dolphins haven't made an appearance, but I captured some good photos of birds and a nice shot of a fish jumping from the sea.

Cillian clears his throat. "Can I ask you a question?"

"Sure," I murmur.

"Where's your mom?"

Something claws at my throat at the question. "Dead."

His jaw works. "I'm sorry."

I shake my head as it stirs confusing emotions. She was run over when I was two years old and died at the scene. My dad said it was an accident, but as I got older, I began to believe perhaps one of his enemies killed her. He has made so many over the years. "I don't remember her. I was two years old when she died. Dad never wants to talk about her. I often wonder if she would have been supportive of my passions or not."

Cillian slides an arm around me and squeezes me against him. "I'm sure she would have been."

My chest aches as he's being so comforting. It's unusual. I never talk about my mom because I have no one to talk about her with. From a young age, my dad would tell me not to talk about her. It's become my default whenever I think of her to bottle it up.

He kisses my cheek and I turn to look into his eyes. I could get lost in his eyes. They're so beautiful. "What are you thinking, princess?"

"I'm thinking I want you to kiss me."

He smirks and I regret saying it because it feeds his ego. "Is that right?"

"Yes," I breathe.

"How about we play a game?"

"What kind of game?"

"Tag."

"What? Are you six years old?"

He shakes his head. "This version a six-year-old would definitely not play."

I frown at him as he leans in close.

"I'm it and you run and try to escape me. I'll be the hunter. You be the prey."

"Right, so I'm not hearing anything different to standard tag."

"The difference is, when I catch you, I fuck you wherever that may be. Even if there are guards right there, I'm going to tear your clothes off and fuck you until you scream so loud they'll hear you in downtown San Diego."

The heat intensifies through my body at the thought. "Why don't you fuck me now?"

"Because the chase will make it more exhilarating."

I can't believe that his suggestion turns me on. He wants to hunt me down like an animal and fuck me. The idea makes my nipples hard and my pussy soak through my panties.

"What do you say, princess?"

I nod in response, unable to find the words.

"Okay, you get a five-second head start."

"What about the camera?" I ask, not wanting to damage it.

He nods at a little hut. "Leave it in there. We will get it later."

I stand and deposit in the hut and turn around.

"Run, princess."

I sprint across the beach and make it up the steps to the garden at the same moment he calls out five. My heart is pounding against my rib cage.

Excitement charges through my stomach like a stampede of elephants. Already I can see the appeal. It's thrilling being chased, knowing once he gets his hands on me, he's going to fuck me like a beast.

I run through the garden, taking a sharp turn between two rows of rosebushes and coming to a sudden stop when I see him right there in front of me.

How the hell did he do that?

He grabs me by my shoulders and throws me onto the ground face first, pulling at my clothes like a crazed animal. He forces my skirt to my hips and then I feel his cock nudging against my soaking wet entrance. My heart is racing in my chest and the adrenaline flowing through my veins heightens my pleasure as he rubs his cock against my throbbing clit. And then, he thrusts inside me, causing sparks to shoot through me like fireworks on the 4th of July. He fucks me without mercy.

"Fuck," he breathes. "You're so wet for me, princess. Do you like being tracked down and then fucked, baby?"

"Yes," I gasp, arching my back as his weight pins me to the grass.

"Good, because it makes me so fucking hard knowing you like to be hunted and captured by a beast like me."

I moan, wishing I could touch my clit as I'm desperate for release.

"It turns you on knowing I want to fuck you so badly that I'm willing to fuck you in front of everyone." He grunts as he pounds in and out of me, stretching me around his cock. "Doesn't it, princess?"

"Yes," I groan, knowing I've never felt so far gone before.

He stops, making me whimper.

Cillian spreads my ass cheeks apart and spits on my hole. I freeze, scared that he's going to fuck it.

I feel his finger dip inside of my ass and my body sets on fire.

"What are you doing?"

"Is this my hole, princess?" he whispers in my ear, nipping the lobe.

"Cillian, you can't fuck it," I say.

He chuckles against my ear. "I can do whatever the fuck I want, but no. I won't fuck it here."

I relax a little as he slides his finger in and out.

"But soon I'm going to stretch it open and fuck it because all of you belongs to me, Gwendolyne."

I shudder at his words and the desire that his finger in my ass ignites. I'm surprised how good it feels.

"Tell me that your ass is mine."

I swallow hard. "It's yours," I breathe.

"Does it feel good?"

I nod in response as I feel his cock still hard and nudging against my dripping wet pussy.

"I'm going to fuck you again."

I suck in a sharp breath and then he slams into me hard. He thrusts inside and I arch my back, moaning as his finger is still in my ass.

"I'm going to fuck you so hard you're going to struggle to walk." He spanks my bruised cheeks and I shudder, drowning in the euphoria he makes me feel.

"You're going to come so hard that I'll have you crawling on all fours and begging me to fuck you again."

"Oh God, Cillian. I'm so close."

He spanks my ass again. "Good girl, I want you to come for me with my finger in your ass and my cock in your perfect little cunt. Can you do that, baby?"

I don't have time to respond as my pussy clenches and my orgasm tears through me. Cillian pushes deeper inside me and I feel his cum shoot deep, filling me up.

Cillian leans over me, his cock still inside me. "You're so perfect, princess," he murmurs, his face against my neck. "I can't get enough of this."

He pulls his cock out of me and I flip over to face him, heat shattering the haze I'd fallen into when I realize we're in the center of the garden on show to anyone.

"Oh my God. I can't believe we did that. What if someone saw us?"

He smirks. "I can, and I fucking loved it. And who gives a shit if someone did?" He plants his lips hard onto mine, kissing me hungrily.

One kiss and I forget everything. This man has cast a spell on me. A spell I don't think I want to break anymore.

26

GWENDOLYNE

I despise him. I want him.

Those two conflicting thoughts ricochet around my head, bouncing off the walls of my mind, spinning around like a tornado. It's been a week since Piero quit his attempt to free me from Cillian so easily. I've been conflicted about it ever since.

On the one hand, I wanted to escape, but not to be with Piero. The appeal has well and truly worn off. Seeing him give up like that was the nail in the coffin. After my experience with mobsters, I'd rather not go near another one in my lifetime.

On the other hand, the thought of escaping this twisted and toxic thing between Cillian and me is as unappealing as being with Piero.

For Piero, the risk wasn't worth the reward—me.

And ever since that night, Cillian has proceeded to tie me up and spank me, insisting I write him a formal apology for trying to throw myself overboard to get to

Piero. I won't bow to his depraved will. The man doesn't deserve an apology.

I know there's another reason I won't do as he says. I crave the pain as well as the pleasure. It's addictive and I don't know what that says about me.

"If you keep scowling like that, your face might stick that way forever."

I narrow my eyes. "Screw you."

He chuckles. "Why do you have to be so stubborn?"

Stubborn.

This man makes my blood boil the longer I'm trapped in this house with him.

"Why don't you write the apology I asked for and the torture can stop?" He brings his glass of scotch to his lips and takes a sip before smirking at me over the rim.

I've never wanted to murder someone as badly as I want to murder him—or fuck him. Again, my mind is so conflicted it's insane. "Or is it because you secretly enjoy me tying you up and spanking you before I fuck you?"

My thighs clench in response. "I can't stand it," I lie. I hate myself for enjoying each every spanking he doles out and the way he makes me climax afterward with his cock. I hate myself for being so twisted in the head.

He's taken to forcing me into the shower afterward to wash me and take care of the bruises on my ass, putting balm on them. As if he cares. It makes no sense.

How can he be so cold in doling out punishment and then so caring afterward? And why the hell does my dumbass like it?

He shakes his head. "Naughty little liar. How else

can you explain why your orgasms are more explosive when I spank you?"

"I don't wish to speak about this at dinner." I spoon myself a helping of potatoes.

The fact is, he's right and I'm in denial.

A tense silence follows because I know what comes next. Like clockwork, he'll drag me to his sex room and tie me down before putting me through a tough spanking that makes me wetter than anything else does. Just the thought makes me wet. Who am I kidding? I've been wet the entire time I've been sitting opposite him. Anticipation wreaking havoc on my desire.

My arousal from pain is something I can't hide from him. Once I'm sure I can't take it anymore, he'll enter me and fuck me like an animal. My ass is getting more bruised by the day, but he doesn't care. Even sitting here at the table is painful. He got me three cushions to sit on, but it still aches.

I drop my fork as all the food is gone, keeping my gaze fixed on the plate.

"Don't worry, princess. You're stubborn and I like that about you, but tonight I'm going to give you a rest from spanking tonight." He winks at me. "We've got somewhere to be."

"Somewhere to be?"

He nods. "Another surprise."

I sigh heavily, as his last surprise was good until it all went to shit. "I'm too tired for that."

His jaw works. "It's not a request. You're coming." He stands and offers me his hand.

I ignore it and get to my feet by myself. "Whatever."

He grabs me by the wrist then and yanks me into his powerful body, chestnut eyes blazing with dominance. "I may be giving you a rest, but I'm still your captain," he murmurs, his hand moving to my SORE ass as he cups it. "Be a good girl and do as you're told."

I clench my fists by my sides as he searches my eyes. "I'd rather punch you in the face."

He laughs. "Come on." He yanks me toward the exit of the dining room, but I manage to swing my arm around and punch him in the back of the neck.

Cillian doesn't flinch, but he turns still. And then, his eyes snap around and the rage burning in them scares me to the core. I think I forgot how crazy he is. He drives me insane with anger, which is an emotion I'm not used to feeling.

"Try that again, princess, and see if I don't give you a real fucking punishment."

My eyes widen. "Are you suggesting what you've been giving me isn't a real punishment?"

"Certainly not, since you enjoy it so much. Now, stop being a brat and come with me." He yanks my wrist and pulls me out of the house. I'm still stunned by the fact he's telling me bruising my ass every night for a week isn't punishment.

A shudder skates down my spine as I try to imagine what he believes is a *real* punishment. He leads me out to the front of the house where his black Ferrari is waiting with the engine running. "My lady." He opens the passenger door for me to get in.

I get into the car, since I've no choice. And the moment he gets into the driver's seat, he puts his hand on my thigh. I can't believe my traitorous body reacts to his touch, making me angrier. The anger isn't directed at him. I'm angry with myself.

"You look like someone pissed in your cereal," Cillian remarks, adding fuel to the bonfire.

"You might as well have."

He chuckles and shifts the stick into gear, pulling out of his driveway at speed. Cillian drives toward the city and I gaze out of the window, not wishing to engage in conversation with him.

After a fifteen minute drive, he parks in front of a warehouse building with bouncers standing outside. "What is this place?" I ask.

"Neverland."

My brow furrows. "What's Neverland?"

"No questions. You'll see." He gets out of the car, and I follow. "Come on." He walks around and grabs my hand, yanking me toward the building.

"This place gives me the creeps."

Cillian chuckles. "You'll be pleasantly surprised."

We walk into the warehouse and I'm shocked that it's opulently decorated on the inside; with velvet curtains, ornate light fixtures, and beautiful artwork. The floor is marble, and in the middle of the room is a large stage with a live band playing jazz music. Everywhere I look, there are scantily clad people dancing and drinking.

"What is this place?" I ask in awe.

"This is my sex club," Cillian says with a smirk. "Welcome to Neverland."

My stomach dips.

Sex Club.

"The real fun is over here," he murmurs, dragging me through a pair of burgundy double doors.

My heart rate accelerates when I notice the booths around the room with clear glass windows. Most of them have people either having sex or participating in various other activities involving torture or pleasure alike.

"Why the hell did you bring me here?" I ask.

"Because I thought you'd enjoy it."

I cross my arms over my chest. "Enjoy what?"

He moves closer, grabbing my arms and forcing me to unfold them. "Enjoy the thrill of being here, or seeing what it's like to watch and be watched."

The way he speaks makes it sound alluring. But I'm not fucking him in front of people.

"You're insane."

Cillian steers me toward a booth. "It's fun to watch, isn't it?"

The scene in front of me makes my thighs clench. A woman hangs from a swing while two men fuck her, one thrusting into her pussy while the other forces his cock down her throat. I'm soaking wet watching them, unable to believe that she doesn't care that people see her being used in that way.

Cillian's warm breath brushes against my earlobe. "Don't you want to learn about your desire for pain? As this is the perfect place to explore it."

I shudder, hating myself for the way my insides flutter and my body heats.

What is wrong with me?

"I'd rather not," I say, swallowing hard. "I already hate myself enough."

He growls and spins me around, his eyes ablaze with what I can describe as rage. "Hate yourself? Are you insane?"

"I'm fucked up for enjoying it."

He yanks me against him and grabs a fistful of my hair, forcing me to look at him. "You're perfect for enjoying it. There's nothing fucked up about you. The only fucked up thing is the fact that society acts like it's taboo to enjoy pain and pleasure, when it's human fucking nature." He presses his lips to my shoulder and bites, making me whimper. "You should love yourself because you're the most amazing woman I've ever met. A fucking goddess I want to worship."

I shudder as he kisses me lower, his lips making goosebumps rise across my flesh. "Cillian," I breathe his name, unable to help it when he's talking to me like this.

"Come into a booth with me," he murmurs.

It's posed as a question, but I sense that it's an order. "And if I refuse?"

"Then we can watch," he murmurs, his teeth grazing my skin. "But it would be a real shame."

"You want other people to watch us?" I ask, finding it a little odd.

"I want everyone in this fucking place to see that I own you. That I possess every fucking part of you, and if anyone ever tries to take you..." He trails off. "Let's say it will get bloody."

I shudder as he talks about murder so easily. And my

sick ass self likes the idea of him killing for me. It's more than Piero was willing to do. The coward wouldn't fight for me the other day, and I've been stewing over it ever since.

"Okay," I say.

"Good girl," he praises, grabbing my hand and yanking me toward a free booth.

There's a man at the door. "Hey boss, you want this one?"

He nods. "Yes."

"And sharing?" he asks.

I stiffen at the mention of sharing. "No," he half growls. "I don't want anyone getting into this booth with us, understood?"

He nods. "You can count on me." The man opens the door and allows us inside the booth, which has a bed with chains affixed and a number of implements hanging from the walls. The lights turn on, illuminating us for everyone outside to watch.

"I don't think I can do this." I glance toward the window, which has drawn a crowd of onlookers.

Cillian yanks me into him. "Free yourself from your own prison, Gwendolyne. Break free and revel in the beauty of sex, pain, and voyeurism." He moves his lips to my ears. "There's no thrill as intense as other people getting off to watching you fuck, trust me."

The last thing in the world I should do is trust this man. And yet, I want to. I want to trust that he's right and that this will be as hot as he says.

"Let go and allow me to lead you into hell. It feels a thousand times better than heaven."

I nod as he pushes the straps of my dress down. He

undresses me. When he unveils the bruises on my ass, he traces them with his fingers. "I'm glad I get to show these off," he breathes, his voice full of fire. "Show everyone you belong to me. These bruises are like a tattoo, Gwendolyne. A mark that binds us together." He pinches the sore skin. "And I couldn't be prouder that you're wearing my mark for all to see."

I shudder. His words are sinful and twisted and everything. The freedom of being able to explore this side of me is refreshing. He slides my bra straps down and unfastens it before tossing it on the floor. People are watching us on the other side of the glass, and I'm filled with a confidence I never knew I possessed.

When my panties are off, Cillian thrusts two fingers into me. "Oh God!"

"That's it, baby. Show them who your God is."

I whimper as he thrusts in and out of me with his fingers, unable to believe how good it feels being watched. As I gaze out at the crowd, I notice two men have their cocks out and are stroking them, eyes fixed on me.

"Those men are walking a dangerous line, stroking themselves while they watch you," he murmurs, fingers thrusting harder as he drives me to the edge. "If they're not careful, I might claw their eyes out with my hook to teach them a lesson."

I shudder at the violence in his tone. "And what lesson is that?"

"That you belong to me and me alone. It was a mistake having you on show, because I'm too fucking possessive of you, Gwendolyne," he purrs.

My stomach tightens and I'm sure I'm going to come, arching my back in anticipation. His fingers slip out of me. "What the hell?"

"You know the rules. No orgasm until I give you permission." He grabs the back of my neck so that I'm arched so far back his mouth is by my ear. "Let's see how rough you can take it." He walks away from me and I glance backward to see he's removing his prosthetic hand and replacing it with his hook, but there's a difference. It's straighter, and the end isn't hooked. It's bulbous.

My eyes clamp shut, wondering what he intends to use that for. When he turns around to face me, the darkness in his eyes should scare me, but it doesn't. It ignites this odd giddiness in me.

"Bend over," he orders.

I glance at the ever-growing crowd. "Cillian," I breathe his name, overwhelmed by the amount of people watching us. "I don't think I can—"

He drags the tip of his hook down my spine. I shudder, starting forward as the metal is cold against my skin. "I don't want you to think. I want you to feel." He moves the hook over my asshole and then to my pussy, lingering there.

"What are you going to do with that?" I ask.

"I'm going to fuck your ass with it."

I try to get away, but Cillian holds me in place.

"Keep calm and trust me. Can you do that?"

"Yes," I breathe.

"Good girl." He unzips his pants, placing his cock against my soaking wet pussy. "So wet for me."

I arch my back, willing him to slide into me. He doesn't move, as I feel the bulbous tip of his hook against my ass. I tense, my body panicking as he squirts lube onto my hole while his cock remains pressed against my throbbing center.

He works the end of the hook into my ass until it's inside me. I've never felt this aroused ever. The sensation is so good and from this angle I can see about four men stroking their cocks while they watch us. I shudder, the need to be fucked building within me.

"Watch those fuckers get off on seeing you like this. If I ever see them again, I'll fucking chop their dicks off and feed them to the wolves," he growls, the hook so deep inside as he starts to thrust between my thighs, rubbing the length of his cock against my clit and driving me insane. "You belong to me. This tight little ass belongs to me. Your pretty little mouth is mine. And that cunt is my heaven and I'm God, got it?"

His filthy words sound delicious. I'm not sure if he's expecting a response, but I nod as best I can.

"Such a good whore. My whore," he growls.

And I know that I won't be able to survive my husband at this rate. He's taking me to places I never knew existed and I can no longer pretend I'm not enjoying every second of the ride.

27

CILLIAN

Rage and desire pulse through me all at once. I severely underestimated how possessive I am over Gwendolyne as about twenty fucking perverts watch us.

This was the intention, and it's not like I can kill those guys stroking their dicks. The club is open for people to watch, for fuck's sake. That's the point. And I'm the owner, but as I slide my cock against her clit and keep my hook in her tight little ass, I'm going insane.

"I need to turn the privacy screen on," I say, pulling away from her and unfastening the hook from my arm, leaving it in her ass.

I walk toward the door to the booth.

"Wait! Isn't the point to be watched?"

I glance back at her over my shoulder. "People are going to wind up dead. I don't like them gawking at you."

She arches a brow. "What did you expect would happen? We're in a sex club in a glass booth!"

I know how insane I'm being right now, but I can't help it. "What does it matter?"

Her cheeks flush then and I realize she's enjoying this.

"Are you enjoying being watched, princess?"

Her throat bobs as she swallows. "Maybe."

I growl. "My dirty little whore likes people watching her, does she?"

She licks her lips. "Yes, captain."

Fuck.

That puts me in a dilemma. As while I want to give her everything she wants, it's driving me insane knowing those men are storing images of her in their perverted wank banks for later.

"I thought you wanted to prove to everyone who I belong to?" She arches her back and grabs her perky tits, rubbing her hard nipples. "Show them, captain."

How the fuck can I refuse that invitation?

"Yes, princess," I say, moving toward her. "Anything for you."

Her eyes widen, surprised by that phrase.

Normally, it's all about what I want, but I can't help it. I want to give Gwendolyne the fucking world.

It's at that minute I realize I'm not wearing my hook or my prosthetic. "Fuck, I'll put my hand on."

"Don't," Gwen says, shaking her head. "You're perfect like this."

I swallow hard as I never go without my prosthetic or hook. It's like my armor and she's asking me to take it off. "Are you sure?"

Gwen nods. "Fuck me, captain," she murmurs,

arching her back. My hook is still embedded in her ass. She looks more tempting than anything I've ever seen, and I can't help myself.

Walking back over to the bench she's bent over, I position the head of my cock between her thighs, coating it in her arousal as I drag it through her slit. "Fuck, baby, you're wetter than you've ever been." I shove into her hard and she moans deeply, arching her back so much it drives me right to the depth of her.

I grab a fistful of her hair and yank her at an awkward angle toward me, leaning down enough to whisper into her ear. "I love how dirty you are, Gwen. I love that you want these people to watch me breed your cunt. Fuck you like the toy you are," I growl, my cock getting harder talking about it. "Because you're my whore and you want everyone to know it, don't you?"

She nods her head. "Yes!"

"Good girl," I praise, forgetting that those bastards out there are getting off watching my pretty angel get fucked. All that matters right now is the two of us, right here and now. "Show them what a good girl you are, taking your husband's cock in your pussy while there's a hook in your ass." I release her hair and she flops forward like a doll.

I spank her and she moans, her pussy clenching me. My hook in her ass tightens her passage and I can feel the metal pressing against my cock. "I'll never get enough of you. I can't wait until you're growing big and round with my baby."

She moans, no longer tensing at the mention of me

getting her pregnant. It's been my desire since the first moment I entered her. "Yes, captain!" She calls out.

Grabbing her hair again, I shove into her harder, losing myself in her. There's a part of me that loves that she wants to be watched, considering she still maintains this bullshit mantra that she doesn't want me. When we both know she's as into this as I am.

"Do you want me to breed you, princess?"

She whimpers, arching more. "Yes, please breed me," she moans.

I love that she's never been this willing. This fucking pliable and submissive, being watched. It cements in me the idea that she's meant for me; made for me.

"Fuck, your pussy is clenching me so fucking hard," I growl, as it's impossible to hold out. "I can tell you're loving this."

"Yes," she moans, pushing her hips backward into me. "Give it to me harder."

"Fuck." I wrap my arm around her throat, drawing her closer. "You want it harder, baby? Is that right?" I'm still inside her as deep as I can go, my cock pulsating and hard as she clenches me like she's trying to milk every last drop of cum from me.

"Yes," she replies, trembling now.

I graze my teeth over the back of her neck and then sink them into it, making her whimper. "Such a dirty whore. My dirty whore. Tell me who you belong to."

"I belong to you," she says, no hesitation whatsoever.

"That's right," I growl into her ear. "And don't ever fucking forget it."

I thrust into her, my balls drawing up as it becomes impossible to slow the oncoming explosion.

"Come for me," I purr into her ear.

"Fuck!" she cries, her cunt getting so tight it's gripping my cock like a vise.

"Good girl," I growl, moving in and out of her with violent force. "Milk my cock. I'm going to breed that pussy."

"Oh God," she moans, her body shudders with force. "Breed me."

"Fuck!" I come apart hearing her say that, my cock exploding deep inside her as I fill her with cum. All I can picture is Gwendolyne, pregnant with my baby. Her stomach is big and round.

It spurs me on; hoping my seed sticks and that vision becomes reality soon.

Once I've emptied every drop of cum inside her, I pull out. And then I remove my hook from her ass.

"Such a good girl, taking my cum like that. And with my hook in your ass. It was sinfully good feeling it rub against my cock."

She stands and licks her bottom lip. "That was crazy..." I notice her attention move to the window, where a larger crowd has gathered. Like the flick of a switch, my possessive side returns.

"Get dressed."

Her brow arches.

"Do as you're told."

She sighs heavily and gets back into her clothes while I tuck myself back into my trousers and put my prosthetic back on.

"Ready?" I ask.

Her cheeks are dark red. "I feel self-conscious about walking out there."

I hold my hand out to her and she takes it. "Don't be. It was fucking beautiful, and don't forget that."

She nods in response, and we make our way out of the booth. One of the assholes that had been jerking off grabs Gwendolyne's wrist.

"Hey baby, how about you suck my cock next?"

I snap. Red floods my vision and I launch myself at him, wrapping my hands around his throat and choking the life out of him. "You don't know who the fuck you're messing with."

His eyes widen as he claws at my fingers, trying to pry them away.

"Gwendolyne is mine," I growl, tightening my grasp as my rage takes over. "Anyone who fucking goes near her dies, do you understand?"

I feel a soft hand on my shoulder, trying to pull me away. "Cillian, stop," her sweet voice calls to me, trying to break through the murderous haze.

I snap out of it, releasing the patron of my club before he passes out.

He groans and falls to the floor, rolling over as he clutches his throat and wretches.

"What the hell was that?" Gwen asks.

I grab her wrist and yank her away from the crowd and into the back. "That asshole put his hands on you."

"And your point is? It's not like I would have agreed to suck his cock."

I narrow my eyes at her. "That's not the point. He touched what's mine, and no one touches what's mine."

"You're crazy."

I grab her throat. "Crazy, huh? And who was it that was begging me to keep the glass unscreened so that everyone can watch me fuck you?"

Her nostrils flare. "You need to take a chill pill."

"When it comes to you, Gwendolyne, I can't. You make me so fucking possessive I'd kill to make sure no one else touches you."

Her throat bobs. "That's the definition of crazy."

"Or perhaps it's the definition of true possession. And let's not pretend that you don't want to be possessed, because you do." I move my lips to her ear and whisper, "You want me to own you and there's no use denying it. I have it all on fucking video."

She tenses then. "What?"

I smirk. "Oh yes, that beautiful session was being recorded. All the booths have recording devices in case the members want a copy."

"You bastard," she says, yanking away from me. "What did you intend to do with that footage?"

"Nothing. Do you think I'd let anyone other than us see it? Your body is for my eyes only."

"Why did you bring me here?"

"I underestimated how possessive I am of you." I close the gap between us. "You make me crazy."

"That ship sailed long before we met." She crosses her arms over her chest as a defense between us.

I reach for her chin so she looks me in the eye.

"You're my anchor, Gwendolyne Tesoro, and without you, I'm lost at sea."

Her eyes widen. "What are you saying?"

Instead of replying, I yank her toward me and kiss her, pouring all the love I feel into it. It's an insane, yet fundamental, truth. I'm in love with my wife.

28

GWENDOLYNE

"*W*hat are you wearing to the event tonight?" Rosa asks.

I finish chewing on my mouthful of meatball sub and swallow. The mention of the charity gala tonight makes my stomach churn. It's the first official function I'm attending with Cillian since our wedding and I'm dreading it. The more time that passes, the more things between us feel normal and that's what scares me. That soon I'll forget all the bad he's done and begin to enjoy being here with him.

"I don't know." I take a bite out of my sub and swallow. "I'd rather not go."

Rosa smiles wistfully. "Are you still struggling to accept your role as Cillian's wife?"

I nod. "Not sure I'll ever accept it. Would you?"

"No. Not considering the way he went about getting you." She stirs a pot of food on the stovetop. "But I've known Cillian eight years and I've never seen him look at anyone the way he looks at you."

"What are you saying?"

She shrugs. "He cares about you in his own twisted way."

"Twisted is an understatement." I sit back and put down my sub. The conversation has killed my appetite. Anytime I talk about Cillian, it makes my insides churn and I know it's because I'm conflicted over my feelings for him.

Ever since we went to his club, Neverland, I can't think of anything else. It was the single most exhilarating experience of my life, and he gave that to me. And the craziest thing about that night wasn't the fact we fucked on display, but when he started to beat that guy for touching me… I know how fucked up it is that I liked it.

I need to see a shrink.

My thoughts are interrupted by the sound of my phone buzzing. Cillian got me a phone which is blocked from making outgoing calls or text messages, but he can message me. It's infuriating.

Captain: Hope you've picked something sexy to wear tonight. I can't wait to show you off.

I roll my eyes, as I can't change the name of his contact. He's made it impossible to edit. I should throw the thing in the trash since it's useless. What's the point of a phone when I can't even reply to his messages, anyway? I toss it onto the table, feeling a sense of rebellion bubble within me.

"The devil himself?" Rosa inquires.

I nod. "Yes, this phone is an insult. I can't text back or ring anyone on it."

"Can you blame Cillian? I heard you tried to throw yourself off his yacht to get back to Piero." She looks hesitant as she says, "You know, Piero's no saint."

The mention of Piero angers me. I hardly know the guy, but after he abandoned my rescue attempt, I started to resent him.

"Neither is Cillian."

"That's true, but..." She clenches her jaw as if deciding whether to continue.

"But, what?"

"I won't say, because it's not my place. All I'll say is, in my eyes, Cillian is a better man than Piero."

I scoff. "Sorry if I beg to differ. Piero didn't stalk me, kidnap me, and then force me down the aisle."

"Fair enough," Rosa says. "I can't argue with that, but Cillian has a reason behind his madness. Let's leave it at that."

Piero has done something to Cillian, but he won't tell me what. It's as if he expects me to take his word for it that Piero isn't a good guy. From my limited experience, he's a gentleman and while he was a little forward, we were engaged to be married. The thing that bugs me is he's supposed to be this powerful mob boss, and he gave up when he came to rescue me.

"I wish he would tell me what the reason is," I say.

She walks toward me and squeezes my hand. "Give him time."

I swallow hard. "It's hard to give anything time when I feel like I'm rotting away in this place."

Rosa raises a brow. "Is it that terrible?"

"Yes and no. I'm used to being locked away. My dad didn't allow me much freedom, but it was different."

She returns to cooking, and I jump from my stool.

"I've got to go and pick something to wear for tonight. Boss's orders."

"See you later," she says.

I walk out of the kitchen, hating that I feel like I'm in no-man's-land. Cillian and Rosa insist that Piero is a bad man, but they're biased. I wish Tilly was still here, as I could have asked her more about Piero and his feud with Cillian. Rosa keeps me company, but I sense I'm a burden to her, hanging around the kitchen when she's trying to get things done.

Sighing heavily, I climb the stairs to our bedroom. I swallow hard as I'm not sure when I started thinking of it as *our* bedroom.

Once I get inside, I jump out of my skin. Cillian is sitting on the edge of the bed, looking irritated. "What are you doing here?"

He arches a brow. "Are you asking what I'm doing in my own bedroom?"

"I thought you were out, working as a mob boss or whatever it is you do."

He chuckles. "I was, but I decided to take off and make sure my princess has the perfect dress for tonight."

I don't know why that nickname makes my insides flutter. It's ridiculous.

"Strip for me," he orders.

I narrow my eyes. "I'm good, thanks."

His jaw works as he rubs his prosthetic hand across

the back of his neck. "Is there any point in being disobedient?"

I cross my arms over my chest, feeling defiant. "I'm not a slave. You can't order me around."

Cillian stands and walks toward me, towering over me. "That's not what you say when I'm fucking you, is it?"

My heart races as he steps closer to me, his breath hot against my ear.

"Strip for me, princess."

I can feel his eyes on me, watching my every move. Hesitantly, I unbutton my blouse.

"That's it." He trails his hand down my back, sending goosebumps rising on every inch of my flesh. "Show me what's mine."

My thighs clench together. It's ridiculous how much I long to be dominated and owned by a man who I *should* despise.

Desire overwhelms me as I continue to undress for him, his eyes never leaving my body.

When I'm naked, he steps back to admire me. "Perfect," he says with a smirk. "I'll never get enough of seeing you naked, princess."

There's a mix of anger and desire fighting for control. "What do you want from me, Cillian?"

He steps closer, grabbing my waist with his hands and yanking me toward him. "Everything," he growls. "I want you to be mine in every sense of the word. I want your fucking heart, and if you keep insisting I'll never have it, I'm going to prove to you why I should."

Intrigued by his words, I shake my head. "How would you prove that?"

"Time," he says, as if that's an explanation.

"You could give me all the time in the world. I'll never give you my heart by choice." There's a twinge in my chest, as I know that's not true. This dark and dangerous man is already sinking his hook into it, and before long he'll own it entirely, but I don't want him to think that. Because how can I give a man who kidnapped me and holds me prisoner my heart? It makes no sense.

His jaw works. "We'll see." He waves his hand. "Now, despite being as hard as a steel rod, we need to pick your dress out for this evening." I can feel his cock evident between us, and it makes me crave him.

"You're not going to fuck me?"

He shakes his head. "Not right now, no."

When he sees the look on my face, he smirks. "Is that disappointment I detect, Gwendolyne?"

I shrug. "Perhaps. It's all you're good at, making me come."

He chuckles. "There are many things that I'm good at. And one of them is teasing a woman to tears. Forcing her not to come as punishment, and I think you need to be taught a lesson, baby."

I gasp as he thrusts two fingers deep between my thighs, finding the spot that turns me into putty in his hands. "Cillian," I moan.

He thrusts them in and out of me, building me toward climax so fast it makes my head spin. "That's right, princess, say my name like that."

I swallow hard, knowing that he's going to push me to the edge and then leave me hanging. And yet I can't help it. I grab onto his arm to anchor myself as his fingers work their magic on me. Before long, I'm panting for oxygen. "Please," I beg, looking into those alluring chestnut eyes of his. "Let me come."

He shakes his head and withdraws his fingers from me. "No chance." He brings his fingers to his mouth and sucks them clean, shutting his eyes. "Delicious."

I swallow hard, feeling needier than ever. "Please, Cillian."

"This is your punishment for telling me all I'm good at is making you come."

I move my hand between my thighs, needing to find release one way or another.

He grabs my wrist. "Don't you dare touch what is mine," he growls, sounding half-feral. "Do I need to get the chastity belt out again?"

My thighs shudder at the thought as I shake my head.

His eyes narrow. "I want to be sure, so I'm going to put it on you. You won't come until we return from this event tonight. I'm going to fuck you so hard you won't know anything once I'm through with you."

I hate that his words excite me.

Cillian walks out of the bedroom and into his depraved sex room and returns with the chastity belt, an evil glimmer in his eyes. "Lie on the bed for me with your legs spread wide."

I hold his gaze, considering defying him. I know he'd

bend me over and spank me, and perhaps that would be enough to send me over the edge.

"No."

He tilts his head. "What was that?"

"I said no. Screw you and your chastity belt."

He smirks. "If you're trying to get me to spank you, I'm not an idiot. I know you get off from the pain."

Damn it.

I was sure that would work.

"This belt is going to be your punishment. No spanking." He tilts his head. "Now am I going to have to force you or will you do as you're told?"

I'm about to open my mouth when he says, "Think before you answer. Your response will determine how long you keep it on for."

I snap my mouth shut and get onto the bed, spreading my thighs for him. It's shameful how wet I am right now, considering he's promising to deny my orgasm for God knows how long.

"Fuck," he breathes, gazing at my pussy. "You're dripping wet."

I bite my bottom lip. "Shame to waste the moment, isn't it?"

He chuckles. "Nice try." I feel him sliding the belt over my ankles and up my thighs. The dildo slides into me, giving me an excruciatingly small amount of satisfaction. And then he locks it in place. "Perfect."

"You're something else."

"I know," he says, a hint of pride in his voice.

"Not in a good way."

He smirks. "You love it." He wraps his palm around

my throat. "You love being dominated and controlled, don't you, Gwendolyne?"

My body reacts to his dominance, driving me mad. Especially when I'm so needy. "Don't touch me," I say, trying to yank away from him.

He tightens his grasp, drawing me closer to him. "I'll touch you anytime and anyplace I want. Do you know why?"

I clench my jaw as I'm not going to answer.

"Because you belong to me. You're mine, Gwendolyne." He traces his fingers along the curve of my breasts, making my nipples ache.

I need release, but this man is cruel. He won't give it to me, no matter how much I beg him. And I have enough self-respect left not to stoop to that level.

"What about this dress, then?" I ask.

He nods and leads me into the walk-in closet. "You have lots of dresses in here, but I have one in particular in mind."

No doubt it's going to be revealing and degrading.

He selects a garment bag from the rack and hooks it on one of the coat hangers on the back of the door. He unzips the bag to reveal a beautiful crimson silk ball gown. With intricate beading and embroidery, work cascading down the bodice and along the skirt. The neckline has an exquisite off-the-shoulder design, and a train that flows gracefully. My mouth drops open in awe at its beauty.

He takes out the dress and hands it to me. "Put it on."

I slip it on, turning my back to Cillian for him to zip me in. "Can you do it up?"

"With pleasure." He moves toward me with a look of admiration in his eyes. His fingers graze against my skin as he zips it up, watching me with desire in his eyes in the reflection in front of me. "You look like a fucking vision. More beautiful than any work of art."

I shake my head, heat blazing into my cheeks. "Don't be silly."

He arches a brow. "It's the truth. Look at you."

I do look, taking in my reflection. And I can't deny that the gown does look stunning.

Cillian walks away and then returns with a pair of expensive pendant drop earrings, which he passes to me. And then he slides a beautiful diamond necklace around my neck and does it up.

Only then does he spin me around and step back to look at me properly. "You look like a princess," he murmurs, yanking me toward him. "My princess."

I can't help but feel the anger melt away. Despite everything he's put me through, Cillian is the only person who has ever made me feel special. As if I'm worth anything other than being a device to bring power to my father.

It's crazy that a man who has kidnapped me and forced me to marry him makes me feel freer than I've ever felt before.

CILLIAN

"*N*ow be a good girl and smile," I murmur into Gwen's ear.

I enjoy the way she shudders, knowing that she's needy for release. She squirmed in her seat the entire ride over here. I'm going to give it to her later, and once I do, she'll thank me for it. Because it's going to feel better drawn out and delayed.

"Screw you," she mutters under her breath.

I smile, placing my hand on the small of her back. "Keep talking like that and I'll leave the belt on you for the rest of the week, not only tonight."

Her jaw clenches and I can tell she takes my warning seriously as she puts on a fake smile. "Fine."

I usher her into the event with my hand on her back, feeling an odd sense of pride to have this beauty next to me. She's exquisite. The most beautiful woman in this place. Scratch that, the most beautiful woman on this planet, and she belongs to me.

"What is this event about?" she asks.

I squeeze her hip softly. "It's a charity event."

"As if you give a shit about charity."

I smile. "I'm not as heartless as you believe, princess."

"What charity is it?"

"A charity for the homeless."

"The people you keep homeless when you supply them with your filthy drugs?"

I narrow my eyes. "Everyone has free will, Gwendolyne. No one forces them to take drugs."

"Whatever. I need a drink." She tries to walk away from me, but I capture her wrist.

"You're not going anywhere without me."

She huffs heavily, but doesn't fight as I lace my fingers with hers and lead her toward the bar.

"What will you have, princess?"

She purses her lips together. "A gin and tonic."

"Is that your favorite drink?"

She shrugs. "I'm not a big drinker."

The bartender gives me a pointed look as if to say hurry up and order. "One gin and tonic and a scotch, please."

She huffs and goes to get our drinks.

"Someone's grumpy."

Gwen smirks. "Me or her?"

"Both of you, but you have a good reason, considering how desperate you are to come."

"Maybe she's got one on, too."

I laugh at that and the air between us shifts. As if we're actually going to have a good time tonight. Ever since I took her to Santa Catalina, that easiness between us has been strained. I guess it doesn't help that I've been spanking her every night, but it resulted in the best sex I've ever experienced.

Gwendolyne loves getting spanked. I think that's the reason she hasn't written an apology. Not that I want it, anyway. I want an excuse to spank her because I love it as well.

"A toast," I say.

She arches her brow, clutching her drink. "To what?"

"To an enjoyable evening."

"Speak for yourself," she murmurs, her thighs clenching. "Nothing about this is enjoyable."

I lean toward her. "Think how fucking good it's going to feel later when I make you come, baby," I murmur into her ear.

When I move back, her cheeks have tinged a deep red as she shakes her head. "You're evil."

"And proud of it."

A small hint of a smile graces her lips. "What exactly is your motive for coming to this event? Surely it must have a political or financial gain for you."

It concerns me that she knows my motives that well. "Am I that predictable?"

"Yep."

"I want to meet with the mayor of San Diego to discuss real estate plans."

"Real estate?"

I nod. "I'm ready to try to get my business on a legit-imate footing rather than a criminal one."

"Isn't real estate corrupt?"

"Baby steps," I murmur, taking a sip of scotch. As she's right, it's borderline criminal considering the amount of corruption and bribery involved. However, I need to increase the safety net of my outfit and real estate is perfect. Unfortunately for me, Piero is already deep into real estate and has been pushing to expand into San Diego, a plan I need to stop in its tracks tonight.

"Where is the mayor?" she asks, glancing around the room.

I spot a group of people in the corner of the room. "Over there." I indicate with a nod. "I need to wait until he's alone to talk to him."

Gwen arches a brow. "Because this real estate venture isn't legal?"

I smirk. "You know me so well."

She rolls her eyes. "How are you going to get a man so popular alone?"

"With the beautiful piece of bait on my arm."

Her eyes narrow. "What do you mean?"

"The mayor has a thing for beautiful young women."

"And you are okay with him touching me?"

I bare my teeth then. "It won't get that far, Gwen, and you know it."

"No, because if that man at your club is anything to go by, you'll probably murder the mayor and then your deal would be dead in the water."

"Exactly." I tilt my head. "I want you to walk past him on the way to the ladies' room. I'll already be there to ensure I head him off before he lays a finger on you."

She glares at me. "Who says I'm going to help you?"

I tap a finger against my lip. "The belt protecting your pussy?"

"God damn it," she huffs.

"I thought so." I lead her in the direction of the mayor with my hand against the small of her back. "You know what to do, princess."

She gives me an irritated look as I leave her alone and head for the restroom. After about two minutes, I hear the clacking of her heels on the hardwood floor before she comes into the corridor and gives me a nod.

"Excuse me, miss," the mayor's voice echoes behind her.

So predictable.

She stops and turns toward him. "Yes?"

I march forward to intercept. "Hello, Joe," I say, placing my hand on Gwen's hip possessively. "What do you want with my wife?"

His jaw opens and closes. "Apologies. I didn't realize she was yours."

The fucker would have if he'd accepted the invite to our wedding.

"I'll tell you how you can apologize."

His eyes narrow. "Do I know you?"

I hold my hand out to him. "Cillian Hook."

His face pales. "Oh, I see." He takes my hand. "I wasn't aware you were attending."

"Why? Have you been avoiding me?"

He swallows hard, his Adam's apple bobbing. It's clear the fucker is scared of me, which is amusing

BIANCA COLE

considering the power he has. "No, but I know I can't give you what you're after."

"And what is that?"

"An entry into real estate in San Diego."

I narrow my eyes at him. "Why the fuck can't you give it to me?"

He purses his lips. "It's Gary Keith. He's the one who is standing in the way."

I know the name, but I've got no idea who he is. "And who is he?"

"A senator in government, but he has the San Diego planning commission in his pocket and when I asked him about it, he flatly refused to entertain your proposal."

I clench my fists. "What you're telling me is that you received my proposal and ignored it?"

"No, I tried everything I could to get a result—"

"Shut it," I snap, feeling the rage begin to bubble beneath the surface. I don't like being ignored, even if this piece of shit is the mayor. "Tell me how to get results. I'm not letting this go."

He quivers with fear. "The only option is to get Gary Keith on your side."

"And where can I find him?"

Gwen shuffles next to me. "Excuse me, I need to use the ladies' room."

I kiss her cheek. "Don't be long."

She nods and turns toward the ladies' restroom.

"Am I right in thinking she was Piero Panarello's fiancé?"

306

"If I were you, I wouldn't say that name in my presence," I growl.

His eyes widen, but he nods in response. "Apologies."

"Answer the question. Where can I find Gary Keith?"

He runs a hand across the back of his neck, eyes darting back toward the party. "There's an event he's hosting next week. I can get you an invitation, but if that woman is who I think, it may be wise to leave her home."

I narrow my eyes. "And why is that?"

"I couldn't be sure whether the person you don't want me to mention will be there or not."

If it's a party hosted by Gary, then it's fifty/fifty whether Piero will attend. "Fine, once I've sorted him out. I'll be knocking on your door again."

His throat bobs as he swallows. "Certainly. May I go now?"

I step out of his way, allowing him to go to the restroom.

Gwen returns a minute later, brow furrowed. "What happened?"

"Nothing important."

I notice the flash of irritation in her eyes. "Fine. Are we leaving now?"

I push her against the wall. "Why? Are you hoping to get me into the sack?"

She licks her lips. "Perhaps." Gwen is vibrating with need and it's intoxicating. She's been like this all night.

"Okay, princess. Anything for you," I murmur,

before kissing her passionately. "I'm going to fuck your ass tonight," I breathe into her ear.

I'm surprised that, instead of telling me no, her eyes dilate and she pushes closer. "Yes, please, captain."

"Fuck," I groan, my cock straining against the zipper of my pants. "You want my cock in your ass?"

She nods in response.

"We're leaving right fucking now."

She smirks and I know she thinks she's won, but I feel like the one with the prize. My delicious wife wants her ass fucked, and I'm happy to oblige. I can't wait to get her home.

30

GWENDOLYNE

There's a strong pulse between my thighs and it's stronger than the pounding of my heart as I follow Cillian to our bedroom. His strong, confident strides contrast with mine as I take two at a time, trying to keep up.

When he mentioned fucking my ass, I thought it would be a turnoff, but ever since he used his hook back there, I've been gagging for more. It was so good.

"You look nervous, princess," he murmurs as he leads me into the bedroom and over to the door to his sex room.

"Maybe I am."

He kisses me passionately, stealing all the air from my lungs. "Don't be. This is going to be the best fucking night of your life, I guarantee it."

My mind races as he wraps his arms around me, and I feel a wave of heat course through me. I've never felt so alive.

He moves me back toward the bed, kissing me still. And then he lowers me to it, eyes alight with pure passion.

His fingers trail over my skin as he pushes the hem of my dress to my hips, revealing the belt that's driving me insane.

Reaching into his pants pocket, he pulls the key out and slides it into the lock at the front, releasing it. Instantly, I feel the pressure lessen.

Cillian pulls the chastity belt out of me and brings it to his nose, inhaling. The sight is primal and yet so sexy. "I'll never get enough of how fucking delicious you taste and smell."

I grip his dark hair in my hands, pulling him close as I kiss him.

"Good girl," he murmurs against my lips as his fingers slip inside me and begin thrusting in and out of me until I'm trembling with pleasure. Every sensation is heightened by the fact that I've been kept on the edge by that belt.

We part for air and a smug smirk appears on Cillian's face. "On your knees now, baby."

"Why?"

"Because I want to get my cock nice and wet from your throat before I fuck your ass." He grabs my hair, forcing me to my knees.

Anticipation builds with every passing second, making me crave him in a way I haven't before. I try to hate this man, but there's something indescribable pulling us together like two powerful magnets.

"Open wide for me, princess."

His cock is as hard as a rock and there's precum dripping from the tip, making my mouth salivate at the thought of licking it off. I unhinge my jaw. Without warning, he guides his cock into my mouth, sending a flood of arousal through my nerves.

I flick my tongue around his tip, savoring the way he trembles and groans as I slide him further into my throat. His delicious pre-cum coats my mouth, making me hungrier.

I draw back, sucking on his crown and reveling in the power I have over him when I'm like this.

He grabs a fistful of my hair and plunges deep into my throat, letting out an animalistic growl as I gag.

"Keep going, princess," he orders gruffly, pushing a little harder into my throat. "Such a good girl."

His words fuel the fire within me and wetness gathers on my inner thighs, dripping onto the bedsheets. The pleasure I get from making him feel so good is unlike anything else. The more he moans and curses, the more intoxicating it becomes.

Before long, he's panting heavily and gripping my hair so tight it feels like he's trying to pull it from my scalp. He pulls away and yanks me to my feet, grabbing my throat.

"You're gonna make me come," he warns in a low voice, tearing at the fabric of my dress as he desperately tries to get rid of it. "And that's not what I need... I need to fuck your ass."

His large hands grip my hips, imprinting his rough

touch on my skin. I know he'll leave me with more bruises when this is over. That dark and twisted part of me he's breathed life into craves it.

Once I'm naked, he forces me onto my knees on the bed and grabs my ass cheeks, parting them. I feel him spit onto my virgin hole, making me tense.

"Cillian," I breathe his name, fear mixing with arousal.

His tongue probes at my tight ring of muscles. All rational thought escapes me. "Ever since I met you, Gwendolyne, I knew I'd possess you in every fucking way. Fuck each one of your holes. And tonight, I will make it a hat trick."

He rubs my clit as he licks my ass, driving me toward oblivion so fast I hardly see it coming.

"Fuck!" My body spasms as I come undone.

"Naughty princess," he mutters, his finger probing at my ass. "Did I tell you to come?"

I purse my lips together and shake my head.

"Time for me to stretch this asshole out ready for my cock," he murmurs, grabbing something off of the nightstand. I feel the coldness of the lube as he squirts it on, followed by the press of something against my hole. Cillian works whatever it is into me and I moan. The sensation is as good as I remember at his club, Neverland. I wasn't sure if it was the aspect of being watched that made it so good.

"This ass looks fucking beautiful stretching around this dildo," he murmurs, beginning to slide the item in and out, sending the most exquisite sensation through my body.

"Oh God." I arch my back.

"Do you like that, princess?"

I sink my teeth into my bottom lip and nod.

He spanks my ass. "Let me hear you say it."

I swallow hard. "I love it, captain." I glance over my shoulder, meeting his dark gaze. "I can't wait until it's your cock."

He growls and I feel the press of his hard cock against my pussy. "Is that right? Well, first I'm going to breed your tight little cunt with this dildo still lodged in your ass."

My pussy gets wetter at the thought and I arch my back.

"Goddamn it, Gwendolyne. You are my fucking whore, aren't you? Getting wet at the thought of being stuffed that fucking full." He slides his hand down my body and rubs my clit, drawing out a wave of pleasure that makes me quiver.

"Do you feel what you do to me?" he asks, as his cock pulses against my entrance. He traces his hands over my front, cupping my breasts. And then one hand slides to cup my throat as he pulls me harder against him. "I can't wait to pop your anal cherry and make that ass mine," he growls.

Without warning, his shaft pushes into my pussy and I scream, knowing I've never felt so stuffed in all my life. It's painful. There's not enough space for the dildo and his cock.

"Ahh!" I grip the comforter below me in an attempt to ground myself.

"My God, you're so wet and ready," he growls, tightening his grasp on my hips. "And so fucking tight with this dildo in your ass. How does it feel?"

I moan helplessly at the combination of pleasure and pain that sweeps through me with each movement of his hips.

"Did you hear my question?" His voice is thick with lust, sending shivers cascading down my spine..

"Good," I gasp, eyes shut from the intensity of sensation coursing through my veins. "Oh God, it feels so good."

He trails light kisses along my neck as he keeps his cock embedded as deep as possible inside me. Slowly, he fucks me. The speed is torturous, as it feels like I'm being torn apart. "Such a good girl," he purrs into my ear, pushing every inch deep.

Each motion drags a soft whimper from my lips.

"Does my princess like being stretched by two cocks?"

I swallow hard as the shameful answer is, I love it.

"Answer me," he barks, spanking my ass.

"Yes. I love it."

"Dirty girl," he murmurs, grabbing the back of my neck and yanking my back against his chest. "I'm going to fuck that ass now, but know that the only real cock ever entering your body is mine, understand? You can have all the dildos you want in every fucking orifice, but mine is the only dick you'll ever have inside you."

I nod in response. "Yes, captain."

"Good girl," he purrs, pulling his cock out of my aching pussy. And then the dildo slips out of my ass, and I know I've never felt emptier in my life.

I feel the tip of his dick against my stretched hole, but he pauses for a moment. "I've been wanting this forever," he growls, pushing through inch by inch until he's buried to the hilt.

The pain is shocking. "It hurts!" I cry out, as he's far bigger than the dildo.

"Relax for me, Princess," he whispers soothingly as his hands caress my body. "It'll feel so good when you do."

I obey, ignoring the pain and remembering the pleasure I felt moments ago. His cock pistons in and out, and each thrust drives him deeper than I believed possible.

Before long, I'm grinding against him, trying to seek that confusing combination of pain and pleasure.

Cillian chuckles. "Fuck, Gwen. I never believed you'd love getting your ass fucked this much." He cups my throat hard.

I attempt to keep my hips still, but can't help myself. "Fuck me harder."

"Don't worry, princess. I'll make sure you experience a true ass fucking." He withdraws all the way out of me, only to push back in so hard I can't help but scream.

My body shudders as I struggle to comprehend all the sensations flooding through me—pain, euphoria, and confusion all merging together like a heady concoction.

"That's it," he growls, no longer sounding human but like an animal instead. "Take that cock in your ass, princess. Let me claim every one of your holes." His lips brush tantalizingly against my earlobe while his rough hand wraps around my throat like a collar made for me. "Mine," he growls. "All fucking mine."

"Yes," I moan, clamping my eyes shut. "All yours."

I feel my body on the edge of shattering like a priceless vase against concrete. His powerful thrusts send pleasure coursing through my veins like hot lava, and I know at this moment I'll never be the same again. He's ruined me for all other men. Turned me into *his* whore as he promised he would. I'm addicted to him and I don't know whether to love it or hate it.

Our bodies fit together like two pieces of a jigsaw puzzle and the sensation is rapturous. I can feel my essence coating my inner thighs so much it's like someone tipped a bucket of water between them.

"Fuck," I gasp, head lolling forward. "I'm so close."

He grunts behind me and grabs a handful of my hair, yanking my neck back. "That's it, princess. Come for me with my cock deep inside your ass." He tightens his grasp, using my hair to shove himself in and out of me with force. "I'm going to fill your ass with my cum and then your pussy, and I won't rest until it's fucking flowing out of you. Until every one of your holes is well and truly bred."

His words alone are enough to send me exploding over the edge. "Yes, captain!" I cry out, pushing back against him as the orgasm tears through me like a rip tide.

Cillian sinks his teeth into the tender skin between my shoulder and neck, growling into my flesh as his own climax comes. I feel him filling me with his cum and it makes me needier. What for? I couldn't say, considering I experienced an earth-shattering orgasm. All I know is that we're in for one crazy night, and I hope he makes good on his promise and breeds all of my holes.

31

GWENDOLYNE

I dig into the delicious stew Cillian's Ma made. She wanted to cook tonight, and Rosa was grateful for the break.

His ma is wary of me, telling Cillian I'm being too nice to her to get her on my side. I'm only being nice to her because she's my mother-in-law and she has dementia. It's clear she's not in her right mind a lot of the time. She keeps calling Cillian, Jonathan. I can only assume that it's his dad's name.

"I'm tired," she announces, standing. "I'm going to bed."

Cillian nods. "Okay, Ma. Sleep well."

The moment she's gone, I can feel the intensity of Cillian's gaze prickling over my skin.

"You've been quiet tonight. Is it because of my ma?"

I shrug. "I prefer not to argue with you in front of her."

He chuckles. "Are you saying we can't talk and not argue?"

"Pretty much."

He puts his cutlery down, stretching his arms above his head. "I'm going out," he announces.

I frown. "Out where?"

"An event. I'll be back later." His eyes gleam with a hint of mischief. "Don't wait up. I'll wake you with my cock when I get back."

"You'd better not," I say, the thought both terrifying and arousing at the same time.

He tilts his head. "I thought you would've learned by now to not tell me what I should and shouldn't do." He walks over to my seat and places his hands on my shoulders, kneading them. "Be a good girl for me, baby," he murmurs, pressing his lips to the shell of my ear. "And spend the night thinking about how good it's going to feel when I slide into you while you sleep."

My skin buzzes with anticipation. "Take your time."

He doesn't respond before striding away, leaving me to contemplate the plan I'd been silently forming since Tilly left. The thought of escape builds inside my mind. If Cillian is out tonight, it's my perfect chance. After all, Tilly is never coming back. I overheard Rosa talking to one of the other staff members who said she handed in her notice and never returned to work.

It means I'm on my own. An odd ache ignites in my chest at the thought of never seeing Cillian again. However, I need to put space between us for my own sanity. I stand and walk through the corridors toward the kitchen, glancing inside. It's empty.

If I'm going to walk to a pay phone to call my dad, then I need supplies. I've got no idea how long it will take me to walk to one. It could take hours, as Cillian's house is at the farthest end of La Jolla from the city center. The kitchen is stocked with plenty of food and drink, so I grab a few snacks, like energy bars, fruit and nuts, as well as a few bottles of water to keep me going. And then I rush out of the kitchen, barreling into Rosa.

She arches a brow. "What's with all the food? Don't tell me you didn't enjoy dinner."

I swallow hard. "It was delicious. I'm always hungry lately. And Cillian is out tonight, so I'm going to watch a movie." Granted, my healthy energy-packed snacks aren't exactly movie food, but she can't judge me for that.

She nods. "Fair enough. Enjoy."

I walk past her toward the home movie theater to maintain the illusion. My heart is hammering at a thousand miles an hour. All I did was get some food and I'm already on the brink of being caught. When I'm sure I won't run into her again, I head up the stairs to our bedroom.

Everything is up in the air, but if I don't take advantage of the fact Cillian isn't here tonight, then I'll never get away. This is the first time he's not been here at night, and I need the cover of darkness to escape.

I open the door to the bedroom and again, that painful twinge hits me. This is the last time I'll be here. I pull off the dress I'm wearing and leave it on the floor, walking into the closet. There are no clothes that are inconspicuous in here, so I head into Cillian's closet instead, grabbing one of his black sweatshirts and pulling it on. My stomach dips as it smells of him, but it's perfect because it's oversize and not what anyone would expect me to wear.

Returning to my closet, I grab a pair of black sweatpants that Cillian supplied me to use in his home gym and put them on. Lastly, I slip into a pair of navy blue trainers also intended for use in the gym.

It's the best disguise I've got. All I can do is hope that the dark of night and this clothing offers me the disguise I need to get out of here.

There's a rucksack stuffed at the bottom of the closet, and I pull it out to stock it with my food and drink. I turn toward the bedroom with a sigh.

This is it.

I'll get out of here tonight or I'll die trying. Either way, I don't want to end up back in this house. Cillian is turning me into someone I don't recognize. What I did the other night at his club was out of character. I hate that I enjoyed it. He makes me certain that if I remain much longer, I'll be glad he stole me... A part of me already is.

Throwing the backpack over my shoulder, I stare at the room we shared. A deep sadness claws at me, knowing I'll never see him again. I've got a serious case of Stockholm syndrome. I need to get some space to clear my head. And then I'm sure this stupid infatuation with the man who kidnapped me will disappear without a trace.

My heart beats like a jackhammer, threatening to burst out of my chest as I scan the bedroom one last time. I slip out of the room, closing the door behind me. My adrenaline spikes as I tiptoe down the stairs with trembling legs, trying not to make a sound. Every step feels like a death sentence as I make my way to the back of the house. The backdoor is the only way out, but an armed guard stands outside it, ready to catch me in my escape attempt.

My pulse pounds in my ears as I assess my options: the side door from the kitchen or risk everything by making a run for it when the guard's back is turned?

I opt for the side door and force the handle down as slowly as possible until I hear a faint click and slip out of the kitchen door, crouching low against the walls to keep out of sight.

The guard's movements are erratic, his gun at-the-ready, his eyes scanning left and right. Then he shifts his stance for a second. It's all the opportunity I need. Without a second thought, I bolt off into the night air like prey being hunted by a predator—desperate for escape. My feet pound hard against the concrete path leading away from Cillian's home toward the beach where freedom awaits.

All the while, the sound of waves crashing on the shore calls to me as I rush down the steps. I search desperately for refuge as my heart races in fear of being caught and returned to my captor. The wind whistles past me as I race through the night without looking back —freedom is a few strides away now.

A man's voice shatters my hopes: "What the fuck?" He shouts. "Cillian's wife is trying to escape!"

Panic grips me as I hear words crackling through on the radio; "All teams to the beach. We've got a runner."

Damn it.

I grit my teeth, sprinting like my life depends on it, ignoring the burning pain in my lungs as freedom draws near.

If I make it to the beach and off his property, I have a chance. With each step, freedom feels like a reality, but more distant at the same time. The thud of heavy boots in the distance warns me that I don't have much time.

I'm about three yards from the neighboring property where a group of people appear to be having a party. I call out to them for help, but their music is too loud. The sound of my voice barely makes it above the thumping bass coming from the speakers. And when I'm at the fence to cross, two heavy hands land on my shoulders and pull me away from freedom. I struggle, but the grip tightening around my body is too strong.

The man who grabbed me is one of Cillian's guards. His grip on me tightens as he speaks, his words dripping with disgust. "Where the fuck do you think you're going, Mrs. Hook? Huh?!"

I swallow hard and look at him. "Please let me go."

He snorts, glaring at me with fierce eyes. "You think I'm going to sacrifice myself on that motherfucker's hook for you? If I let you go, Cillian will kill every guard working tonight for negligence." A chill consumes me as I consider how many lives could have been lost if I'd escaped.

He drags me back into Cillian's house, throwing me onto the floor like an unwanted toy. Two guards remain behind me. Their malignant stares are like daggers piercing through my skin. "Wait here," he growls. "Cillian will be back to deal with you." And then he stomps off in silence, leaving two armed guards behind me.

I've never felt more helpless as I remain on the floor, broken and defeated. It was a good plan in my mind, but clearly I underestimated how many guards Cillian has patrolling the grounds.

Time ticks by at an agonizingly slow speed, or perhaps it's because I know what's awaiting me when Cillian gets back. A punishment far worse than he's subjected me to so far.

Each tick of time intensifies my fear until I can hardly breathe when the door finally swings open. This is it. My reckoning.

I fear I may not survive my husband's wrath this time.

32

CILLIAN

I hate that I have to attend this event without Gwen, but there's the tiniest chance Piero could be here tonight, so I couldn't risk her coming. But I couldn't miss it. Especially not when I don't trust my men to get the job done.

Smyth stands next to me. "What's the plan, boss?"

I glare at him, suspicious still of every fucker I employ. "The plan is we mingle and when the time is right, we strike."

He arches a brow. "How exactly?"

"You monitor him and when he heads for the restroom, you tell me. Got it?"

Smyth nods. "Yes, sir. And do you want me to follow as backup?"

I am considering whether I'll need backup confronting a fucking politician. A politician who's firmly in Piero's pocket and the reason the mayor won't consider my proposal, giving Piero an upper hand in my own goddamn city. The man controls the funding for the planning commission and, in turn, Piero has the entire San Diego real estate in his pocket. I need to ensure that changes tonight, as he's overstepping into my territory.

"No, I'll do this alone."

Smyth's jaw clenches, but he respects my wishes and turns to head toward the sidelines.

I grab his arm. "And Smyth?"

He looks at my hand around his wrist, a pained expression on his face before he glances at me. "Sir?"

"Make sure you don't get in the way."

He nods, but I see an odd glimmer in his eyes. Ever since I found out someone is working against me, I can't shift my suspicion from Smyth. I'm not sure why he'd betray me, other than the fact I don't treat him well despite ten years of working together.

Walking around the outskirts of the room, I keep my eyes on Gary Lewis. The politician I'm here to blackmail into getting the planning commission on my side instead of Piero's.

Thankfully, I haven't seen Piero or his men. If he does show up, then all bets are off. I won't hesitate to murder him, and I doubt he would hesitate to murder me. It would be a fight to the fucking death, and the idea excites me. I've been wanting to get my hands on that son of a bitch ever since that conversation the night the news broke.

I follow Gary's movements for the next half an hour, not wanting to approach him with a crowd. I need to get him alone. This time I don't have the assistance of my beautiful wife.

"How are you going to get him alone?" I hear Smyth in my earpiece.

It only winds me up. "Leave it to me," I growl.

I hear a heavy sigh on the other end as I walk toward the group of people he's currently with. If the fucker isn't going to go anywhere that I can get him alone, I'm going to have to approach him in a group.

"Gary, can I have a word?" I ask, interrupting his conversation and forcing him to look at me.

His brow furrows. "Do I know you?"

"By reputation, I'm sure you do."

His jaw works and he nods. "Excuse me, please," he says to the couple he had been chatting with for twenty minutes.

Once we're out of earshot, he turns to me. "I don't know who you are, but thank you. I needed a way to get away from them."

I smirk as he won't be thanking me when he realizes who I am. "No worries, can we chat somewhere private?"

He looks unsure, but nods. "Follow me." The idiot leads me into a small study and turns to face me. "How can I help you?"

"My name is Cillian Hook."

His face pales the moment I tell him who I am. "Oh."

"Yes, and I hear you're in the way of my buying shares in San Diego real estate, in my city, because Piero has you in his pocket. Is that right?"

I love seeing the fear in his eyes, as it means my name instills fear in men like him.

"Correct. I don't think we have anything to discuss." He tries to move around me, but I put my arm out to stop him.

"Wrong. We have plenty to discuss." I glare at him. He may be a politician, but I don't give a shit who he is. If he stands in my way, I won't hesitate to remove him.

"I can't do anything for you. My hands are tied."

I clench my jaw. "I assume you know who I am?"

He nods. "Of course."

"In that case, you also know what I'm capable of."

His throat bobs. "Are you threatening me?"

"Of course, and if you don't stop jacking about with Piero, I'll ensure you won't be breathing for much longer."

"Piero said the same thing. Who am I supposed to trust?"

Bastard.

"Me. As Piero won't be a problem for much longer."

The flash in his eyes tells me he knows what I mean, but he shakes his head. "I've accepted his deal."

"Whatever he's paying you, I'll double it."

His eyes light up at the mention of money, the motherfucker. It's all that talks in this world; money and power. If you can't offer either, then violence is the only way to get to the top. I know because that's how I got back to the top after Piero sunk me to the depth of the ocean.

"That sounds fair…" he murmurs, rubbing a hand across the back of his neck. "However, Piero might pay more."

I narrow my eyes. "Are you trying to play me off against Piero?" I crack my knuckles. "You don't realize the kind of men you're playing with."

His throat bobs and he takes a step backward.

I step forward, feeling the darkness well within me, and rise toward the surface. "What do you think? I'm in control of this city, not Piero." Clenching my fists, I keep advancing. "You think that you can side with a man like him in my own city and I won't react?"

The asshole quivers, fear clear in his eyes. He's a goddamn coward and I hate cowards.

"Of course not. I accept your offer."

I clap my hands. "Perfect. My lawyer is waiting outside. Have a seat." I gesture to the chair behind him.

There's a moment of hesitation. I sense he would prefer to do business with Piero, probably because he takes a softer approach.

"Boss, we've got a problem not related to this asshole."

I press my finger to my ear. "What is it?"

"The men have caught Gwendolyne trying to escape. She was close, apparently."

My entire body turns numb. My world spins a little and I begin to shake.

I've been gone a matter of two hours and she's already trying to flee my home. Rage hits me as I thought we were getting past the whole kidnapping and forced marriage thing. She'd been submitting to me and enjoying the sex like no woman I'd ever been with before.

"Fine, you handle this piece of shit and get the

contract signed." I glare at the man before me. "I'll head back now."

Smyth clears his throat on the other end. "Sir, it's in hand. You don't need to—"

"Don't tell me what I need to do, Smyth," I snap, knowing that there's no way in hell I'm staying here after he broke that news to me. I have a princess to punish, and I won't be kept from her by a sniveling excuse of a politician who thinks he can play God and mess about with two mob bosses.

Smyth comes in through the door to the study. "Sir."

"Make sure he signs the document Karl is coming in with." I say, pinning him with a stern glare. "I need to deal with my wife."

I march out of the room, entrusting Smyth to deliver, even though I trust no one. The detective hasn't worked out who is behind the leak in my outfit, so it goes against every instinct to leave this to someone else. My wife is making me do things I'd never normally do.

I will deal with her harshly for trying to escape. Although taking the harsh route hasn't been working to my advantage with her. Gwendolyne fights our connection every step of the way when all I want is for her to feel the way I do.

33

CILLIAN

*P*ain claws at my insides as if I'm being torn apart from the inside out. Gwendolyne stands in front of me. Her head hung because my guards caught her trying to escape. I could have lost her tonight.

And here I was thinking she was beginning to feel what I felt.

"Leave us," I say, glaring at the man who manhandled her. "And don't ever touch my wife like that again, or you may end up with a hook for both hands yourself."

He pales and bows his head. "Apologies, sir. It won't happen again." He leaves the room and shuts the door.

"Have a seat," I say.

Gwendolyne looks at me, eyes dazzling with unshed tears. "Why don't you let me go, Cillian?"

My nostrils flare as too many emotions swirl around inside me that I can hardly work out which one is most prominent. "Because you're mine, Gwendolyne."

She shakes her head. "You took me captive. I can never be yours, because I never chose to be."

I clench my hand. "And you chose to be Piero's?" I snap. The mere thought of him touching her driving me to the brink of a psychotic break. If she told me she wanted him, I'm not sure I could contain my rage. Fuck knows what I'd do, but I'd cause fucking carnage.

"At least he didn't force me to marry him, take me against my will and then expect me to feel something other than disgust toward him."

I march toward her and grab her chin.

"Piero is no fucking hero, Gwendolyne. And you may see me as a villain, but who the fuck wants the prince, anyway?" I grind my teeth. "A prince will pick saving the day over saving you, but the villain... Me," I confirm. "I'd do anything to ensure that you remain safe. You're all that fucking matters to me. Do you understand?" I search those eyes for a flicker of emotion. "And if I remember rightly, that piece of shit, Piero, has no time for you."

Her expression softens a little. "Before you took me captive, I couldn't stop thinking about you. Those two weeks before you struck and became my captor, my mind was consumed with thoughts of you..."

Hope flares to life. If that's the case, all is not lost. There was something between us from the start and I refuse to believe it's gone.

"And then you fucked it all up. You took me captive, forced me to marry you at gunpoint, and then took my virginity like a cave man claiming his right." Her throat bobs as she swallows. "If you'd had any sense, you wouldn't have done any of it. Maybe you would have won my heart fair and square."

I release her chin and pace the floor of my study, trying to work out how to fix this. The fact is, I'm not a hero. She's right, I'm one of the villains of the story, but I want her. I want her more than anything—even more than getting revenge on that piece of shit Piero. And despite wanting her love, I can't let her go because I can't risk Piero using her against me. He doesn't care about her, and the quicker she learns it, the better.

"All hope can't be lost," I say, looking at her.

Her brow furrows. "If you let me go, it won't be."

I shake my head. "That's what people say when they want to get away and never look back."

"And would that be so terrible?"

I march toward her and grab her throat, looking into her eyes deeply. "It would end me, Gwendolyne. You're my world now and I won't let you go. Not for anything."

Her eyes widen. "Not if someone offered you a billion dollars?"

I shake my head. "There's no treasure on this earth that means more to me than you."

She narrows her eyes. "If that's the case, then you should let me go."

"And allow that piece of shit, Piero, to lay his hands on you?" I shake my head. "No fucking chance."

She reaches for my face and cups it, the gesture gentle. "Tell me what happened between you two."

I know that if I want a chance at salvaging this twisted mess I've made, then I have to come clean. I've not spoken of Piero's betrayal to anyone but Smyth and Ma since it happened. "It's hard for me to get into it."

"Is he the reason you have one hand?" she presses.

I shake my head. "Do you think I'd go to these lengths to destroy a man, all because he chopped my hand off?"

She shrugs. "You're a little crazy."

I can't help but smile at that. "No, that's another story all together."

"Tell me both."

"My da chopped my hand off when I was ten years old because I broke his grandma's vase."

She gasps, holding a hand over her mouth. "Your dad?"

I nod in response.

"What kind of father would——"

"He was nothing but a sperm donor. I wouldn't call him a father."

"That's terrible."

I shrug as I got over that a long time ago, but it was the seed that turned me into the twisted, dark individual I am today.

"Why did you say it was a crocodile?"

"It was. My dad's nickname was the crocodile. He was ruthless and would snap a man's fucking head off for looking at him the wrong way."

Gwendolyne shudders. "What about Piero?"

I look into her emerald green eyes, knowing that I want to tell her everything. I want to bare my soul to her and hope that she accepts me; every dark and warped part of me. As I search those eyes, I know that she won't accept me. I'm too broken and damaged for her.

"I can't get into that."

"Why not?"

I swallow hard, feeling myself disappearing into my memories of the day I found out what Piero had done.

My da and sister are dead. Suddenly, my cell phone rings and I pick it up.

"Cillian," my ma's tearful voice sounds on the other end. "T-they're dead."

Numbness spreads through me, as I can't wrap my head around what is happening. "Ma, where are you?"

"I'm in Palm Springs visiting my sister," she says, her voice strained. "How has this happened?"

I shake my head, as I have no idea. "I don't know. Stay put and don't go out. You could be in danger." I swallow hard, unsure how I'm keeping it together. "I'll call you back." I end the call, my heart pounding in my ears. "Who can I call about this?" I ask, looking at Smyth.

"Piero?" he suggests.

I nod and dial his number on my cell. After the third dial tone, he answers. "Cillian." His voice is cold and devoid of all emotion.

"Have you seen the news?" I ask.

He laughs. "Of course, I fucking made it."

Sickness coils in my stomach. "What do you mean?"

"While you were off making deals behind my back, I've taken everything from you. The Murphy empire no longer exists and if you step foot in Los Angeles again, I'll personally see to your demise."

My world spins. "You did this?" I confirm.

"Yes, Daddy begged for his life at the end. A sign of a weak

man." I can't say that I disagree with him, and a part of me is relieved he's gone. "And Kira..." He laughs. "Don't get me started on her." Rage slams into me, as Kira, on the other hand, was my world. My little sister and I couldn't protect her.

"You're sick," I say, shaking my head. "We're supposed to be friends."

"We could never be friends, Cillian. We're rivals. And now, you're nothing. It's a shame your mummy wasn't here, so I could end her, too."

I growl on the other end of the phone. "Careful, Piero." My fists clench, but there's always that ache where my limb used to be, a painful reminder that I'm no longer a whole man, the prosthetic never feeling the same.

Smyth watches me with a confused look on his face.

"You may be a killer, but so am I. I won't rest until your heart is no longer beating."

"Cillian?" I feel a hand on my arm, shaking me.

I grab it, anger flooding me. It takes me a second to realize it's Gwen. I release her throat which I've wrapped my palms around.

Her eyes are wide as she rubs her neck. "Where did you go?"

I shake my head, ignoring her question. "What Piero did to me, I can never forgive, but it's hard for me to talk about."

Gwen looks hurt by that, and I know I can't keep ignoring her questions forever.

I sigh. "But I'll tell you what you want to know." I know this is my chance at salvaging our relationship. A relationship that I've gone about entirely the wrong way from the start. "Piero and I were best friends growing up. He was there before I lost my hand and after."

Her eyes widen slightly hearing that we were friends. "What the hell happened then?"

"We were both the heirs of two criminal organizations operating out of L.A. Our families had always remained on good terms." I run my good hand across the back of my neck. "Until ten years ago, when Piero took control and his father stepped back because of bad health."

I clench my fists, thinking about it inspires a rage I can't control. "I was out of town negotiating a deal with a new supplier when I saw the news on the TV. My da and sister had been murdered. In turn, the Murphy family ousted."

"Piero did that?" She asks, a hint of disbelief in her tone, which makes me angrier. She's as blind to who he truly is as I was all those years ago.

"Yes, I rang him when I saw the news and he told me it was him and that if I showed my face in Los Angeles again, he'd murder me." I grind my teeth. "I've fought my way back to the top in San Diego with one goal in mind. Destroy Piero."

Gwen looks like she's struggling to process everything I'm telling her. "Piero murdered your family?"

"Yes. My sister was eighteen, and what Piero and his men did to her is unspeakable."

Her face pales. "What did he do?"

My mind strays to the moment three of my loyal men managed to break into the morgue and make it back to the yacht with her body before we fled.

"We've got Kira, sir."

I swallow hard, walking onto the deck to gaze upon her body. And I remember bending over and throwing up. Her body mutilated. Evidence that the men had raped her is clear as day. Her clothes were ripped. Her face was bruised and graying.

"Cillian?"

Ma's voice.

I shrug off my jacket and place it over Kira's body, turning around to block Ma's view

"Ma, stay back. The men have Kira's body and…" I shake *my head. "You don't want to see."*

Tears flood down her face. "I have to see my baby."

"Ma. Are you sure?"

"Certain." Her eyes fill with determination and I know nothing will stop her. I step aside, allowing her to see her daughter.

A shrill scream pierces the night air.

"Cillian?" she presses.

I shake my head, trying to erase the dark images from my mind. "I'd rather not talk about that in detail, but it's as bad as you can imagine."

"Is she the one who loved reading?"

The pain in my chest intensifies. "Yes."

Her throat bobs as she swallows. "And I was going to marry him," she mutters.

"Don't let my stories change your mind about your beloved Piero," I say, shaking my head. "I wanted you to see it for yourself."

"See what?"

"Who the better man is out of the two of us?"

Gwen's jaw tightens. "How do I know that you didn't start it? I'm hearing one side of the story."

My rage bubbles up because I hate that she's not accepting my story. She doubts me. "His dad died of old age and his siblings and mother are still alive. He remains in his childhood home, whereas mine is a pile of rubble after Piero tore it down." I narrow my eyes. "He's still in Los Angeles and I was forced to start again. What else could there be to the story?"

"Sorry," she murmurs, shaking her head. "I didn't mean to offend you."

The fact that she doesn't trust me does offend me, even if I don't have the right to expect her trust after what I've done.

I cup her cheeks in my hands. "I promise you, what I'm telling you is the truth."

She searches my eyes for a couple of infinitely long seconds before nodding. "I believe you."

Those three words I needed to hear. "Thank you."

"But it doesn't change anything. I wasn't trying to escape to be with Piero. I was trying to escape because I'll never be free here." She narrows her eyes. "Don't you understand that?"

I do understand, but I don't want to dwell on it because it means she can never be mine in the way I want. "Gwendolyne, please," I say, hating how desperate I sound.

She tilts her head. "Please, what?"

"Try to find it in your heart to look past what I've done."

She shakes her head. "I can't."

I move toward her and grab her hand. "I love you," I gasp, finding it hard to breathe in that moment. The moment I bare my heart and soul to her. Something I've never done for anyone.

"Love me?" she says, an odd look in her eyes. "This isn't love, Cillian. It's toxic and broken."

Rage overwhelms me as she's rejecting my love, something I've not given to anyone before—not in the romantic sense. I love Ma, of course, and I loved Kira.

"Toxic?" I rush toward her and grab her throat, squeezing. "That's what you think of my love for you?"

She arches a brow. "You have me in a chokehold and you're questioning whether I think this is toxic. That's rather ironic, don't you think?"

Her words slice through me and I release her throat, turning my back on her.

"I love you, Gwendolyne. I've never felt this way about another person in my thirty years of life." I can't look at her because inside I'm breaking. Cillian Hook is supposed to be untouchable, unbreakable, and yet this sweet angel has broken me. "If you can't believe that, then that's your problem." I walk away without another word.

Deep down, I know what I've got to do, but it's going to hurt like a bitch. I have to let her go.

34

CILLIAN

"*Y*ou've got news for me?" I ask as I walk into the detective's home.

He turns around and smiles at me. "Yes. I've found the rat."

"Spit it out, then," I say.

"Frank Henderson. He's the one who has been working against you."

My brow furrows. Out of my guys, Frank is probably the last person I would've expected. "Are you sure?"

"Positive." He gestures for me to join him. "Here. I've got all the evidence. Frank is the one selling you out to your enemy."

Motherfucker.

The detective does indeed have the evidence. Not only paperwork, but photos of him meeting with both Piero and Jovani. "God damn it."

He tilts his head. "About payment."

I hold my hand up. "You'll get your fucking payment. Don't worry about that."

"When can I expect it to clear?"

I draw in a deep breath and pull my cell phone out, logging onto my banking app. I wire a million dollars to the bastard. "As soon as the bank has processed it." I show him the transfer on my phone. "I have a fucking rat to kill."

He smirks widely. "Enjoy. Pleasure doing business with you." He holds out his hand for me to shake.

I narrow my eyes, but take it and shake. "And you."

While one thing is resolved, another is turning to shit. My lawyer is working on my divorce papers for Gwendolyne. It's been three days since I opened up to her and I've not returned to the house, crashing at Neverland ever since. Later tonight, I intend to give the papers to her and offer her the freedom she's been desperate for. A part of me hopes she'll refuse, but I'm not stupid. I know she'll take them and run.

I've been perpetually angry—angrier than I normally am—ever since she refused to believe I love her. My actions toward her haven't been that loving. I maintain the mantra that love is complicated. It's not something you can control. There's no way in hell I expected to fall for my wife, even though what I felt for her when I first saw her was electric.

"If you need any more help, don't hesitate to give me a call."

I arch a brow, as this is the first time I've ever had to deal with a rat in my outfit. "I hope I won't need your help again."

He nods. "Indeed, hopefully not."

"I've got to get going." I turn away and walk toward the door.

"Cillian," he calls my name, forcing me to come to a halt.

"Yeah?"

"Make him pay."

I narrow my eyes. "You don't have to tell me that." I walk out of his home, thankful I don't have to go back there. The place and the guy give me the creeps.

Pulling my cell phone out of my jacket pocket, I call Smyth.

"Sir?" he answers after the second dial tone.

"Call a meeting at Neverland in two hours. I've found the rat." I don't let him answer and end the call, walking toward my Porsche. Violence is brewing like a thunderstorm within me, and by the time I make it back to San Diego, I know that Frank will wish he had never been born.

I STAND in front of my men, pacing back and forth. The weight of my hook feels good like an anchor, while part of me wants to implode with the rage coursing through my veins and annihilate everything in my path.

All of them are unaware of what's about to happen.

"Frank, can you step forward, please?"

My hook is firmly in place, and my phantom limb aches in anticipation. This man is going to be gutted and carved up like a fucking pig on the butcher's table.

Frank steps forward, brow furrowed, as if he has no idea why I'm calling him out. "Yes, sir?"

"I have evidence that you've been working against me."

Frank's expression turns to fear so fast and the blood drains from his face. I notice the way he looks toward Smyth, as if he can save him from this. No one can save this sniveling excuse of a man.

"All of you know what happens to men who betray me, don't you?" I ask, still pacing in front of them.

"Sir, I didn't—"

"Silence." I glare at Frank. "I don't want to hear pleas of innocence, or I'll slice your tongue out."

Frank's mouth snaps shut so fast. They all know how depraved I can be when it comes to torture. I learned from the best, my father—the crocodile, as his men called him, because he wouldn't hesitate snapping a man in two if that man crossed him like a crocodile would. The memory draws me right back to the moment he called himself that, after he'd chopped my hand clean off.

"How did you explain this as an accident?" I ask, holding my arm up.

His eyes flash with wicked delight at the question. "You were being naughty and playing in your da's study, where you're not allowed to go, and you stumbled upon my decorative machete."

"What, and I chopped my own hand off?"

He tilts his head. "It was a terrible accident, as we've said."

"You're a monster," I say.

He arches his brow. "A crocodile. May it be a lesson to you both." He signals to me and Kira. "This is what happens when you cross me." His gaze lands on my ma. "You too, love."

"Cillian?" Smyth says my name, drawing me back to the present. "Do you want me to strap him down?"

I stare at the rat before me. "No."

Frank's Adam's apple bobs and he watches me like a deer caught in headlights. He could run. I enjoy chasing my prey. Depravity runs deep. It's a part of who I am and that'll never change. I'll never apologize for my darkness. I wonder if that's why Gwendolyne can't love me. She's too sweet and innocent, and I'm too broken and damaged.

I take off my suit jacket, rolling my shirt sleeves to my forearm and stalking toward Frank. He cowers against the wall, knowing there's no escape. I grab him by the neck, throwing him onto the floor.

"You should have known better than to cross me," I say loud and clear for all my men to hear. "But now you're going to pay." I slide the hook under his chin, forcing him to look into my eyes. "You all know what happens when someone gets on the wrong side of me."

"Sir, I—"

I increase the force of my hook and slice into his skin, making him cry in agony. I pull it away and bash the edge of it into his face, knocking him flat to the floor with a crack as his cheekbone fractures from the force.

I drag the hook through his shirt, tearing it apart and grazing his chest as blood pools at the surface.

The coward screams and I've hardly started yet.

His eyes are wide with terror as I keep cutting until

his body is covered in bloody lines. Blood pools around him as he cries for mercy. But I refuse to show emotion or compassion—that would be a sign of weakness, something that I cannot afford to do if I want to maintain my power over these men. The one decent lesson I was taught by my father.

Once he's been sufficiently tortured and he's struggling to keep his heart beating from the loss of blood, I stand and kick him in the stomach to ensure he won't survive his injuries. He collapses in a bloody heap on the floor like a broken doll, limp and lifeless; he takes his last wheezing breath of air and then his chest stops moving as he bleeds out onto the cold stone floor.

Another victim of my wrath.

The men around me stare at me in shock before averting their gaze, backing away from me in fear while others look away in disgust. They know what kind of man Cillian Hook truly is—ruthless and unforgiving when it comes to traitors such as Frank who dare cross me.

35

GWENDOLYNE

I wake and glance at the other side of the bed,
finding it empty.

Cillian didn't sleep here last night, not after our
fight.

My stomach churns as I sit up, certain I'm going to
puke. I rush into the bathroom, my head spinning.
Lifting the toilet lid, I hurl what little contents are left in
my stomach into the bowl.

Groaning, I slump to the floor and clutch my stomach. I have been trying desperately to ignore the glar-
ingly obvious fact. My period is two weeks late. I can't
go out and buy a test, but I don't need to.

The aching breasts, feeling so tired as though I've
run a marathon, and throwing up every morning tells
me all I need to know. Not to mention, I've had weird
fucking cravings for pickles and ice cream.

I'm pregnant.

Pregnant with Cillian Hook's baby.

It's a fact I've tried to ignore for a while, the idea

nagging at my brain. Since he keeps telling me he's going to breed me. It's as if this was his aim. To get me pregnant and trap me with him, so that I have to remain here.

What would my dad say if I made it out of here?

He'd probably make me get rid of it, and that's not something I think I could do. Clawing myself off the floor, I return to the bedroom and fall back into bed, shutting my eyes. I can't be bothered to get out of bed today.

THE WORDS on the page don't register as I fail miserably to read the book I was into four days ago. Ever since Cillian told me he loved me and I admitted to myself I'm pregnant, I've been unable to focus on anything.

I can't work out if that's because of him admitting his feelings for me or because I haven't seen him since. For four days he's not returned to the house, at least, not that I'm aware of. It's driving me crazy.

Ironic considering seeing him drove me crazy most of the time, but now that he's not here... I can't dwell on my fucked up emotions right now and what they mean.

I've felt guilty for hurting him, which is ridiculous. I shouldn't feel guilty for refusing his love, considering the way he went about everything.

My feelings for the man are complicated. There was

a spark before he kidnapped me and it hasn't extinguished. If anything, it's grown stronger.

I sigh and toss my book onto the sofa, knowing that no matter how badly I want to divert my thoughts from Cillian, it's impossible.

"What did the book do to you?" That voice sends shivers down my spine. It's even more striking having not heard it for four days.

"Cillian," I breathe his name, my heart pounding erratically beneath my skin. Heat spreads through my body, despite myself, as I turn to face him. "Where have you been?"

He tilts his head to the side, an odd glimmer in his eyes. "Why? Have you missed me?"

I swallow hard and shake my head. "Of course not."

He chuckles. "Answer the question. What did the book do to you?"

I glance at the novel and shake my head. "Nothing, I'm bored with reading."

"You love reading."

I swallow hard, hating that he knows that about me. "What do you want?" I ask, trying to divert the conversation away from the fact that I can't read because all I'm thinking about is him and our baby.

He moves toward me and all I can think about is how beautiful he looks. The man is striking up close and those chestnut eyes never cease to amaze me, even when his expression is solemn.

"That's no way to greet your husband, is it?" he says, the normal playfulness in his tone gone.

Did I break Cillian Hook with my rejection of his love?

And if so, why the hell does that idea make guilt worm its way deeper? He's the one that kidnapped me, for God's sake.

I swallow hard as he moves closer, anticipation coiling in my stomach. Four days and I can't deny that I've missed him. I've missed his touch, his voice, his scent—everything about him.

"I've got something for you," he announces, and that's when I notice the papers in his hands. He stops a few feet away from me and doesn't try to touch me, which is unlike him. I'm used to his touch when we're this close.

"What is it?" I ask.

His jaw works before he hands the papers to me. "Divorce papers. You're free to leave when you want."

A lead weight settles in my stomach as I stare at him blankly for a few seconds, pretty sure my brain is misfiring. "What?"

"I said, here are the divorce papers. They're signed." He tries to thrust the papers into my hand, but I can't function right now. Cillian told me he would never let me go, and now... It feels like this is a practical joke.

Instead of taking the papers, I step back and meet his beautiful gaze, searching his eyes for the truth. The anguish in them is as clear as day. "You said—"

"—Forget what I said, princess. It's clear you're never going to feel the same way I feel for you, and I'm not the kind of man to stand by and wait for you to realize we belong together."

I don't know why my stomach flips. Perhaps because I've been wondering if that's true.

"You've made it clear there's no chance you'll ever feel that way for me unless I give you your freedom." He tries again to put the papers in my hand, and this time I take them. "So here."

Why now?

I want to ask, but I fear that if I speak, I may say the wrong thing. And yet, I have to question it. Cillian doesn't strike me as the kind of man who gives up. "But—"

"Look, princess, you've been begging me for this since I kidnapped you, so take it and leave." His jaw clenches when he says that, those eyes flickering with what I can only describe as heartbreak. And while I did say this is what I wanted, now I'm hesitating to snatch the thing I've been begging him for since he stole me.

What is my problem?

I'm at war with myself. My head is screaming at me to snatch them and run for my life. My heart is aching at the thought. Reluctance is the last thing I imagined I'd feel at that moment. I can't tell what the reason is, but perhaps it's because I'm carrying his baby. Something he's talked about since day fucking one—getting me pregnant. I wonder if he'd still let me leave if he knew I'm pregnant.

"What was all of this for, then?"

"I've told you how I feel about you, Gwendolyne. Nothing has changed, but you persistently tell me you'll never feel the same." He rubs a hand across the back of his neck. "I'm a greedy man and I need all of you, not just your body. I need your heart and soul." His voice is husky. "I crave it more than anything on this planet."

"More than revenge on Piero?" I ask.

"A million times more."

Damn it.

I want to tell him he can have it. That I've already started to fall for him, but I know that nothing good can come from this twisted thing between us. Stockholm Syndrome is the only answer to what this is. My feelings seem deep and profound, but they can't be, because I've never been given a choice. Freedom will help me get perspective on the situation.

"I can walk out of here a free woman?" I confirm.

Cillian nods.

"And what happened to your revenge plan?"

"That's still going ahead. It doesn't involve you anymore." His jaw clenches. "If you marry that bastard, I can't promise you won't become collateral damage."

"Spoken from a man who claims to love me."

"I do love you, but what can I do if you won't accept my love?"

I study him for a moment, taking in his chiseled jaw and piercing eyes. It's clear he's hurting, and although I'm still confused about his sudden change of heart, I realize that I don't need to understand it. All I need to do is sign those papers and walk out the door to be free.

"Alright," I say. "I'll check them over with my lawyer."

"Do what you need to do," Cillian says, stepping back to let me leave. "Remember that I'll always love you, no matter where you are."

I swallow hard as I look into those dark eyes of his, knowing that it will be the last time. My feelings are too confused and the only way I'm going to sort them out is to get space from him and this place. Time to clear my head and process the fact that I'm carrying this baby.

"Goodbye, Cillian."

His jaw clenches. "Goodbye, princess."

I walk out of the room, knowing that leaving is the right thing to do. Space is what I need.

Why does it hurt so damn much?

36

GWENDOLYNE

I step into my childhood home, and the numbness inside me heightens. A cold chill runs up my spine. The walls close in on me like prison bars, threatening to take away my freedom.

"Gwendolyne," Dad calls my name as he rushes down the stairs. "Thank God. You're okay." He envelopes me in his arms.

I clutch onto him, but resentment flows through me like a river. "You didn't come to save me."

"We tried, but Cillian is smart."

I shudder at the sound of his name because ever since I left him, something resembling regret has been burrowing its way deep in my gut. "You should have tried harder."

"I know you're upset, but we did all we could."

"We?"

"Piero and me. He has been frantic and wants to see you so badly." He pauses. "He's on his way over now."

I stiffen, glaring at him as the rage within me wells up. "Are you joking?"

"No, he's been out of his mind with worry and desperate to see you."

Fury boils within the depths of my soul learning Dad thinks it appropriate to ask him here the moment I get free from over a month in captivity. "I've been away for over a month and you call someone to come over when I need to rest and recover from the ordeal?"

"Piero is your fiancé. It's right he be here."

A bitter laugh erupts from my lips. "I'm married to another man," I spit, clenching my fists until my knuckles turn white.

"It won't stand legally." He shakes his head. "I've had lawyers working on a way to annul it since the day he married you."

The papers in my purse are burning a hole through the leather, but I don't mention them. Cillian freed me, but I'm not going to be hasty and give my dad the perfect way out. It would mean that there's nothing stopping him from marrying me off to Piero.

"I don't want to marry Piero." I shake my head. "After what I've been through, I want nothing to do with him or any mob boss ever again."

His jaw clenches in response. "I'm afraid you don't have an option, Gwendolyne," he says. "The deal is done with Piero. And now you're back…"

"Now I'm back from being forced against my will. You want to thrust me into another predator's arms?" I confirm.

His eyes soften and he reaches for my shoulder, but I

don't want his pity. I shrug him off and turn away from him as tears of frustration gather in my eyes. "I'm going to my room." I rush away from him without another word, taking two steps at a time as I ascend the stairs.

"Gwendolyne!" He calls after me, but I don't stop. I sprint for my room, needing time alone.

I slam the door behind me, locking it firmly to ensure no one will enter without permission. I hope he doesn't have a copy of the key, because all I want is solace process and reflect on all the emotions swirling inside me like a raging storm.

The moment he gets word of my return, he has the wolves descending. If it isn't bad enough that I've been kidnapped for the past month, my dad brings another mob boss here to greet me. One who wants to fuck me and use me like Cillian did. A thought that makes me sick to my stomach. The idea of being with Piero used to be appealing.

A knock on my door sets me on high alert. "Sweetheart, open the door and we can talk."

All I want to do is tell him to go away, but I've never been brave enough to stand up to him. With a sigh, I open the door. "What do you want?"

"I've called Piero to tell him you're not ready for visitors."

At least he listened. "Thank you."

"I can't imagine what you've been through at the hands of that monster." Every muscle in his body tenses and he clenches his fists so hard I hear the popping of his knuckles. "Trust me when I say I'm going to make him pay." His voice is raw with anger and determination, and all I can think of is what he'd do to Cillian if he had the chance.

"Please don't do anything," I beg. "It'll cause problems." I place a hand on his arm, unsure why I'm begging him to spare Cillian. "It's best if you leave it alone."

"Leave it alone?" he scoffs, shaking his head. "What kind of man would I be if I left it alone?"

"The bigger one."

Seconds pass by, thick and heavy with anxiety, until he breaks the silence. "There's no way I can ignore the fact that he kidnapped you... That he did God knows what to you." His face darkens and I feel hot at the mention of what Cillian did to me.

If my father knew everything Cillian did, he'd go ballistic and murder him without a second thought. The thought scares me. I don't want any harm to come to Cillian, but perhaps that's still the after effects of Stockholm Syndrome.

"I would rather you buried the hatchet and moved on, but I can't tell you what to do."

My father steps closer to me and places a hand on my shoulder. "Are you okay?"

His eyes search mine for an answer, but I'm too overwhelmed with conflicting emotions to give him one.

"I...I don't know," I whisper, realizing that the truth has slipped out. I don't know if I will ever be the same. Not because of what Cillian did to me as such, but because I fear I've fallen for him.

"I'm happy you're home and safe," he says softly. "Is there anything I can do for you? Anything you need?"

I shake my head, as there's nothing he can do for me. "I need rest and time alone."

He nods in response and gives me a kiss on the cheek. "Take all the time you need, sweetheart. The staff will take care of your needs while you rest."

I attempt a small nod as he pulls away, and his gaze lingers on me for a second before he walks out, leaving me alone.

I curl into a ball on the bed and pull the covers over myself, desperately wishing I could escape from my own thoughts.

Cillian had been like oxygen in my world—and now that he's gone, I'm suffocating again in my life here at home. I'd been so used to being alone. I realize how lonely my life has been all these years.

"GWENDOLYNE!"

My eyes shoot open at the sound of my dad's voice. "Dad?"

"You've been sleeping for twenty-four hours, sweetheart." He sits on the edge of my bed, moving a strand of hair out of my face. "I need you to grab a shower and get dressed for dinner with Piero."

My brow furrows. "I told you, I don't want to—"

"Enough, Gwendolyne. Piero is your fiance. Nothing on that front has changed."

"That's the grace I get? Twenty-four hours to recover from being kidnapped."

My father's jaw clenches. "I've apologized for not getting you out sooner, but it's important that you and Piero get married and show a united front."

I roll my eyes. "Important for who? You and your wallet?"

His jaw clenches. "I won't argue with you about this, Gwendolyne." He crosses his arms over his chest. "Before Hook took you, you were happy to marry Piero. Nothing should have changed."

Everything has changed. I was kidnapped by my fiancé's rival and I'm pregnant with his baby. It freaks me out the more I think about it, so I've been trying my best not to.

Not a great way to solve a problem, but I've never been good at solving anything. Perhaps that's the result of my father making sure I never have to. All my life I've been wrapped in cotton wool and had everything done for me, something I never noticed until I was kidnapped.

"I won't ask again. Get dressed for dinner and be in the living room in an hour."

I glare at him but don't reply. My instincts were right. I've walked from one prison into another. The question is which one was better?

I sigh as he slams my bedroom door behind him. The thought of sitting at a table with Piero and pretending like everything is okay makes me sick to the stomach after I learned what he did to Cillian's family.

He's a murderer.

I make my way to the bathroom. I shower and dress in an old pair of jeans and a T-shirt, despite knowing my father will expect me to make an effort with my appearance. I couldn't give a shit. I head toward the dining room. The sense of unease lingers in my bones, making it hard to breathe as I walk through the corridors.

When I reach the dining hall, my father and Piero are seated at the table. They both stand when I enter, but Piero speaks first.

"Gwendolyne! You look beautiful this evening." He smiles, but there's a predatory look in his eyes at the same time as his gaze roams the length of my body, which is well covered by the baggy clothes.

I force a tight smile, even though I can feel my stomach churning with revulsion. This man is a killer and dishonorable and he thinks we can go back to before? The thought of marrying him makes me want to run in the opposite direction, but for now, I have to be civil.

I take my usual seat without a word, and my father and Piero sit, staring at me expectantly. What they expect me to say after what happened, I don't know. If they thought I'd be all sunshine and rainbows, then they'll be disappointed.

"So, Gwendolyne," Piero speaks after a moment of awkward silence. "How are you doing?"

I clench my jaw and meet those hazel eyes that used to intrigue me. "How do you think?" I snap back, unable to keep the sarcasm from my voice.

"I'm sorry we weren't able to get you away from him sooner."

Empty apologies. He had his chance, and he chickened out.

"Right, because you were too much of a coward to call Cillian's bluff. I know for a fact he hadn't called any of his men. You had him outnumbered, and you turned and fled."

My dad stiffens. "What? You had the chance to rescue Gwendolyne and didn't mention that to me?" His face reddens.

Piero remains unfazed by my accusation and my father's face turning the color of beetroot. "It wasn't important to mention since I failed." He draws in a deep breath. "As for me being a coward, as you say, I couldn't take the risk that he may have been telling the truth."

Dad looks irritated. "You still should have told me. We're supposed to be partners in all of this."

There's a flash of something in Piero's eyes, but it's gone too quickly for me to evaluate it. A sense of dread sweeps over me like a freezing cold winter wind, making me shudder. If what Cillian says Piero did to him is true, then no one can trust this man.

37

CILLIAN

Smyth stands before me, looking like he wants to puke. The rest of my senior men look equally pale.

"Spit it out, Smyth. What's this meeting about?" I snap.

"Sir, it's bad…"

"Just tell me!"

He moves forward with a piece of paper and passes it into my hand. "An informant on the inside gave us this, a transcript of a conversation he overhead between Piero and one of his men."

I scan the paper and the more I read, the more the rage within me threatens to decimate everything in my path. Now I know why they look so worried.

I try to calm the storm brewing within me as I've let Gwendolyne go and now they uncover a plot by Piero to kill her and her father! "Is this a sick joke?!" I'm about ready to explode. "How did you not find this out sooner?"

Smyth pales slightly. "It was only yesterday evening when the informant and I met."

"Fuck's sake, Smyth." I clench my fists. "And you didn't consider calling me last night?" It may have been too late to tell Gwendolyne, but leaving it until the next afternoon is fucking stupid. "It's not good enough. You're supposed to be my second in command!"

He pales. When I'm like this, there's no knowing what I'll do. "When is he going to do it?"

Jake steps forward. "We don't know for sure, but the informant believes he's going to strike at the wedding party."

Smyth holds a hand up. "At least, that was his original plan. Apparently, the wedding is back on."

If I wasn't pissed off enough to find out that Piero intends to murder Jovani Tesoro and take everything he owns, they have to mention the thorn in my side. Gwendolyne. She's going to marry that bastard after everything I told her about him.

The question is, is it her choice or is she being forced to marry him?

I hope it's the latter.

"I let her go and now he's going to destroy everything."

Jake clears his throat. "How do we stop him?"

Smyth tilts his head. "Do we want to stop him, considering he'll take out our competition?"

"Definitely," I say, shaking my head. "If we don't, he becomes our new competition. Piero would be unstoppable and you know it." I can't help but wonder why Smyth would ask such a stupid fucking question.

Not to mention, if he takes out Jovani, I know that Gwendolyne would be devastated. It's clear she cares about her father, despite the fact he's been her prison warden all these years.

And I care about how she feels, even if she chose to leave me and even if she chooses to marry that snake, Piero.

"When is the wedding?"

"I think they're planning it in two weeks."

I grind my teeth. "We'll make sure that the wedding doesn't go ahead, and that Piero is unveiled for the piece of shit he is."

Smyth narrows his eyes. "How will you do that?"

"I'll figure it out. Leave it to me." I clap him on the shoulder. "If there's no other business to discuss, I've got a plan to make."

Jake, Tim, Oliver and Jeremy all nod. "No, that's all," Jake confirms.

"Great."

"Can I have a word in private, sir?"

I nod and we move away as the other four men file out of the room. "What is it, Smyth? I've got to get working on this plan."

"I wanted to offer my help with the plan. Aren't two heads better than one?"

I narrow my eyes. Smyth doesn't normally go out of his way to offer help, at least not lately. "I've got it covered, thanks."

A muscle in his jaw clenches. "Fair enough. Give me a call if you need anything."

I nod and he walks away. As I watch him, I still can't

shake that niggling doubt that this man is working against me.

THE THUNDER CRASHES above our house, making me shudder with terror as I remain curled in bed. It's not the storm that has me on edge, it's the storm I'm awaiting when Da finally returns.

Kira and I did something stupid today, and the look on my ma's face was what scared me most of all. We broke our da's priceless antique vase in his study. A room we are explicitly restricted from entering, and yet we did anyway.

A flash of lightning illuminates my room for a second and then another crack of thunder shakes the windows. I can feel the vibration of the glass with each rumble, as if my whole house is trembling in anticipation. The wind is howling outside, like a lost soul searching for a path home.

Taking a deep breath, I close my eyes and try to steady my nerves.

The sound of the front door slamming immediately snaps me out of my trance and I feel my stomach drop. I can hear my da's heavy footsteps as he marches into the house, shaking the walls with each footfall. His voice echoes through the hallway as he greets Ma.

And then I hear his voice get louder than usual and full of a menacing power that leaves me feeling frozen in fear.

"Cillian!" Da shouts, only calling to me since I told Ma it was me who broke it to protect Kira.

My heart races faster and faster as I try to find the courage to answer him. Taking one last deep breath, I slowly make my way downstairs. I'm at the mercy of a crocodile. That is what his men call him, because he's ruthless and unforgiving. He won't hesitate carving a man up if he crosses him like a crocodile would. That's what I've heard. Ma tries to shield me and Kira from the truth about what he does for a living, but I've known for a while.

Walking into his study, I notice he's pacing the room, his face red hot with anger. "Yes, Da?" Raindrops pound on the study windows, reminding me of the chaos outside.

"What the fuck is that?" He points at the smashed pieces of the vase we had picked up and placed on his desk.

"I'm sorry, I was playing here and it was an accident—"

He rushes toward me and lifts me off my feet with the collar of my shirt. "How many times have I told you not to play in here?"

My heart thunders and all I can hear is the heavy ticking of a clock in the background.

Tick-Tock, Tick-Tock.

I bolt upright in bed, sweat covering my face. It's been years since I relived that dreaded moment in my dreams. But every morning since I let Gwendolyne go, the same nightmare has woken me sometime after 4am.

I'm surprised I slept at all, considering today she's supposed to marry Piero. What she doesn't realize is that Piero is going to double cross her and Jovani like he did to me ten years ago.

If I have any hand in it, then I won't allow history to repeat itself. The plan is relatively insane, but it has to work.

I rub my hand across my face and force myself not to think about what would happen if it didn't. Horrific images of Gwendolyne's lifeless body have plagued my mind ever since I learned of Piero's plan. Two painful weeks of planning and scheming, making sure that whatever intention Piero has toward Jovani and his family is stopped before it's too late.

Gwendolyne has been unreachable. I've tried to follow her and reach her, but the security team her dad and Piero have surrounding her is ridiculous. She's barely out in public since I let her go, making catching a glimpse of her impossible.

It's ironic. My first attempt at doing the right thing and it royally backfired. Letting Gwendolyne go was something I had to do, but now I fear it might have damned us both.

I get out of bed and walk to my closet, getting dressed in my finest suit, grabbing my favorite gun from my gun cabinet. I check it's loaded and slip it into the inside jacket pocket. My heart pounds as I wonder whether to wear my hook today, as instinct tells me I'll need it. But it makes me less conspicuous and easier to spot.

I grab it and screw it on, deciding that it will come in use if I come face to face with Piero. The satisfaction I'd get thrusting this hook into his gut and watching the life drain from his eyes would be unparalleled.

I stare at myself in my body-length mirror. The darkness within me is evident as I look into my own eyes. When Gwendolyne was near, I felt like the darkness was tempered by her light. Ever since she's been away... I fear that I'm going to be lost to it forever, drowning in it with no way out. And yet it's worth it if it means I save her. I'd lay my own life on the line a thousand times over to keep her alive.

Men chatting echoes through the corridor from my study. I walk that direction to find the men I'd invited gathered, including Smyth.

"Morning, gentlemen."

They all fall silent the moment I step into the room.

"Morning, sir." They say in chorus.

"As most of you know, we're going to try to pull off my most ambitious plan yet to stop this wedding and Piero's operation in one swoop."

I pause for a moment, looking around at each of their faces. They're on board, but I can see the fear lurking in their eyes. This is no small feat we're about to attempt, and failure means death.

"We've done our best to gather information on Piero's plans and gather our resources. Today we strike, and we do whatever it takes to keep Gwendolyne and Jovani safe."

There's a determined nod from my men, and I can feel the energy in the room shift. We're ready to do what needs to be done.

"Now," I say, taking a deep breath. "Let's get to work."

We all disperse, each taking on a different task in the plan. Smyth comes to me, his face serious.

"Are you sure about this, sir? It's not too late to back out now."

I look him dead in the eye. "This is our only option. We have to try."

He nods, but I can tell he has his doubts. Smyth

hasn't been as supportive as he usually is ever since I snatched Gwendolyne from Piero.

"See you at the venue."

Smyth nods. "Do you still plan to visit her beforehand?"

"Yes, it's the only way to ensure she stalls the wedding and gives us as much time as possible."

"What if she refuses?"

It's possible, but something in my gut tells me she won't. Despite the way I've treated her, I know she cares for me.

I turn to leave the room, my heart racing with antici- pation. This is it. This is the moment we've been building toward for years.

I step out into the sun, the wind blowing through my hair. The sky is a brilliant blue, the sun shining bright and warm. A cruel joke that such a beautiful day could be the backdrop for the most dangerous plan my outfit has ever tried to orchestrate.

While Piero is distracted by his wedding, I will be dissembling his entire empire behind his back. My men are stationed and ready to carry out a series of attacks on his establishments.

I open the door to my Porsche and sit in the driver's seat, cracking my knuckles. It's time for me to put an end to this rivalry and win back my soul mate. I will burn the world to the ground before I let Piero harm a hair on her head.

38

GWENDOLYNE

I stand in front of the mirror, a shudder running through me as I brush a hand across the slight bump. The wedding is in twenty minutes. Neither my dad nor Piero know I'm pregnant, and I'm too scared to tell them. I fear they'd make me get an abortion, but I don't want one—even if the man who got me pregnant was the one who kidnapped me.

Shaking my head, I tear my mind away from the baby in my belly. The ache in my chest won't fade, it only grows stronger as the minutes tick down until the wedding ceremony. The bathroom adjoining the dressing room is the only place I could try to lock myself in to ensure the wedding doesn't happen, and yet I know it's futile.

Dad would have his men break the door down rather than postpone or cancel this wedding. Walking into the room, the cold, hard tile beneath my bare feet is welcoming. I glance around, taking in the details of my surroundings. The walls are painted a pale pink and decorated with small silhouettes of birds, their wings spread in flight. In one corner, a large mirror hangs above a marble sink. On the counter, a glass vase is filled with white lilies standing in contrast to the grey tile behind.

I step closer to the sink, letting my fingertips trace the smooth surface of the marble. Sadness digs through my veins, as the loneliness I've felt all my life is much more poignant now. Even before my wedding, I feel utterly alone. No friends to share the moment with or my mother, since she has been dead for so long. My two cousins, who are bridesmaids, don't even like me. Dad has spent my entire life isolating me, and this is the result.

A thump from the dressing room startles me from my thoughts as I spin around, marching toward the door. It can't be time yet. There's still at least fifteen minutes until it should start.

Creeping toward the door, I open it a crack and my heart thuds erratically in my chest at the image before me.

Cillian.

Butterflies flutter to life in my stomach and the clawing desire to burst out of the bathroom and straight into his arms is both absurd and impossible to ignore.

Opening the door further, I step out to see him brushing leaves from his jacket. He's dressed as impeccably as always in an expensive suit with his dark hair perfectly styled. Today he hasn't got his prosthetic on, instead a sharp-looking hook is affixed to his left arm. "Cillian," I breathe his name.

His shoulders turn rigid as he turns to face me. Those eyes undo me as I look into them, knowing that no dream I've had since we parted ways ever did the intensity of them justice.

"Hey, princess."

That voice breaks me as I feel weak suddenly, clutching the doorframe to keep myself upright.

"What are you doing here?"

His Adam's apple bobs, and I realize at that moment that he's nervous. Cillian Hook is nervous, something I never believed I'd see.

"I'm here to save you," he says, stepping closer.

"Save me?"

He keeps moving, closing the gap until he's inches from me. His hands land on my hips and he groans. "I've missed you so damn much."

I shut my eyes, tears welling behind my eyelids. "I hate to say it, but I've missed you, too."

He chuckles. "Good."

I shake my head, forcing myself to look at him. "But that doesn't change the fact I'm about to get married."

"Did you file the papers?" he asks, searching my eyes.

I shake my head. "I couldn't bring myself—"

He kisses me, his lips forceful against my own, followed by his tongue delving inside. I claw at him, desperate to draw him closer, as if he's my oxygen and I'm running out. A moan escapes my lips as I feel the press of his erection against my abdomen. "Cillian, anyone could walk in."

He grabs a fistful of my hair and yanks my head

back, glaring at me. "And what? See me kissing my lawfully wedded wife? They can't annul our marriage. This wedding can't go ahead."

I lick my lips. "And how exactly are you going to stop it?"

"First of all, I want to hear you tell me you want me to stop it." His eyes narrow.

I nod frantically. "I want you to stop it, please."

He smirks. "Why?"

He wants me to tell him the truth. The feelings I had for him while his captive were never Stockholm Syndrome. I love him. No matter how ridiculous that may be. I opt for a different angle.

"Because I'm pregnant," I say.

His eyes widen and then darken. "You knew when I let you go?" His voice is lethally calm—too calm.

I swallow hard as his eyes burn holes in me. "Yes, but I knew you wouldn't let me go, if—"

He yanks me even closer, his warm breath tickling my face. "You left with our fucking unborn baby growing in you, Gwendolyne. I had a right to know about it." His eyes are full of dark and dangerous fury. "I wouldn't have let you go."

"That's why I couldn't tell you."

He growls, wrapping his hand gently around my throat. "That's a foolish thing to say. I'd protect the two of you with my life, but if your father or Piero had learned of the baby…" He shudders. "You know what they would have done."

I nod, as I know they would have forced me to get rid of it.. "I didn't think about that at the time. All I knew was that I needed space away from you to be sure the way I felt was real."

There's an unmistakable flash of hope in his eyes. One that makes my heart race and butterflies erupt in my stomach. "And what is it that you feel, princess?"

The crazy thing is the way I feel about this man shouldn't be possible. I shouldn't love someone who has done the things he has to me, but there's no denying the truth. I'm in love with Cillian Hook. Every complex and dark part of him that makes him who he is. He may have captured me and locked me in a prison, but I'd never felt freer than when I was with him.

I've been a prisoner all my life. Locked away for fear that something could happen to me, like it happened to my mom. I don't remember her as she died when I was two years old. Dad lost sight of what was important in life the moment she died and he's never been the same again.

"I love you," I breathe, my voice so quiet I'm not sure he'll hear me.

"Princess, you don't know how badly I've wanted to hear those words." He wraps his hand around the back of my neck and pulls me to him, crashing his lips against mine in the most intense kiss I've experienced.

It's emotional, fierce, passionate. A throb ignites between my thighs. The ache in my chest deepens because I'm going to be married off to another man in ten minutes. Cillian may believe he can stop the wedding, but I fear he's likely to end up dead facing Piero and my dad.

I slide my hands up his chest and dig my nails into

his skin, pulling him closer. He groans in response. The kiss becomes desperate. The sounds we make together are animalistic, and we haven't even got our clothes off. I'm panting for him, begging for more, when he breaks the kiss. He runs his nose along my neck and my whole body shudders in response.

"We need to stop right now," he says. "I can barely control myself when it comes to you. If I keep this up, I'm going to forget why I'm here."

"No, I don't want you to stop," I gasp, clawing at his shirt. "I need you, Cillian."

He growls, a pained look crossing his face. "You don't know how badly I want to sink my cock deep inside your cunt and remain there for the rest of my goddamn life, but that's not why I'm here. We don't have time."

I groan in frustration as he pulls away from me. His body heat is gone, leaving me cold and unsatisfied. I feel the loss of him keenly. It's like my soul is crying out for him. I want him. I've never wanted anything as much as I want him right now. "Maybe we can lock the—"

He groans. "We can't." He runs his hands through his hair. "Not yet. We don't have much time until everything crashes around us, Gwen."

"I still don't understand why you're here."

His eyes darken again. "As I told you before, I'm here to save you."

"From what exactly?"

"From this damn wedding and meeting the same fate as my sister."

"What?"

His eyes are frantic as I search them. "My men uncovered Piero's plan for you and your father." A muscle flexes in his jaw. "He intends to murder both of you and take everything."

I gasp, wondering if he's telling the truth. "Are you certain?"

"I've been going fucking insane trying to get to you ever since I found out. The day after I let you go..."

I move closer to him, pressing my hand against his muscular chest. "How are you intending to stop him?"

He grabs my hand and kisses the back of it. "Let me worry about that. I need you to do something for me."

"Anything," I breathe.

"Stall this wedding for as long as physically possible." His nostrils flare as he takes a step back. "I need all the time you can buy me."

I give him a nod, as my stomach twists with nerves. I need to know what he plans to do, but before I can ask, he pulls himself out of the window and is gone as quickly as he appeared. My head is spinning with the news.

Never in my wildest dreams could I have imagined Piero intended to kill me... It makes me feel so sick, as he always acted like he wanted me.

All I am is a vessel for him to take over my father's territory. If he did that, then he would be unstoppable.

39

CILLIAN

I haul myself out of the window as fast as I can, knowing I'm on the brink of turning around and sinking my cock into Gwendolyne. She drives me insane and two weeks without her makes it impossible to think straight when she's looking at me like I'm her fucking God.

The last thing I need is a distraction from the plan. Right now, my men should be orchestrating attacks on Piero's establishments. The longer he's stuck here waiting to get married, the better.

Learning she's pregnant only makes success vital. It has to go right. I've wanted to get her pregnant since the moment I set eyes on her, but I've never considered the implications. I'll be a father. Something I have no idea how to be.

While my men are causing a nightmare for Piero back in Los Angeles, I'll be waiting in the limousine as the driver for the *happy* couple.

The intention is that I will drive away with Gwendolyne before Piero gets a chance to climb inside. That's if he doesn't head back to Los Angeles immediately to clear up the carnage my men will leave in their wake.

Straightening up, I brush the leaves from my jacket. The click of a gun behind me makes me tense.

"Well, well, I didn't expect to see you here, Cillian."

That voice.

My jaw clenches and I slowly turn around to face my arch nemesis. All the blood drains from my body when I see *who* is standing next to him.

Smyth.

I should have listened to my instincts.

How did the detective not figure this out?

"What the fuck, Smyth?"

"My name is Darren, not Smyth," he growls.

I shake my head, struggling to believe all this time he's been working against me. "How long?"

On the other side of Piero is Tilly. She quit not long after I caught her and Gwendolyne in the library... There are fucking snakes everywhere.

"That's right, he's had enough of the way you treat him." Piero's eyes narrow. "You should have treated your loyal staff a little better, shouldn't you?"

I clench my fist and move forward. "You bastard—"

The click of another gun cocking forces me to an abrupt halt, as Smyth points his gun at my head—and he never misses. "One step and I'll murder you."

Piero chuckles and places a hand on his arm, lowering it. "Remember the deal, Smyth. He's mine."

Smyth's eye twitches.

"Why?" I ask him, my eyes fixed on my former second-in-command.

He laughs, but it's humorless. "You've treated me like shit since the day we met." He shakes his head. "All I ever did was love you—" His voice cracks on those words and my brow furrows.

"Love me?" I say, arching a brow. "What the fuck are you on about?"

Piero chuckles. "It appears that your second in command wanted more than friendship from you, Cillian."

I swallow hard, as I've always known Smyth is into men, but I never imagined that he had feelings for me. If I had, I would have set the record straight years ago. Despite Smyth being a valuable asset and a friend, or the closest thing I had to one after Piero annihilated my trust in humans, I could never have felt the same for him.

It makes sense now why he hated me sleeping with all the staff at Neverland.

"I don't know what to say."

Smyth shakes his head. "I knew you'd never see me in that way and I was fine with that, but you treated me like shit the entire time we worked together. Over ten fucking years."

It's true. I didn't treat him well. He was always there and loyal, and I never thought much of it.

"Why now?" I ask, feeling sick to my stomach. I never thought Smyth would betray me to Piero.

"Money," Piero says with a wave of his hand. "When someone has had enough, money talks."

Glancing at Tilly, I clear my throat. "And you?"

She smirks, and it's full of malice. "I was never loyal to you. Piero hired me to work for you."

My brow furrows. "But, you've worked for me for—"

"Five years," Piero finishes my sentence. "I've known about your presence for a while, Cillian."

My blood runs cold. I can't believe he's been one step ahead of me. Again, I've underestimated Piero, which may be my downfall.

"What do you want?"

Piero chuckles. "I want your head on a fucking platter, of course." He tightens his grasp on his gun. "But I'm going to take my time with you. Make sure it hurts."

I tilt my head to the side. "Why don't you put down the gun and fight me like a man?"

He arches a brow. "The hook gives you an unfair advantage. It wouldn't exactly be fair, would it?"

"Too scared, as always," I say, shaking my head. "You were always a coward."

Piero's eyes narrow. "If you want to fight, take off the hook."

I clench my jaw because the hook is my safety net. The idea of fighting with nothing makes my phantom limb ache, and yet I've got no choice. If I manage to fight hard enough and beat Piero with one hand, there's nothing to stop Tilly or Smyth from shooting at me. I look Smyth in the eye, but he doesn't meet my gaze.

How much of my plan has he fucked with?

I don't even know if my men are doing as I instructed right now. They're supposed to be attacking

Piero's establishments and damaging his operation while he's getting ready for this wedding. I know Piero well enough to know that any damage to his image will be more important to him than this wedding.

I notice a flash of movement by the window I'd climbed out of and realize Gwendolyne is watching us.

Fuck.

"Fine, I'll remove it and fight you." I don't have to think about it for a second when I realize Gwen is going to do something stupid.

Unfastening my hook, I place it to one side, leaning toward the window where Gwen is watching us. "Don't," I breathe, giving her a warning glare.

Her responding glare tells me she's not going to listen.

Turning around, I bring my fist up. "Give it your best shot."

Piero smirks. "I'll easily best half a man."

I grind my teeth as he knows how much losing my hand affected me as a kid. The idiot thinks one insult is going to rile me, but he doesn't know me, not anymore.

He approaches and all I can think about is saving Gwen and our baby. "Let's see what you've got," I say, goading him into making the first move.

Piero bites like the predictable asshole he is. He jabs toward my left, knowing I haven't got the cover on that side. A move I could see coming before he even jabbed. Dodging to my right, I evade it and then punch him with my right hand in the chest.

He grunts, eyes flaring with rage.

Good.

I know from experience that he gets sloppier the angrier he gets.

Piero growls as he launches forward, trying to land a punch on the right side of my face. I dodge out of the way and bring my fist into his gut, forcing him to double over in pain.

His jaw tightens as he straightens back up, the rage in his eyes flaring brighter.

That's right, you stupid son of a bitch. Get angry and make a mistake.

He comes at me without much thought, every movement easy to read. I let him come, darting out of the way of each lazy blow. Until I see an opportunity and punch him in the throat, making his eyes flare wide as he chokes.

"You've gotten too lazy, Piero. Too much sitting behind a desk pulling political strings," I say, circling around him.

He can't get any air in his lungs to speak, so he glares at me with murder in his eyes instead.

Good.

He's close to making a mistake. Like I predicted, he lunges forward, taking a big swing. I block it and head-butt him across his nose. He stumbles back, hand clutching his face. Blood pours from between his fingers.

He swipes at my face but misses his target. I've already punched him in the jaw, my knuckles connecting with a satisfying crack.

He falls to the floor, struggling to claw himself to his feet as I walk toward him. The click of a gun stops me in my tracks.

I turn to glance at Smyth and Tilly. Both of them have guns pointed at me.

"Not a step further," Smyth warns.

I smirk as I expected them to stick their noses in. "A fight is a fight. You two are breaking the rules."

"Fuck the rules," Tilly says.

Smyth glares at me with a hatred I struggle to understand, even after his explanation. Piero's the one to intervene, surprisingly. "He's right. Lower your weapons." He struggles to his feet, glaring at me.

"What's going on here?" Jovani's voice booms and when I turn to face him, I see Gwen by his side.

Fuck.

I had this, and Gwen had to intervene. Now she's walked herself and her father into a dangerous situation and I'm not sure yet how I'm going to get myself out, let alone them.

"What's going on is the man you sold your daughter to is a two-faced liar," I announce, glaring at Piero, who has managed to peel himself off the floor. "His plan is to murder both you and Gwen after the wedding."

Jovani's eyes narrow as he glances between me and Piero. "Piero and I have an agreement. You can't go banding around accusations without proof."

Piero chuckles as blood gushes from his nose. "Gullible to a fault. Aren't you, Jovani?"

Jovani's brow furrows. "What?"

Piero points at him. "Of course I'm going to kill you both. With you out of the picture, I'd have control of both San Diego and Los Angeles." He smirks at them both. "No one would be able to stop me, including Cillian Murphy."

"Murphy?" Jovani asks, eyes narrowing.

It's clear he has no idea what is going on here.

Gwen steps closer, making my blood pressure skyrocket as she's in danger right now and I'm too far away. "And why would you have to kill me?" She demands.

"I can't deal with the hysterics of a wife whose father I murdered. It would be doing us both a kindness."

"You're a monster," she says, her eyes glowing with hatred.

He shrugs. "Never professed to be anything other. It's people around me expecting too much from me that gets them in trouble, isn't it, Cillian?"

Clenching my jaw, I ignore his dig. "Trusting anyone is what gets you into trouble. I learned that the hard way."

I don't see a safe way out of this for any of us. Gwen is too far from me for my liking, and Piero is unpredictable. He could kill her at any second.

"You were a fool to trust a rival. Your entire family were idiots," he says, glaring at me.

I'll never understand why he did what he did. Life was good the way we had it, and he fucked it up. Taking a few steps closer to Gwen, I shake my head. "No, you were an idiot. There's more to life than money and power. Friendship and love are more important and you have neither."

Piero laughs. "Says the man who drove his closest friend into the arms of his enemy?"

He's right. I treated Smyth like a servant beneath me when he's been there from the start. My rage has eaten away at me for years, blinding me to any good around me. Until Gwen. She's brought me back from the dead and given me a second chance if I can get us out of this mess.

I take a few steps, hoping he doesn't notice my intention. And that's when a gunshot stops me in my tracks. I glance behind Piero to see Tilly's eyes narrow and smoke coming from the barrel.

"What the fuck did you do that for?" Piero asks, sounding irritated. "You know he was mine to finish!"

"Cillian!" Gwen screams my name.

Pain ricochets through my body as I grab the side of my abdomen and stumble, my legs no longer able to hold me as I fall to the concrete beneath me. My head bouncing off the sidewalk.

Darkness descends and I feel everything slipping away.

40

GWENDOLYNE

*I*t all happens in a blur.

One moment he's standing there, the next he's on the ground.

My world spins around me. My heart beats at a thousand miles an hour. The blood pooling around him is horrific. He's not moving and all I can think is the worst.

What if he's dead?

My hand instinctively moves to my stomach, where his baby is growing inside me. A tear trickles down my cheek as I wonder if he or she will grow up fatherless.

Piero smirks at me. "Shedding a tear for your husband, I see," He chuckles. "He did get under your skin, didn't he?"

I swallow hard, my hatred for this man swelling within me. He's a complete and utter asshole.

"It's time to tie up loose ends. I may not get your empire through marriage, but with Cillian gone and you and your father dead, there'll be no one to fight my takeover of San Diego."

My father shakes his head. "How much would it take for you to walk away and leave us alone?"

He laughs. "There's no price that can be paid. I'm taking everything and this time I won't leave loose ends as they come back to bite you on the ass." He nods at Cillian's body. "Here's a prime example."

Tilly won't look me in the eye as she stands behind Piero. I believed that she genuinely wanted to help me, when all along she intended to return me to Piero so he could murder me and my father.

It's hard to believe someone could be so cold, but I find that my dad has sheltered me from real life for far too long. I've become too innocent and gullible, and I hate that about myself.

The flash of metal catches my eye first as Cillian miraculously claws himself to his feet, his hook firmly fixed in place. He's still bleeding from the abdomen and it makes my heart thunder. He shouldn't be standing, he should get help as soon as possible before he loses too much blood.

Tilly and Smyth are both looking in our direction too, which gives him the air of surprise.

He places the hook around Tilly's throat and her eyes go wide. "I would rethink your entire plan unless you want her to die," Cillian says, his voice stable considering the amount of blood he's lost.

Piero turns around and panic flashes across his face. He cares for her. A woman he pushed away to stalk his enemy for five years.

"What makes you think I give a shit whether you slit her throat?"

Cillian smirks and there's a darkness in his eyes that scares me. "You wouldn't trust just anyone to watch me. You'd choose the person closest to you in this world, because you don't trust."

Piero's jaw works and Tilly is begging him with her eyes. "That's bullshit," he breathes.

"It's the truth and you know it. If I'm wrong, I'll kill her and you won't bat an eye." Cillian draws the sharp tip of his hook across her throat, blood pooling there.

"Stop!" Piero growls, nostrils flaring. "What do you want?"

Cillian laughs, shaking his head. "What do I want?" He wobbles, and I can tell he's struggling to remain upright. "What I wanted was to destroy you the way you destroyed me, but I don't care about that anymore."

Piero's brow furrows. "You don't?"

"No, I want you to fuck off and stay in Los Angeles. Never step foot on San Diego territory again and leave my wife and her family alone. In turn, I'll leave you and your pretty little Tilly alone."

Piero falls silent, and that's when my dad speaks. "Are you expecting me to be okay with you keeping my daughter as your wife?"

I set my hand gently on his arm. "I want to be with Cillian, Dad."

His nose wrinkles in disgust. "I'll never understand how that's possible. He kidnapped you, sweetheart."

I shake my head, my stomach swirling with

405

emotion. "It's not that simple. I know he made a mistake, but we love each other. He's the father of my baby."

My dad looks like I've slapped him. "What baby?"

"I'm pregnant, Dad."

Silence fills the air as my dad's eyes widen, and then he looks at Cillian. "You got my daughter pregnant? You son of a bitch."

Cillian holds up his hand and hook. "It wasn't planned, but I love her and I'll take care of them both."

Piero clears his throat, drawing our attention toward him. "I agree with your terms, Cillian. We'll stay out of each other's way, and I'll leave you, your wife, and your child alone." He nods to Tilly. "As long as you let her go."

Cillian doesn't show any sign of relief. "And Smyth?" he asks.

Piero waves his hand dismissively. "Kill him if you want. I don't give a shit."

Cillian shakes his head. "No, that would be too easy, but I don't want him working for you." His eyes narrow. "Leave the fucking state or I will kill you."

Smyth's expression softens, and he nods. "Of course."

"Leave now," Cillian orders, pushing Tilly into Piero's arms.

He ushers her away and Smyth follows them.

And that's when he collapses and my heart aches.

Is he going to make it out of here alive?

"Dad, call an ambulance now!"

He does as I say, dialing 911 despite the fact he's in

shock over my declaration of love for my kidnapper and pregnancy.

"They're coming. E.T.A is five minutes. They said to keep a compress over the gunshot wound to stem the bleeding."

I kneel at Cillian's side and place my hand on his jacket, covering the wound.

He winces. "You could be a bit gentler, princess."

"I'm trying to save your life," I say, emotion sticking in my throat. "You can't die." Tears escape my eyes and trickle down my face as he looks so pale.

"It'll take more than that to kill me."

"I know you like to think you're a God, but the truth is your flesh and blood."

He smiles and rests his head back, eyes shutting. "I never said I was a God. I said I'm your God, Gwendolyne."

Heat radiates through me as I realize my dad is listening. He clears his throat. "They said to make sure the victim doesn't speak too much. He needs to conserve as much energy as possible."

"How much longer?" I ask, as blood oozes through the fabric and onto my dress.

"They should be here any minute."

As if on cue, the sirens wail in the distance. "Thank God."

The ambulance pulls up a few seconds later and two paramedics jump out, rushing to the scene.

"What happened?"

"Gunshot to the abdomen," I say.

"Sir, are you still conscious?"

Cillian opens his eyes. "Just about," he mumbles.

"It's a miracle. Look how much blood he's lost!"

"We need to get you onto a stretcher and into the ambulance, fast."

Another paramedic rolls the stretcher over and then together they lift him onto it, rushing him into the back of the ambulance.

"Can I go with him?"

"What's your relationship?" The paramedic asks.

"His wife."

Her brow furrows, considering I'm wearing a wedding dress. "Just now?"

I nod, as the truth is too complicated. "Yes."

"Come on, you can ride in the back."

My dad watches as I jump into the back of the ambulance with him. "I'll meet you at the hospital, Gwendolyne."

I sit next to him and squeeze his hand. "Stay with me, Cillian."

"Always, princess," he murmurs, but his voice is weak and he can barely keep his eyes open.

"We need to get to the hospital fast," the paramedic says to the driver. "He's losing too much blood and needs a transfusion."

My stomach dips and I sit back out of their way, watching as they try to stop the bleeding. Another paramedic places an oxygen mask on his face. They're speaking among each other frantically, but I barely hear anything above the roaring in my ears.

The heart rate monitor they've connected him to is getting slower and slower.

I've fallen into a nightmare I can't wake from.

Cillian might die. The father of my baby and the man I love. I can't help the guilt that floods through me that I ever left. If I'd admitted what I felt instead of denying it, then I never would have left and none of this would have happened.

If he dies, I'll never forgive myself.

41

CILLIAN

ive weeks later…

"Is he going to wake up?" An angelic voice speaks in the distance.

"We can't say for certain. He lost so much blood and, in turn, we don't know whether there was any damage to the brain. It all depends how long he was without enough oxygen."

I groan, my body aching all over as I am slowly being pulled back to the land of the living.

Are they talking about me?

"Is he waking?" Her voice is the only thing guiding me.

My eyelids feel heavy as I force them open and immediately shut them at the blinding light burning my irises.

"He blinked!" I feel soft skin against my hand. "Cillian, can you hear me?"

"Miss, please step back. He's—"

"Don't you dare step anywhere," I murmur, grabbing her hand and holding it as hard as I can. "Do you understand, princess?" I open my eyes, squinting to see her face.

Tears steak down her cheeks as she nods her head frantically. "You are awake."

"Did you ever doubt me?"

"I need to go and get the doctor. Avoid overstimulating him. We don't know what brain injuries he may have sustained."

I glare at the nurse with the clipboard. "I'll tell you who might be sustaining brain injuries in a minute."

The nurse looks a little concerned as she scurries away to find the doctor.

"Why do you look so pale, princess?"

She swallows hard, her throat bobbing. "It's been a tough five weeks waiting to find out—"

"Five weeks?"

She nods. "Yes, you slipped into a coma from blood loss before we made it to the hospital."

I try to sit up, but my body is weak. She places a hand on my chest, pushing me back gently. "Please, Cillian, you need to rest."

"I'm fine," I say through gritted teeth as pain shoots through my body. "What about The Rogues?"

Gwendolyne gives me a soft smile. "Don't worry. Everything is okay with your men. They banded together after what happened. My dad helped too."

"You dad?" I can't believe Jovani changed his mind and helped out the opposing outfit in the city.

"Yes, we announced our wedding and the joining of our two families." She bites the inside of her cheek.

"I hope that's okay. It's the only way we could have helped bridge the gap while you were…" Her lip wobbles as if she can't bring herself to say another word.

I grab her hand and squeeze. "It's fine. Thank you." When I made the deal with Piero, I never considered what it meant for The Rogues and The Tesoro Mafia. It has to work out since I'm now married to the sole heir of the Tesoro family.

"And Piero?" I question, wondering if that bastard decided to go back on his word.

She shakes her head. "We've not heard a word from him. Your men had orchestrated your plan, and I think he's trying to pick up the pieces."

"I don't expect him to adhere to the agreement. He will hate his plan being foiled, so we have to be careful. And he'll be pissed at the damage I did to his reputation."

"We have taken extra steps to fortify our security. Having The Rogues and the Tesoro Mafia working side by side has made us far stronger." Her lips purse together. "Maybe the danger he put Tilly in has made him reconsider his actions."

I think my angel is too gullible. Piero cares for Tilly, that I'm sure of, but I'm not sure it's enough for him to put aside his thirst for power and money.

A doctor enters the room and clears his throat. "It's good to see you awake, Mr. Hook."

I try to sit up, but he shakes his head. "Please don't move. How are you feeling?"

"Oh, I'm feeling great," I infuse my tone with

sarcasm, as it's a stupid question. I just woke from a fucking coma.

"Any amnesia?" he asks, as he shines a light into my eyes.

I glare at him. "No, other than being in a shit ton of pain. I feel my normal self."

"We'll increase your pain meds. Where are you feeling the pain?"

I consider the question, feeling the aches and pains everywhere. "Everywhere, doc. It feels like I got hit by a truck."

He nods, scribbling something on his notepad. "That's expected. Your injury was severe and the loss of blood would have taken it out of you. But I'm happy to report that your vital signs are stable and initially I don't notice any signs of brain damage." His jaw works. "We will do a routine MRI scan to confirm, most likely this afternoon."

I sigh. "How long will I be here?"

The doctor's brow furrows. "Let's see what the results of your MRI are and we can give you an accurate estimate."

"Worst-case scenario?"

His jaw works. "Months," he says, before turning and walking out.

"He's got to be kidding," I say, glaring after him. "I'm not staying here for months."

Gwen grabs my hand again and squeezes it. "You'll stay here however long the doctor says is necessary. You almost died, Cillian."

The emotion in her voice draws my attention back

to her. My beautiful wife. "How often have you been here?"

"Every single day. I only went home to sleep and shower now and then."

"Home being?"

"Our home," she says softly.

"Our home," I repeat, letting the words sink in. It's surreal to think that she actually wants this. When I let her go, I was sure she'd never come back to me. That I was destined to live a life of solitude because it's all I deserved. And while I told her Piero doesn't deserve her, I know I don't deserve her either. No one is good enough for her.

"I don't deserve you," I murmur.

She shakes her head. "You do. Of course you do. You deserve to be happy, Cillian."

"I'm not sure that's true. If you knew all the things I've done... I'm not a good man, princess."

"I don't care," she says, looking at me with determination blazing in her eyes. "You're mine."

I smirk at that, as those are the words I've said to her countless times since we met. "Is that right?"

"Yes, and you deserve to heal from the darkness of your past. I want to help you."

My jaw works as I'm not sure there's any coming back from the darkness I've lived most of my life in. "The darkness is a part of me now," I warn.

"And I'll embrace it. I love you, Cillian. Every part of you. Especially your darkness."

My lips feel dry hearing her tell me she loves me. It's

going to take a while to get used to. "Say that again," I breathe.

She rolls her eyes. "I love you."

"I think I could spend the rest of my life listening to you say those three words to me."

She smiles and leans over to kiss me, her mouth soft against mine. "I love you," she whispers again when she pulls back.

"I love you too, princess."

I give her a stern look. "Now go home and get a proper night's sleep and a home-cooked meal. You look like you've barely slept."

Her expression turns irritated. "Are you saying that I look like shit?"

I press a hand to my chest. "I'd never say that, but you look tired. Get some rest."

"But you've only just woken up."

"And I'll be here when you get back. Be a good girl for me and do as you're told."

"Fine," she breathes. I can tell that she's relieved that I'm letting her get some rest. "But I'll text you to check in later." She nods at the nightstand. "Your phone is there and charged."

I smile at her. "Thanks, princess."

She gives me a long look, as if she's still reluctant to leave, before turning around and sauntering out of my room.

Her ass swaying arouses me even though I'm in a shit ton of pain and there's no way in hell I can do anything about it. I groan as I rest my head back and shut my eyes, knowing that despite feeling terrible physically, that I've never felt better emotionally. Gwendolyne loves me and that makes all of this worth it a thousand times over.

Two months later...

I sit opposite my arch nemesis, struggling to believe that we're putting this into a legally binding agreement.

Not that legality means shit to either of us, but it makes it harder for him to go back on his word. Maybe Gwen was right. I sense that Piero does care for Tilly and he's worried I'll come after her. I will if he's stupid enough to cross me.

"Surprised you survived, considering how much blood you lost," Piero says, as his lawyer takes a seat next to him.

Jovani is also present, along with mine and his lawyer.

"I'm invincible," I say simply, flexing my prosthetic hand. "Now let's cut the bullshit chit-chat and get to business."

Piero's jaw clenches. It kills him to sign on the dotted line of this agreement. I know him well enough to know this is a little too close to defeat. "Fine. My lawyers have gone over the paperwork and believe everything is in order."

I nod. "Of course it is."

Jovani clears his throat. "All that is left is for the three of us to sign it."

My relationship with my father-in-law is an uneasy one. However, things have never been better for The Rogues in San Diego. Our power has increased with the merging of the Tesoro mafia. In my eyes, we'll always be The Rogues. A group of misfits who banded together and rivaled powerful mafia families.

"Jovani is right. So what do you say?"

Piero watches me for a few seconds, eyes narrowed. And then he pulls the contract in front of him and unfastens the lid on his pen. "I say, let's get it over and done with."

I smirk, knowing this is a huge win for me. Not only have I secured a ceasefire between our two cities, but I've also managed to secure the safety of Gwendolyne and my child. It's been two months since I woke from the coma and Gwen is now four months pregnant.

"Excellent," I say, taking the pen from Piero and signing the contract. And then Jovani signs the contract, too. I feel a sense of relief wash over me as I realize that this is over—at least for now. I wouldn't say with complete certainty that Piero won't go back on his word or the contract.

Piero stands and I do the same, eyeing him warily. "This doesn't mean that we're friends, Cillian," he says, his tone icy.

"That'll never fucking happen," I reply, my voice calm. "I'd rather shoot myself in the balls than be friends with you. But at least it means we stay out of each other's way."

He snorts. "We'll see about that."

"You signed the agreement."

His jaw works and he doesn't say another word. Instead, he nods to his lawyer and marches out of the boardroom. My hatred toward him simmers deep within me at the mere sight of him. The end game was always him dead. It's a miracle I didn't claw his fucking eyes out. Kira hasn't been avenged, but getting so close to losing my life and putting Gwendolyne in danger made me realize something.

Revenge won't fill the hole in my heart. Only Gwendolyne and our unborn child can do that. I know if Kira could speak to me beyond the grave, she'd tell me to be happy.

I turn to Jovani. "Thanks for all your help, Jovani. I couldn't have done this without you."

His jaw is hard set, but he nods. "You are family now, Cillian. We take care of our own."

I swallow the lump in my throat. "You could have killed me for snatching your daughter."

"I could have," he admits, shaking his head. "But she loves you and this arrangement works for both of us, doesn't it?"

"Yes," I say, nodding.

"Then that's all there is to it. Gwen is outside. Let's go and join her." He walks out of the boardroom and I follow, to find Gwen in the waiting area.

She looks worried, her hand resting on the small bump of her stomach. "How did it go?"

"It went as planned," I say simply.

"Everything is going to be fine, sweetheart," Jovani says, giving her a quick hug. "I guess I must be going—"

"We were going to grab dinner at Giuseppe's if you want to tag along?"

Jovani looks surprised.

"A little celebration," I add.

His gaze softens. "Yes, sounds perfect. If you don't mind me joining?" He glances at Gwen, who looks equally surprised at my suggestion.

"Definitely not. We'd love to have you join us, Dad."

"Great, I'll go inform my driver and meet you both there." He walks away, leaving us together.

"Thank you," she breathes.

I look into her emerald eyes, wondering how I got this lucky to call this woman mine. "What for, princess?"

"Including him, it means a lot to me."

I grab her hips and yank her toward me. "I know it does. Why do you think I did it? Because I want to make you happy." I kiss her. "Let's get to the car before I do something that'll make us late."

Her eyes flash with fire, but she knows when to heed my warning as she grabs my hand and leads me to the elevator. She smiles at me. "I'm going to give you a reward later," she murmurs.

"What kind of reward?"

There's a playful look in her eyes. "It's a secret."

I grab her then, pulling her back against my chest. "You can't tease me, princess. Tell me now."

She leans toward me and whispers, "I've got the biggest anal plug in my ass right now. I'm stretched and ready to be fucked."

I growl, my cock getting painfully hard. "Dirty girl," I breathe into her ear. "You made a big mistake telling me because I'm going to fuck it in the back of the limousine on the way to the restaurant and then put the plug back in and know that you are full of my cum while we eat dinner with your dad." I spank her ass and she yelps, a small smile visible on her lips as I watch her in the mirror of the elevator. "You dirty little minx. That was your plan all along, wasn't it?"

"Perhaps," she breathes.

How did I get this lucky to get to keep the most precious treasure on this earth?

All I know is I'm never letting her go.

42

EPILOGUE

GWENDOLYNE

en months later…

A piercing cry shatters the peacefulness in the room, forcing me to my feet for the fourth time since I put Alex to bed an hour ago.

Before I can take a step, a heavy hand lands on my shoulder, forcing me onto the sofa. I turn around to see Cillian standing over me. "Rest, princess. I'm home," he says softly, his voice like silk.

The tension in my body softens and warmth fills my heart as I look into Cillian's eyes. He's been gone all day for work and now that he's here, everything is better.

"It's been a tough day." I force a smile, gesturing to the monitor screen on the coffee table where Alex is crying "He's been suffering from colic."

Cillian squeezes my shoulder and leans down to place a gentle kiss on my cheek. His lips are soft against my skin and the touch sends an electric current running through my body.

"I told you we can get a nanny," he says, straightening to his full height.

I shake my head. "No, I'm his mom, and that means I'm going to take care of him."

He chuckles softly at my vehemence. "Okay, but you could have someone help out a bit while I'm at work. Especially since you need to get back to your photography."

I open my mouth to protest, as Cillian has been pushing me to pursue wildlife photography as a career, but he silences me with a look. "We'll discuss it over dinner." He turns and walks away toward Alex's nursery.

I watch the monitor as he lifts Alex from his crib. Cillian never fails to amaze me as he took to fatherhood with such ease, despite having grown up in an abusive home.

He speaks softly to our baby boy and sways him gently until he's lulled into a peaceful slumber. My chest clenches as I know I've never known what love looked like before I met him.

Cillian tenderly returns our baby to the crib and then stands over our son for a moment, a look of pure adoration in his eyes. His devotion to both me and Alex swells my heart. I can't help but be amazed by how much he loves us both.

It's moments like these when I realize how deeply I love my husband. I'm amazed that something so pure and beautiful as our family could blossom from such dark and toxic beginnings.

Cillian admitted to me that the moment he set eyes

on me, he knew that he'd marry me and I'd be the mother of his children.

Sadly, Cillian's mom was not around to meet her grandson—she passed away due to a stroke linked to her dementia the month before Alex was born. It eats at him because she was so desperate to meet her grandchild.

The sound of his voice snaps me out of my thoughts. "Can I get you anything?" Cillian asks, standing in the doorway looking devilishly handsome in his tailored suit.

I force away the lump in my throat. "No, I'm alright."

He slides into the chair next to me, never taking those chestnut eyes off of me. I place the book I'd been reading onto the coffee table and smile at my husband. "How was your day?"

He shrugs. "Same old. Not sure about Jake yet."

Jake is his newly appointed second-in-command after Smyth's betrayal. He was under immense pressure to appoint someone for months before finally deciding to pick Jake.

"He won't betray you like Smyth did."

His shoulders bunch at the mention of his former right-hand man. "How do you know that?"

My lips curl into a subtle smirk. "Because he's not madly in love with you." Tilting my head to the side, I gaze deep into his chestnut eyes—the ones that have always made me swoon. "Love makes people do crazy things."

I hear his teeth grind together. "Don't I know it?"

I elbow him in the ribs. "What's that supposed to mean?"

He smirks. "Loving you made me fucking crazy."

"I think that ship had sailed long before we met."

He arches a brow. "Perhaps." Those chestnut eyes of his burn with fire as he grabs my hand and yanks me onto his lap. "But I became truly crazy the moment we met. So crazy that I'd do anything to keep you safe." He grabs my wrist and yanks me onto his lap. "You know I'm not done with breeding you, princess. I want to keep filling that pretty little cunt and getting you pregnant with my babies."

I groan as an ache ignites between my legs. "I'm not sure I'd survive raising more right now."

He nips at my earlobe. "I told you, we'll get a nanny."

Sighing heavily, I roll my eyes. "And I told you—"

"Quiet, listen to your captain and be a good girl."

My nipples harden at the demanding tone of his voice. He knows how to turn me on with a few simple words. "Cillian," I breathe his name as he kisses my neck softly. "

"Yes, princess?"

I cup his face in my hands and look him in the eyes. "I love you," I say, feeling my chest ache at how deeply I feel it.

He grabs my wrists and pushes them behind my back, restraining me. "I love you too." A wicked smirk slashes across his face. "And I'm going to show you how much."

I groan as he grinds the hard length of his cock between my legs, making me needy without much effort.

"Is my princess ready to be bred by her captain?"

I moan. Cillian's dirty talk can turn me on as much as anything he does to me. "Yes, captain."

"Good girl," he purrs, lifting me off his lap and pushing me onto my back on the sofa.

He towers over me, looking at me with such love in his eyes it makes my insides flutter. "Do you want your captain's cock?" He teases, unfastening his pants and dropping them to the floor.

My eyes drop to the bulge in his briefs and I feel my mouth water. "Fuck, yes," I breathe.

"Tell me where you want it, princess."

I shudder, the ache between my thighs growing unbearable. "My ass, please."

"Fuck," he groans, squeezing himself. "Such a dirty girl, aren't you?"

"Yes, I'm your dirty girl," I breathe.

He smirks and lifts the hem of my skirt to my thighs, eyes darkening when they fix on my bare pussy and the plug in my ass. "Looks like you were anticipating this, weren't you?"

I bite my lip as I was feeling particularly horny earlier and worked a butt plug into my ass, so I was stretched for him when he got home. "Perhaps?"

"Mmm," he croons, rubbing his fingers through my pussy. "I fucking love how you're always so ready for me."

He kisses me as if I'm the most precious thing in the world.

My breath hitches as he wraps his fingers around the handle of the butt plug, giving it a little tug. "Such a filthy girl."

He pulls it out and I groan, feeling so empty. I feel the tip of his cock nudging at my stretched, eager hole.

He gazes at me with hooded eyes. "You still want this?"

"Fuck yes."

"You have such a dirty mouth, princess."

"Fuck me," I breathe, spreading my legs further apart and trying to push closer to him.

He chuckles as he tosses the plug onto the floor and grabs hold of my hips, pulling me toward the edge of the sofa. "Such a greedy little thing, aren't you?"

"I am—" He silences me, driving his cock deep into my ass without warning.

I scream, growing wetter at the feel of his cock filling me. "Oh God, yes!"

"You like that, princess?" He asks, pulling out until only the tip is left inside and then driving in again, making me groan as exquisite pleasure builds within me.

"Yes, fuck yes," I moan as he rolls his hips against mine.

He sits back, pulling out completely. I look at him, confused as to why he stopped.

"What are you doing?!" I ask.

"I want you to beg your God for more," he breathes.

I swallow hard, as he knows how much making me beg drives me insane.

"I need it, Cillian, please. I need you to fuck me hard and fast."

I feel his cock pressing tight against my ass, slowly pushing in until the tip is just inside. "Make me believe you."

Tears of desperation spring to my eyes. "Please fuck me. I want your cock so damn bad it feels like I'm dying without it."

He smirks. "Not bad."

And then he drives into me so hard I feel it in every nerve ending. My entire body tenses because the pleasure is hard to handle.

"That's it," he growls, his hips moving faster. "Come all over my cock, princess."

I scream his name, my body twitching as he makes me come so hard I see stars.

"Look at you," he breathes, leaning over and kissing my neck. "So fucking beautiful."

"Cillian..." I breathe, feeling the pleasure heightening again before I've recovered from my last orgasm.

His thrusts grow wild and erratic, and I can feel the heat of his cock as he nears his release. "Come with me again, princess. Come while I breed you."

I grip his shoulders tighter as he pounds into me, reaching between us and rolling my clit between my fingers. "Cillian," I moan, feeling my body begin to shake again.

"Fuck," he groans, burying his face in my neck as he comes.

"Yes," I moan, my ass spasming around him and milking his cock for everything it's worth.

I'm still riding the waves of pleasure as I pull him onto the couch and he lies on top of me, his face buried in my neck. I bite my lip as he slides out of me, missing the feel of him right away.

"You're such a good girl," he murmurs in my ear, his fingers tracing patterns across my skin.

I grin against his shoulder, feeling so loved. "I love you, Cillian."

He kisses me deeply and then lifts up, propping himself on his elbow. "And I love you."

I stare into his beautiful, endless eyes and feel my heart swell to the point it may burst.

My fingertips trace the rippling contours of his back, and I can feel him stiffen in response. "Again?" I whisper against his neck.

A deep groan echoes from his throat before he rolls us over so I'm above him. His heated gaze burns into my soul, and I part my thighs invitingly for him.

"I don't need to be asked twice," he growls as he guides himself into me.

The air around us shifts as I lower myself onto his hard length, and we both know this is more than pleasure. It's a surrender of our souls, a connection that transcends physical boundaries.

"Fuck me, captain," I murmur, looking into his eyes —smoldering pools of desire that make my heart skip a beat.

"That," he whispers with a devilish smile as he begins to move inside me, "is the only prayer I answer to, princess."

THANK you so much for reading Hook, the second book in the Once Upon a Villain Series. I hope you enjoyed following Gwendolyne and Cillian on their journey.

If you enjoyed this book, you will enjoy the next one, Wicked. It's on pre order with a current release date of October 31st.

It's a dark step-dad mafia romance, and here is the cover and blurb.

Wicked: A Dark Forbidden Mafia Romance

My step-dad is as wicked as they come, and he wants to claim me.

Three months after Mom married Remy Morrone, she's killed by his enemy.

Leaving me at the mercy of my step-dad.

A cold, ruthless, and wicked man who decides I'll make good money at auction.

I make a wish for Prince Charming to buy me and whisk me away.

And at a pre-auction dinner, I meet him.

Alex Vishekov is sweet and charming, and he vows to rescue me.

My step-dad doesn't like it.

He keeps looking at me in the most primal way.

And then everything changes.

He calls it off and tells me I'm his.

Remy will have me, no matter how wrong that is.

I wished for my Prince Charming to save me.

Instead, I'm being claimed by my villainous step-*daddy*.

But perhaps I've got it all wrong.

What if the prince is actually the villain, and my wicked step-*daddy* is my knight in shining armor?

ALSO BY BIANCA COLE

Once Upon a Villian

Pride: A Dark Arranged Marriage Romance

Hook: A Dark Forced Marriage Romance

Wicked: A Dark Forbidden Mafia Romance

The Syndicate Academy

Corrupt Educator: A Dark Forbidden Mafia Academy
Romance

Cruel Bully: A Dark Mafia Academy Romance

Sinful Lessons: A Dark Forbidden Mafia Academy Romance

Playing Dirty: A Dark Enemies to Lovers Forbidden Mafia
Academy Romance

Chicago Mafia Dons

Merciless Defender: A Dark Forbidden Mafia Romance

Violent Leader: A Dark Enemies to Lovers Captive Mafia
Romance

Evil Prince: A Dark Arranged Marriage Romance

Brutal Daddy: A Dark Captive Mafia Romance

Cruel Vows: A Dark Forced Marriage Mafia Romance

Dirty Secret: A Dark Enemies to Loves Mafia Romance

Dark Crown: A Dark Arranged Marriage Romance

Boston Mafia Dons Series

Empire of Carnage: A Dark Captive Mafia Romance

Cruel Daddy: A Dark Mafia Arranged Marriage Romance

Savage Daddy: A Dark Captive Mafia Roamnce

Ruthless Daddy: A Dark Forbidden Mafia Romance

Vicious Daddy: A Dark Brother's Best Friend Mafia Romance

Wicked Daddy: A Dark Captive Mafia Romance

New York Mafia Doms Series

Her Irish Daddy: A Dark Mafia Romance

Her Russian Daddy: A Dark Mafia Romance

Her Italian Daddy: A Dark Mafia Romance

Her Cartel Daddy: A Dark Mafia Romance

Romano Mafia Brother's Series

Her Mafia Daddy: A Dark Daddy Romance

Her Mafia Boss: A Dark Romance

Her Mafia King: A Dark Romance

Bratva Brotherhood Series

Bought by the Bratva: A Dark Mafia Romance

Captured by the Bratva: A Dark Mafia Romance

Claimed by the Bratva: A Dark Mafia Romance

Bound by the Bratva: A Dark Mafia Romance

Taken by the Bratva: A Dark Mafia Romance

Forbidden Series

Filthy Boss: A Forbidden Office Romance

Filthy Professor: A First Time Professor And Student Romance

Filthy Lawyer: A Forbidden Hate to Love Romance

Filthy Doctor: A Fordbidden Romance

<u>Royally Mated Series</u>

Her Faerie King: A Faerie Royalty Paranormal Romance

Her Alpha King: A Royal Wolf Shifter Paranormal Romance

Her Dragon King: A Dragon Shifter Paranormal Romance

Her Vampire King: A Dark Vampire Romance

ABOUT THE AUTHOR

I love to write stories about over the top alpha bad boys who have heart beneath it all, fiery heroines, and happily-ever-after endings with heart and heat. My stories have twists and turns that will keep you flipping the pages and heat to set your kindle on fire.

For as long as I can remember, I've been a sucker for a good romance story. I've always loved to read. Suddenly, I realized why not combine my love of two things, books and romance?

My love of writing has grown over the past four years and I now publish on Amazon exclusively, weaving stories about dirty mafia bad boys and the women they fall head over heels in love with.

If you enjoyed this book please follow me on Amazon, Bookbub or any of the below social media platforms for alerts when more books are released.

Made in the USA
Monee, IL
07 August 2024

63399783R00260